LAST CLEAR CHANCE

Bob Tripp

Copyright ©2008 by Robert Tripp

Acknowledgment is made to Sony/ATV Music Publishing Company for permission to reprint excerpts from "Pearls" by Adu Sade and Hale Andrew.

All rights reserved. Used by permission.

Library of Congress Control Number: 2008901786

ISBN 978-0-9817447-3-5

Cover illustration by Marionette

Cover design by Digital Arts of Waimea

AUTHORS NOTE

Though it is not necessary for enjoyment of the novel, for those who are curious, technical aviation terms and colloquial Hawaiian words are explained in a glossary at the end of the book. These are not the same definitions you might find in a technical text or dictionary but are plain language interpretations. The Halepio Valley does not exist on the island of Molokai. Those that know the real valley will recognize it by its description. Otherwise, you are left to find it on your own.

ACKNOWLEDGEMENTS

Many agents, editors, and readers over the years helped to shape the final form of the story. I am indebted to all of them, and if I missed your name, you have my sincere apologies.

Ian Boyington, Jenny Wagner, Angela Dracott, and James Wade took part in the early editing phases.

Alice Acheson, not only advised me on publicity, but always kept me pointed in the right direction.

Richard and Sabryna produced more results than they will ever know.

Aletha Kaohi was my kapuna for the Hawaiian section, and John Humphrey covered the pidgin portion.

Susan Remoaldo always was able to find the library references I needed, and sometimes ones I didn't even know I needed.

Lowry McFerrin, of ProForma, guided me through the process of turning a novel into a book.

Without Cynthia this book would probably not exist. She read and corrected every version and was there for me in both the good times and the bad.

LAST CLEAR CHANCE

CHAPTER 1

Dawn. Sunlight strikes the rows of high-rise buildings lofting toward the clouds covering Victoria Peak. When Dan Swanton opened the curtains to their hotel room, nothing seemed unusual. Seldom are any of us aware of the abyss that waits at the edge of an ordinary day. He looked at the clock next to the bed. Good, his internal clock had awakened him before the alarm. Back in bed, he stretched and felt the warmth of Manalani's body next to him. In spite of that familiar closeness, a sense of unease rubbed against his thoughts. He slipped out of bed and into the bathroom trying to locate the source of that feeling.

It wasn't because this was his first flight out of Hong Kong. He had confidence in his abilities from his years of flying. Maybe it was because of last night's conversation. Manalani had insights that sometimes were foreign to his way of thinking. She got into him again about their son's sexual orientation. Dan couldn't come to terms with it and its implications. Why couldn't she understand that he just wanted to make things easier for Mark? Being a teenager was a tough enough job in any case.

When he first met Manalani, she was flying for Air Micronesia and on her way to Honolulu. To him, she was an exotic, pungent mystery that shunted aside his usual reticence. She encountered him as a musician, not as a pilot. In those days, when he was home from flying, he played tenor sax in Torrance at a club called Monk's Room, named that because Thelonius Monk played gigs there when he was in the city. On that fateful night, the quartet was in sync and swinging hard and fast. She stepped up to the stand and requested "Round Midnight." Dan was surprised. *Who is this gorgeous lady who knows Monk's tunes? She looks like she dropped in here from some exotic slice of heaven.*

He wanted to impress her and put all of his emotion through the horn, extending the last phrase out to the point it brought a standing ovation. When she again approached the stand to thank him, he felt the spark of frisson between them. He asked her out for coffee when their gig was done. Afterwards, at Chez Mélange, they were not very far into their conversation before she found out he was a pilot. She laughed, tossing her halo of dark hair, but looked into his eyes intently and said, "You're lucky we met this way. I don't date pilots, but a pilot with a musician's soul, I could handle that."

She had maturity and insight, and a personality that complemented his. Because of this, when his infatuation with her began to fade, their relationship became deeper. He became dependent on her in ways he only partly understood. Sometimes she would tease him into doing things he would never have tried on his own.

***

As he shaved, Dan felt that even though last night's conversation, and the surrounding issue of Mark's problem, were probably the sources of his unease, it would just have to wait. His focus was narrowing down to the flight coming up. Manalani knew him well enough to understand. She called it getting into his mechanical man act. Twenty-minutes before their pickup time he was down in the lobby with his bags packed. Manalani would follow in a few minutes. The crew slowly assembled. They counted heads, ten flight attendants and four pilots plus Manalani. They were ready to go on the long taxi ride out.

The ride to Kai Tak confirmed Dan's observations from the air on their arrival. The harbor supported a vast flotilla of waterborne equipment, darting, lumbering, and charging into any open space available. Commerce was the lifeblood of this city, as it had been from the start when the British wrested it away from the Chinese during the opium wars. Hong Kong was now the portal through which billions of dollars in cash and products flowed to and from mainland China. This was one area where the Japanese had no direct entry. Memories in China extended back to World War II, and the hatred generated by the conquering Japanese armies still festered close to the surface in the older generation.

On the way, rain and wind began to beat on the windows of the limo. Dan wondered, *Is the typhoon in the weather forecast moving faster than predicted? Better take a good look at the trend in the forecast.*

At the airport terminal, passengers in the lounge were looking at him. He shrugged it off. They seldom tried to speak to him due to his rank and appearance. The planes of his face all angled forward, dominated by a beak of a nose, with his eyes deeply set beneath bushy eyebrows. Manalani once said he looked like a bird of prey, an eagle or a hawk. She was right;

he could present a fearsome visage, particularly when he was angry. They made an unlikely yet striking couple. She was all soft brown curves, smooth and seal-like; he was all angles and attitude.

As the rest of the crew descended the stairs to the operations level, Manalani and Dan paused. He gave her a kiss on the cheek and squeezed her hand. "See you on board in a bit, angel."

She smiled, "Love you, big boy," and walked out to the departure gate.

Just before Dan started down the long dark passageway to operations, he looked back at her and found her looking back at him. A small tremor passed through him. He stuffed the feeling into the recesses of his mind. He had to get down to work.

In the briefing room, he and his three crewmembers began their preflight briefing, surrounded by route charts, weather faxes, special procedures, and notices to airmen (NOTAMS). During their discussions, Dan received some compliments that pleased him. Greg Allred led off. "Dan, I was impressed when you let me fly the first leg. A lot of captains would insist on flying it themselves, just to show they could do it. I've seen some pretty hair-ball approaches by new captains on this route because of that."

"Well, like I told you then, I could learn a lot by observing you. Besides, I haven't given up my captain's prerogative."

Dick Borman, the relief captain, chimed in, "Yeah, and I appreciate your asking for my views. I can tell some of the guys new to this route get their feathers ruffled when I try to give advice."

"Well, I figure I need all the help I can get, stumbling around through the skies in a giant airliner."

They spent the next fifty minutes checking navigation points on the plotting chart, discussing fuel burn, minimum acceptable fuel over destination, and weather conditions. That done, they gathered their flight bags, and strode through a maze of corridors leading out to the planes.

At the gate, there was a jetway that required the use of a magnetically striped authorization card followed by a coded PIN. None of the pilots' cards would work. Dick grumbled, "Great security, huh? Can't even get through to go to work. Someday when this happens, I'm just going to turn around and go home; let them call me when they're serious about letting me get to my airplane."

Dan looked at him while he was commenting. He had his head and shoulders thrust forward and had approached the subject with his usual bulldog tenacity. His short compact body and swarthy face complemented an aggressive stance that he said was the best way to avoid fights in the tough neighborhood where he grew up. At that moment, a gate agent came through the door from the other direction. They slipped on through.

At the door to the MD-11 cockpit, they ran into another delay. A ship cleaner, working on the lavatories that were next to the door, had left her trash cart in the aisle. Two mechanics in the cockpit were running byte checks on the computers, and one was writing in the logbook. A flight attendant was making a change to the passenger service panel facing the cockpit area.

"That's it," Dick exploded, "I'm going home. Now they will blame us if we don't get out on time, even though we can't get to our seats until fifteen minutes before departure. Lucky you, Dan, you get to rush through the cockpit set up on your first flight home."

They all laughed, but Dan replied, "There won't be any rushing in my cockpit. If you rush or skip around through the checklist, the feds got you cold because it's on the voice recorder."

The crew settled into the routine of preflight checking. Dan and Greg cross-checked the flight plan and ICAO clearance. Dick verified fuel burns and fuel loading, and carefully checked weight and balance and performance data since they were close to maximum weight for take-off.

Dan turned to the pages of the meteorological report.

Dick asked, "How does the weather look on the charts? Think we should be worried about the typhoon?"

Dan replied, "No, it's not a problem. It's drifting in from the China Sea, but it won't arrive until tomorrow. We will have to use wet runway data though for take-off. We'll have a lower V_1 speed, but the quartering head wind will help to compensate."

Twelve flight attendants were on board. Though Dan encouraged them to visit the cockpit during slack periods, he often did not meet those working aft in tourist class until they were on the bus going to the hotel or back to the parking lot. Everyone had duties that would keep them busy until they had been in cruise for several hours. Dan took advantage of a boarding delay to have a short briefing with the lead flight attendant. To avoid towering over her, he sat on an armrest. "Ann, it's going to be rough on climb-out. I want you to remain seated. When Manalani boards, I want to know her seat number."

"No problem. So you want us to stay seated until the seat belt sign is turned off?"

"This time, I think that would be best."

"Thanks for letting us know."

"I try to keep the crew happy. Don't want Manalani getting on my case."

Back in the cockpit, he could see Greg, his lanky frame folded awkwardly in his seat, typing the flight plan information into the Flight Management System (FMS) computer keyboard. When programmed correctly, this computer, through the autoflight system and autothrottles, would set engine power, control airspeed, and could navigate the MD-11 all the way to a landing. Only half-jokingly, Greg said that typing skills were as important as flying.

From his left side seat, Dan checked the logbook for write ups. He placed his charts and pencils on a clipboard on top of his flight bag, sunglasses hung from a clip on the side window. He called it, "Making my nest." The familiar glow of the panel, the hum of the gyros and fans, the slight smell of old leather, oil, and ozone, helped Dan in this process. Each pilot had a routine that was part of the process of settling in. In this day of standard procedures and enforced conformity, it was one way of stamping his identity in the cockpit. Then he looked over the instrument panels to be sure that each switch and gauge was correct for the before-start checklist.

From his hermetically sealed cockpit, Dan peered down to the ramp filled with charging trucks and buses, taxiing airplanes, and towering buildings. This disrupted his feeling for the larger world outside and produced a sense of dislocation. He realized, with a sense of longing, that he preferred the small airports he used to fly into on the Lockheed Electra and the Boeing 737. Places like Bozeman, pervaded by the smell of new mown hay in the summer; Jackson Hole, marked by the huge valley,

Grand Tetons, and pine trees. Tucson exuded the ozone and creosote-sharp smell of the desert, often accompanied by towering cumulus build-ups in the afternoon. At all of these small airports he could step out on the ramp and get a sense of the weather that went beyond the symbols on charts and weather faxes. He realized this intuitive knowledge came from his years on the farm. Observing the weather and predicting its whims were part of the lessons of survival if you were a farmer. At Kai Tak and all of the big hubs, the fumes and chaos on the ground prevented him from gaining any of this innate feeling.

The relief first officer, Tom Spanger, returned with his usual announcement, "Walk around's done and everything's okay."

Dan noticed that Tom had done the check without putting on his coat. When he threw his hat into the overhead bin, his hair dangled over his ears and collar. Dan knew he was one of those pilots who pushed the dress code. Sort of a dandy too, always primping a bit before he went aft into the passenger cabin. Dan didn't really care; he was a good pilot, but Dan warned him again, "Tom, someday a check pilot will nail you."

"Yeah, yeah," Tom replied, "but I'm going to see how long I can push it. Then maybe I'll get a buzz cut. See how they like that."

Just as they finished the checklist, an agent appeared at the cockpit door. "Sorry guys. There's a power outage or computer glitch. Your final flight release and weight and balance papers are delayed."

Dick said, "Typical. Hurry up and wait. I'm going back to the galley. You guys want something to drink?" He took their orders and left.

Tom made an observation. "Have you seen how they run

their utilities here? Wire bundles and conduit strung across streets between buildings supported by bamboo frames. Sewage barely contained. Water running everywhere. It's a wonder anything works and that people aren't electrocuted every day."

"It probably does happen and nobody cares," Greg replied. "Have you even peered into some of the rat warren slums here? No streets, just dark tunnels and alleys diving into eight-story high piles of rooms. No law, the police won't even go in there. Gangs set the codes and make their own justice. How do ordinary people survive? Why would they even live there or move there?"

Dan said, "If they came here from the villages and are willing to live like this, can you imagine what kind of condition they left? Makes me really appreciate what we've got."

"You're right," Greg said. "Flying here or to Bombay or Delhi is a real eye opener. Do you know the three real signs of civilization?"

"No, tell me."

"Hot showers, cold drinks, and flush toilets. And most of the people in the world are missing one of those."

"Which one would you give up first?" Dan asked.

"Flush toilets," Greg replied. "I can take a dump anywhere, but I sure love my cold drinks and hot showers."

Tom changed their train of thought with a new comment. "Do you know what my girlfriend said is wrong with pilots?"

"Wrong with pilots?" replied Greg. "There ain't nothing wrong with pilots. Let me set you straight on this. Didn't anybody tell you? We are livings gods, sent down by Zeus as gifts to this planet."

"Yeah, I know. I gave her a line like that and she said, 'You guys all think you hit a home run, but you started on third base.'"

At the cockpit door with their drinks, Dick replied, "No offense, but that's bullshit. I paid my dues more than once, Korea and Viet Nam. Lucky to get out with my ass in one piece. Flying with the non-scheds wasn't much safer. What she doesn't appreciate is that this is one of the few jobs where you can die in your seat, sitting in your office, and take a bunch of people with you."

"Hey, you're preaching to the choir," Tom replied. "But I sure wouldn't want to live here."

"No arguments there. I've lived in a lot of shit holes since I was a kid. I love my wife, home, and kids, except for my stupid second son."

"What's happening now?" Dan asked.

"Well, you know he didn't want to go to college. Now he just quit another job, or got fired. I'm not sure which. He's got no drive, no ambition. I think he's been on easy street too long. I should have kicked him out of the house."

"Let me ask you a couple of questions, Dick, then see if your outlook changes."

"Okay, shoot."

"Does he do a lot of drugs? Does he like girls?"

"No, he's clean. Scared himself bad with drugs a few years ago. Too many girls are part of the problem. Spends too much time and money on them."

"Dick, in this day and age, if your son doesn't do drugs and he likes girls, you are halfway home. Appreciate him for what he is. You can't run his life for him. I lost my oldest son, Lyle.

It seems like I fought with him since he was a kid. He and I never got along, but when he died, man, it hit me real hard that I never really appreciated him. I loved him, but I never liked him, and then I lost him, and that hurt double hard."

Dick paused, his face creased in a scowl. Then he smiled. "I know you are right, Dan, it's probably a good warning to me. He's not really a bad kid. Just rubs me the wrong way. If I lost him, how would I feel?"

The paperwork arrived, and Dan and Greg covered the fifty-six items of the before-start checklist. The agent closed the entry door. The tug pushed them back, engines started, taxi permission was received from ground control, taxi checklist completed, and they rolled out along the taxiway to Runway 13. On the way, after they had done the control surface checks, Dan reinforced one final instruction. "Since we are at max weight, if we get to V_1 minus ten, we are going on unless the airplane is coming apart. Dick, since you are in the center jump seat, monitor us for screw-ups, and if we lose an engine, you are pre-commanded to dump fuel. When we get up to three-thousand feet, you can read the appropriate checklists to us. Are we all together on this?"

Everyone agreed. They were cleared into position on the runway and ran the last few items of the before take-off checklist. As they waited for their take-off clearance, the mood was one of quiet anticipation. With the engines far aft of the cockpit, and everything sealed up tightly, the sound level was very low. The period from brake release, until the wheels were in the wells and the flaps and slats were up, was their most vulnerable state. In a sense, they weren't really flying until the plane was all cleaned up and they were accelerating and climbing away. If anything went wrong in that three-minute period, they would all earn their whole year's pay in a matter of seconds. At the weight they were flying there was very little margin for error.

"I'll hold on the lights until we're on the runway and cleared for take-off," Dan said. He turned on the radar to see if he could separate the rain showers from the ground clutter of the surrounding terrain. After a Cathay Pacific 747 loomed out of the rainy mist and touched down, the tower cleared them, "Intercontinental 80, line up and wait."

As they moved out onto the runway, Dan asked Greg, "Can you clean up the radar returns?"

Greg said, "Don't think so Dan. Even with ten-degree tilt, we seem to be getting ground returns. Dick, when we get in the air, would you keep working on it. Should clear up pretty quick. It looks like some rain out there, but at this time of year, there is always some around."

The typhoon in the China Sea, though no direct threat to Hong Kong, was gathering its energy and sending out waves of rain from its expanding core. One of these waves contained a strong rain cell moving out from the hills toward the end of the runway two miles away, but the pilots could not separate it from the ground returns reflecting off the mountains on each side of their flight path. In the office of the Royal Meteorological Society, the weather radar, spinning out its lonely sweep, detected this cell, but there was no repeater scope in the tower to make this information immediately available. The radar operator, on a short break from his duties, was talking to an attractive secretary a floor below. That eliminated the human element in the warning chain.

The rain cell resembled an ugly black cauliflower shouldering its way thousands of feet into the humid air, but its mass was hidden in the mists and rain surrounding it. Driven by the high altitude winds, and fed by the heat and water vapor of the sea, it sucked in energy and eased its way into the projected path of Intercontinental 80. The cell now reached the mature stage where the uplift energy could no longer hold all the water in its upper levels. The mass of water droplets in its core began to fall, gathering more water and momentum as it continued. This formed what meteorologists call a microburst, a downdraft of air and water less than a mile in diameter. People on the ground receive this as a blast of cold air and pounding rain. To a pilot, it is a column of negative energy pushing his airplane toward the ground.

As this was happening, they received their clearance, "Intercontinental 80 is cleared for take-off. Wind is 105 at 20."

Dan said, "Okay, that gives us a quartering left headwind. Shouldn't be a problem. I'll keep some rudder in. Okay, here we go. Looking for 1.60 on the EPR gage."

"Airspeed's alive on both sides."

"Eighty knots, take-off clamp, power looks good."

A long pause followed as the airplane gathered itself and accelerated at an increasing rate toward its V_1 commit point. The cockpit insulation muted the scream of the turbines to a single buzzing tone. Vibrations transmitted by bumps in the runway created the sensation of speed. As speed picked up, the initial wallowing sensations became sharper, until at take-off they were distinct jolts. Since Dan's attention was entirely devoted to the instruments and the remaining runway, he had very little visual perception of increasing speed.

"V_1"

"We got an overheat on number two." This came from Dick Borman who was monitoring the engines.

"That's all right," Dan replied. "We're going on. We can fix it in the air."

"Rotate"

"V_2"

"Positive rate"

"Gear up"

"Hey, number two is spinning down, we're losing power."

Dan was shocked. "What the hell! Give me max power. Start dumping fuel, What's going on?"

"You've got the power; can't tell why it shut down. No fire. I'm hitting ignition override."

"Fuel dumps are open. You should see all the failure messages I'm getting!"

"Screw that," Dan said. "But go through the memory items."

Dan was concerned about their situation, but it was under control. They were climbing four-hundred feet-per-minute. That was all he could expect with an engine out at this heavy weight. Dan's attention focused on scanning his flight instruments, but Tom Spanger, sitting behind him, could see the dark mass of rain ahead of them. "It looks like we are about to get dumped on." Immediately, the view outside turned black. Rain pounded on the surface of the plane with an intensity that the pilots felt and heard inside. The MD-11 shuddered as it encountered the wind shift in the rain shaft. Dan saw his vertical speed indicator start a deadly trend downward to zero.

A loud synthesized voice broke into his concentration:

WINDSHEAR WINDSHEAR WINDSHEAR.

"God damn it! Firewall those engines!"

"You've got it already."

He knew what was happening, but his options were limited. They were penetrating a mass of sinking air in the core of the rain shaft. On the far side of this core, the outflow was producing a tailwind component. This combination robbed the airplane of energy needed for climb. This would make the situation critical if all engines were operating. With one engine out it could be disastrous.

Following the movement of the flight director bars, Dan pulled the nose of the MD-11 upwards. The sophisticated sensors and program of the windshear guidance system confirmed his instincts and training. It was designed to lead the airplane through the event by conserving the maximum amount of energy. In this case, Dan already knew what had to happen. He had to trade off airspeed for altitude, and he didn't have much left to use. The engines were now at their maximum output. Except for the callouts of the emergency checklist and the concern on each of the pilots faces, a casual observer in the cockpit at this moment would have little clue as to their desperate situation.

As the plane began to sink toward the water, the ground proximity warning system gave out another warning: DON'T SINK DON'T SINK.

"I know! Damn it! I'm trying," was Dan's response. The last thing he wanted was superfluous advice from a machine.

"Stickshaker!" Greg called out. The control column vibrated a tactile warning to the pilots that they were within twenty knots of stall speed. Dan now was in a tight box that was shrinking. If he released the backpressure on the yoke to stay out of the stick shaker, the usual response, the airplane would sink toward the water. He had to stay at that fine line between stall and sink.

"Fly it, Dan, fly it," came from Dick in the jump seat.

By now, Dan had pitched the nose up to eighteen degrees. He was talking to himself, as he always did when things became critical. "Steady, steady. Keep it there. Come on baby, we can do it." The airplane was wallowing around in turbulence forcing him to vary his control inputs just to hold the airplane where he wanted it.

"100 feet" Greg called out, reading from the radio altimeter. For a few seconds they held their altitude. The airplane now was occasionally shuddering as the gusts of air caused the airplane to nibble at the edge of a stall. Then quite noticeably, like a huge animal, which had given everything it could, and now was resigned to its fate, the airplane began to settle.

For the first time, all the pilots in the cockpit faced the incomprehensible possibility that they were going into the water. Until now, it was as though a simulator exercise had gotten out of control. If they just came up with the right actions, the right moves, they could pull it off. Each pilot searched desperately for one more thing that could save the day. Nothing was left. Their only hope was that they would make it out to the other side of the windshear before they hit the water.

Tom Spanger raised himself up in his seat behind Dan, partly as an unconscious effort to lift the airplane, and also to see out. Forward visibility improved, and he was shocked to see boats and ships flashing by them in the mist. Suddenly a tanker loomed up on their left. Its superstructure was above them!

He thought, "Oh God, if we hit one of those, it's all over," but he didn't say anything because he knew they had no room to maneuver, and any comment from him about ships would just distract Dan.

"50 feet...shit! We are still sinking."

"20 feet...damn it! Climb, damn it!"

Without being commanded, Greg reached up and hit the ditching switch that would close all the external openings in the fuselage to help keep it watertight. It was an overt admission on his part that he felt they were about to go in.

On the jump seat Dick reached down for the public address microphone to give the command, "Brace—brace for impact."

At this moment, Dan felt the tail contact the water. A few seconds earlier a small part of his mind had said, "You're going in. You're not going to make it." He immediately squashed this thought with a response of, "No, we're not going in. I'm not giving up. I won't let it happen. Fly the airplane, fly the airplane." Simultaneously, at a more subtle level of his mind, part of Dan was pulling back, becoming an impartial observer of all the chaos and tension that was occurring. This part had no vested interest in the outcome and acted only as a witness.

At this speed, when the MD-11 contacted the water, it was solid, not the soft medium that most humans encounter. The fuselage aft of the wing fractured. The airplane began to pitch downward. Next, the wing engines hit. In two seconds, they went from full speed to zero as water rushed through them. The combination of gyroscopic loads and impact tore them loose from their pylons. The pylons dug in. The sudden deceleration and impact loads caused the fuel tanks in the wing to rupture. The right wing contacted the water slightly ahead of the left causing the airplane to lurch to the right. This made the fuselage forward of the wing break off to the left when it hit. The downward angle also made the nose penetrate the water first and then break upwards.

Inside the plane, the forces involved were enormous. Rows of seats broke loose and collapsed on each other. Lucky passengers ejected outside the airframe into the water through openings. The only portion of the fuselage left relatively intact was the center section above the wing and main gear. No fire erupted, but Jet A-1 fuel spread over the surface of the water from the ruptured tanks.

The plane impacted one small fishing boat and obliterated it and its occupants. When the family turned up missing at their usual dock site in Aberdeen, that was the first clue that they were involved. Several other small fishing boats and one tug narrowly missed the same fate.

In the cockpit, as the airplane began to break up on impact, Dan grappled with an event that was too monstrous to comprehend. As the nose of the airplane hit, the sound and forces involved were so great that his mind snapped inward to that secret place all humans have when shock becomes so great the brain and senses cannot encompass it.

His first conscious awareness was of sounds—hissing, crackling, gurgling, and a low groaning sound like an animal in pain. He could see; light was coming from the emergency cockpit lights, powered by their own batteries.

For the first time, he realized he was alive. He looked to his right where he could see Greg slumped in his seat. His posture and lack of movement indicated he was dead. In the debris covering the center pedestal he could barely recognize Dick's head and shoulders. He was shocked to see the blood pooling there and running down to the floor of the cockpit. He realized that when Dick had reached for the mike, the impact had twisted him out of his harness and driven his head into the power levers. He called out to Tom Spanger but received no reply. He looked down to his left and saw the upper half of Tom's body twisted and jammed between Dan's seat and the sidewall. When he reached down to touch him, he received no response.

Dan now was dimly aware of pain in his own body but had a hard time locating its source. Finally, he centralized it to his chest and his left leg. A cold numbness spread upwards toward his chest. Suddenly, his mind jerked in fear. Of course! They were in the water and sinking slowly. He reached down to unbuckle his harness. It took three tries before he felt it release. He attempted to raise himself out of his seat, but his left foot was pinned in the wreckage under and ahead of the rudder pedal.

Now, the metallic taste of panic began to fill his mouth. He pulled, jerked, and twisted in desperation. The pain became inconsequential. The idea that he would survive the impact only to be dragged to his death in the wreckage was unacceptable.

And yet, it was happening.

The water was up to his neck; his breath came in rapid gasps.

That was good; hyperventilation would allow him to hold his breath longer.

But what difference did that make? He was going to die anyway. It would just take longer. As the water closed over his head, he gave another series of jerks on his leg.

He felt overcome by an immense sense of loss. The fear of death was not the fear of the unknown; it was the loss of everything he knew. His entire life, every act, every thought, was disappearing into the void. That void surged up toward him, an immense empty otherness; his death rising to meet him.

CHAPTER 2

He blacked out for a short period. Then, inexplicably, he found himself floating on the surface of the water. The smell and taste of jet fuel were everywhere. He was holding onto a piece of the wreckage that jutted up through the surface of the water. His mind, numbed by the cataclysmic events of the last few minutes, hardly questioned this revelation. It was impossible, though no more so than everything else that had happened, but there was no time for reflection, only time for survival. Later, he would realize that a mystery, hidden in that blacked-out period, would change his life.

His rational mind clicked back into operation. The checklist called for him to organize his crew and passengers to await rescue, but all he could see was chaos. His eyes hurt; his vision was blurred, but he could make out people amid the debris in the water, some moving, some not. He tried to call out, but his chest hurt so much that all he could do was gasp. What could he do? He could not swim over to help them. Then it hit him like a hammer blow between the shoulder blades—Manalani. Manalani was on board. How could he forget? He was not used to her being on his trips. In his shocked state, he didn't remember. Oh God, she had to be alive. It couldn't be any other way. Things like that didn't happen, couldn't happen. Where was she sitting? Business class, seat 19C. That would be over the wing. That was good. That area was the strongest structurally. He had to find her.

To his relief, he could hear the sound of engines approaching and saw powerful searchlight beams sweeping the water. He realized that they had hit the water a short way out from the end of the runway. This must be the rescue crew arriving.

He was hearing the sound of the twin diesels of Thunderbird, the rescue catamaran that had set out within one minute of impact. Shift commander Aaron Drang was on duty at the auxiliary fire station located eight hundred feet from the end of the runway. He had observed thousands of heavily laden airplanes take-off on Runway 13 and had an instinctive feeling of the rotation point, the engine sound, and climb rate of a normal take-off.

When Intercontinental Flight 80 went by, he knew it was in trouble. It didn't sound right, and it wasn't climbing as it should. He snatched up his field glasses to observe it as it flew into the rain shaft. The plane was not climbing at all; in fact, it appeared to be sinking. He hesitated a few seconds considering his options. He glanced down at his men that he could see on the tarmac inside the station. Some of them were looking up at him questioningly. They also could sense trouble. He made his decision to hit the crash bell. He had a gut feeling, that short of a miracle, this airplane was going in. Wrong, and he would be criticized for causing disruption and thousands of dollars of expense on a false alarm, but if he guessed right, precious seconds would be saved.

The second he hit the bell, his men jumped into their gear and rushed toward the catamaran. The rest of the men at the station who were on duty would supplement the eight men who manned the cat. The main station received the crash signal. The men on duty there immediately ran to their positions from which they would organize the recovery operation and triage process. Commander Bei Duck Chan, from this position, could relay requests for support equipment and personnel as needed.

In the tower, the relay of the crash signal prompted the tower chief to hit a single button on a computer-controlled phone. This phone automatically dialed a series of numbers alerting hospitals, ambulance services, the navy, police, fireboat stations, and others to initiate their crash procedures and await further orders on clear radio or telephone channels. Since this was a water impact outside the airport boundaries, they initiated a separate plan for that contingency.

In spite of the efficiency of these operations, the rescue crews were not the first at the accident scene. The tugboat captain, when he recovered from the shock of the near miss, turned his boat into the area. Though a tug might not appear to be big when viewed from a large ship, it's very big compared to the survivors in the water and also not designed to pick up people out of the water. Knowing this, the skipper put his drive in neutral and drifted in. He gave his men orders to help those survivors that could swim to the tires hanging over the sides and stern or could grab the poles that the men extended to them. He knew his crew would not go into the water to rescue anyone. He had rescued seven passengers when he could see and hear the catamaran approaching. Now his only problem was transferring them without running over anyone enroute.

On his small fishing junk, Sai Ho, had other considerations. In his mind, the crash was a sign that the wheel of life and death had finally turned in his favor. He was no stranger to violent death. Some of his earliest boyhood memories were of the bombing and subsequent occupation of Shanghai by the Japanese in World War II. Except for one sister, his entire family was killed or lost in that event. When the Maoist revolution swept into the area, his sister disappeared into a forced commune, and he escaped to Hong Kong. Through hard work and a good sense of timing, he was able to gain his own boat and establish his own family. Though fishing was a precarious living, he had moderate success. Just a few months ago though, he lost a son-in-law. He had been drinking beer while cleaning fish, lost his balance, and fell overboard into the waiting jaws of one of the sharks that often follow the boats.

Sai Ho looked upon the crash as a gift from the gods. It was fate that people would die in the crash, and it was fate that he would be there to pick up the booty that would be floating on the surface. The dead would no longer have need of their possessions. He quickly turned his boat into the chaos and ordered his two sons to use the gaffs to retrieve anything of value. His wife and daughter had a sharp eye for these things and could quickly decide those to keep.

Two bodies and a dismembered arm yielded up rings and watches and some cash. A briefcase was a disappointment, but two suitcases contained a treasure trove of jewelry. All of this they accomplished before the catamaran arrived on the scene. Rather than risk trouble by being greedy, Sai Ho slipped away in the opposite direction. No passengers had approached his boat so he did not need to worry about their ghosts affecting his future luck. He took this as a sign that the gods were truly with him.

He would have to sell these items to the broker, Hao Lam, who would claim his too large share. Even so, there should be enough to buy a bigger boat, put his number one son into school, have enough left over for pleasure, and buy his wife some of the silly things she was always badgering him about. Ah yes, he would definitely need to improve the family shrine and possibly go to the Man Mo temple to make an offering to Kovan Kung, the family patriarch.

As the catamaran made its way toward him, Dan could see there were water level ramps extended at the sides. When they came near, the catamaran slowed almost to a stop, and divers leaped off to assist survivors. He slipped down into the water to cover the few feet remaining. Someone reached for him and said, "Okay captain, we have you now." On board, he temporarily forgot his damaged leg, and when he tried to stand, he almost fainted from the pain.

A firefighter said, "You had better lie down, captain. You are hurt and in shock. We will take care of things."

"How bad are things?" Dan asked. "I have to try and keep my crew together."

"We will keep you posted. Haven't picked up any crew members yet."

Dan started to shake uncontrollably. He felt his energy slipping rapidly away. Hard to concentrate. Couldn't remember…in the cockpit…Greg…Greg was dead, but what about everybody else? What about the flight attendants? What about Manalani?

He pulled himself upright, holding on to a stanchion. He could barely stand; no way could he walk. Confusion, noise, firemen rushing about. He gave up; sat back down. He would talk to them; explain when they were under way.

He must have blacked out. Not only were they underway, he could see the fire station looming up ahead. Someone, an officer, was standing over him. He had to explain, "My wife, my wife, Manalani, she was on board, in business class, 19C. Where is she? Is she all right?"

The officer looked at him grimly, "I'm sorry, sir. There weren't many survivors. I'm not sure about your wife. We recovered two flight attendants alive. No pilots. Don't know how many passengers yet. We'll be docking in one minute. They will help you find your wife there. Sorry about all this."

Dan was staggered. He didn't know how to respond. He was responsible for his crew. Two flight attendants, which meant ten were missing. "Is there any chance there might be more survivors?"

"Almost none, sir. We are fairly certain we picked up everyone that was floating. Anyone under water this long would be dead. But we do have divers still checking out there now with the boats."

They reached the dock. Immediately, more personnel swept over the catamaran. Firefighters carried passengers off. Another officer came down to speak to him. "We will have you out of here shortly, sir. I think that…"

Dan cut him off. "No! No! I don't want to leave until all the passengers are taken care of. I want my crew isolated if possible, and I must find my wife; she was on board, seat 19C. I want her with us."

The officer blinked several times. "Sorry, sir; so far we have only found two flight attendants. We didn't know about your wife. Your senior agent has sent us a copy of your manifest.

Most passengers that can talk have been identified. Everyone will be taken to Queen Elizabeth Hospital. You will need to go too; your leg looks bad, and you are obviously in shock."

"Hell yes, I'm in shock, but I'm not going anywhere until I have found my wife."

"What I'm trying to tell you, sir, is that she is probably already on her way to the hospital."

"But you don't know; you can't be sure."

"We have not been able to identify everyone, but they're all on their way. No one is remaining behind."

Dan looked around and realized that he was almost the last person remaining on board. "All right. Take me up there, but I tell you, I've got to find my wife."

The officer replied, "We'll do our best, sir; we really will."

But Dan noticed that he looked away as he said it.

At ground level, amidst all the noise, glaring lights, and seeming confusion, Dan could see there was a group of stretchers set aside with blankets over them. The significance was obvious. There was no hurry to move them. He asked again about Manalani and the two flight attendants. The guarded reply was that they were checking for him, and that she would probably turn up at the hospital.

Temporarily he gave up. He was overwhelmed, could not concentrate, shaking. The pain now flooded his body, each breath a short painful gasp. He could not spit out the taste of jet fuel. As they lifted him into the ambulance, it became the predominate smell. He thought he might throw up. He felt the prick of a needle in his arm. The ambulance was warm. He was losing focus. The trip to the hospital was a nightmare of drifting into unconsciousness and then suddenly snapping out into the dread and anxiety of reality. There was part of him that just wanted to stay in that warm, dark, empty place forever.

But he couldn't.

He had responsibilities for crew and passengers.

And he had to find Manalani.

CHAPTER 3

By the time they arrived at the hospital, Dan was worried again about his own survival. He could only breathe in shallow panting gasps. He was afraid that his lungs might be collapsing. As they rolled him in on a gurney, this fear helped to keep his mind focused. A round Asian face suddenly appeared in his field of vision. "Well, hello Captain. Sorry about all this mess. How are you feeling?"

"I can hardly breathe. Lung, something wrong. Foot hurts."

"Ah, we can fix your breathing problem. You probably have a pneumothorax; part of your chest cavity is filled with air and fluid. Just a minute."

The face disappeared. He felt a cold sensation, then a sudden sharp pain in his chest, followed immediately by a sense of relief as though someone had released a band from around his chest.

The face appeared again. "Is that better?"

"Yes, what did you do?"

"We inserted a hollow needle in there to release the pressure. We will shortly put you on a machine to suck out the rest of the fluid. You also have badly bruised or broken a couple of ribs but you will recover from that."

"Look, I need to know…"

"Quiet here for a few minutes. We need to run more tests.

Then we can talk."

Dan could hear the doctor and his aides discussing his heart rate, blood pressure, and some other terms he couldn't understand. They hooked him up to several machines. One that hovered over him for a few minutes was a portable x-ray. They talked about a c-spine series, pelvic screen, and urinalysis. They asked him to wiggle his toes and fingers and log rolled him onto his stomach. Eventually, they inserted a finger-sized tube between his chest wall and lung and connected it to a machine that provided suction to draw out more air and fluid.

The doctor leaned over him again. "You have a bi-malleolar fracture of your left ankle. I am going to relocate it. Then we will splint it. You will need some surgery later, but don't worry about it now."

Dan felt a shock in his ankle followed by a reduction in pain. He summoned up enough energy to ask the doctor, "What does bi-malleolar mean?"

"In laymen's terms you could just say you broke it rather badly. It will probably require pins or some other metal support, and there may be some restriction, but an orthopedic surgeon will need to make that decision."

Dan could feel himself slipping away toward unconsciousness. He knew he had to ask again, "What about my wife? What about Manalani? What about the other crew members?"

The doctor paused a moment and then hesitantly replied, "Ah, yes, your wife. We are trying to find her. You understand that survivors have been taken to several hospitals so that is not an easy task. I think that…"

Dan interrupted him, "Look, you can understand my concern can't you? Let me know as soon as you find her. I would like her moved to my room. What about the other crew members?"

Again, the doctor hesitated. He rolled a pencil between his fingertips. "Ah, you understand, in all the confusion it is hard to confirm. Ah, I believe there are two flight attendants at this hospital who are survivors. At this point the others are dead or missing."

Dan was stunned. He didn't want to ask again but he had to, "What about the other pilots?"

"I am afraid they are casualties, sir."

"What do you mean casualties? Does that mean they are dead?" Dan was afraid he knew the answer.

"Yes, I'm afraid so, sir." The doctor's voice was low and soothing, but he hunched his shoulders, his fingers fluttered about, and he would not look Dan in the eye.

The information hit Dan like someone had struck him. He could feel his body tense and shake. "Oh, God. No."

It felt as though he was speaking with some other person's voice. The enormity of what had happened was overwhelming. He couldn't handle it. His mind retreated, his thoughts circled endlessly into a pattern he could not decipher. They were wheeling him into another room. He no longer cared what they did to him. The one thought that he held onto was that they must find Manalani.

A nurse spoke to him. "You must rest now. You are in shock. We have given you a sedative. When you wake up, we should have more information for you. Presently we have you on an I.V. drip providing electrolytes and morphine for pain, and you are hooked up to a Pluerovac, which is clearing out your chest."

He summoned the energy to make one last request. "Find my wife. Find Manalani." Then he let himself slip into unconsciousness.

Hours later, he began to rise out of that warm encompassing darkness toward waking consciousness. He had to climb a long staircase, and the effort was too much for his first few attempts. Finally, he could sense himself on the bed and the pain coursing through his body. For a few minutes, he was content simply to lie there, his mind idling along registering only sensory impressions. Slowly, a vague sense of dread gathered focus, until with a jolt he could feel in his body, he came back to the realization of his situation—in a hospital bed, crew dead or injured, passengers the same, there was a crash—Manalani, where is Manalani? Someone had to tell him. He didn't know. Why hadn't they told him? Didn't they know? They said they didn't. Were they hiding something from him?

His eyes fluttered open. The light hurt. He could see a woman in the room. Manalani? He had a hard time focusing. No, a nurse. She should know. "Nurse, can you tell me about my wife, Manalani? Where is she?"

The nurse crossed over to him. "You should rest some more."

"To hell with resting. I'll rest after I find out."

The effort of speaking sent sharp pains through his chest. He could sense the nurse's concern but her reply was oblique, "I will get the doctor for you."

The effort was all Dan could muster, and he sank back into a semiconscious state. When the doctor arrived, Dan had not seen him before. It didn't matter; he just wanted to know from anyone, "I need to know what happened to my wife. Where is she?" He looked into the doctor's eyes, and suddenly he knew, even before the doctor began to speak.

"I am sorry to inform you of this…"

Dan gathered all his strength, "NO, NO, DON'T SAY IT! Don't say it." Somehow, if he didn't say it, it might not be true. But in his heart, in the deepest recesses of his soul, he knew the truth, but he couldn't accept it. Not now. Not on top of everything else.

"Don't take that from me. Oh God, don't take her from me. She's all I had left. Now you have taken it all. Don't do it. How could you? It's not right. You know it. It's not right."

Who was he talking to? He didn't know. It didn't matter. Nothing mattered anymore. Why wasn't he dead? It wasn't right. She was dead. The crew was dead. All those people dead. Why couldn't he be dead? Something was terribly wrong that this could happen.

They were talking to him. What were they saying? What did it matter? A low moan, a sob escaped through his lips. He sank back into oblivion. Now he welcomed it. Oblivion. He was slipping away. Oblivion. He wanted it; he did not want to come back. The darkness enveloped him. Time slipped away.

Then the darkness released him. It released him into a hellish pit. He was falling. Down a mineshaft? Air tore at his body and the walls rushed by at an increasing rate. At the bottom of the pit was noise, a primeval noise, a roar, a hiss of incredible volume. At the bottom, he would be consumed by the noise—devoured, swallowed alive.

In desperation, he jerked awake, gasping for air, body sweating and shaking. The full impact of his situation flooded into his mind. He couldn't take it. He shouldn't be here. He wanted to be with Manalani, and if she was dead then that was where he wanted to be. Nobody was in the room. The box beside his bed, which control was the morphine? He couldn't tell. Didn't matter. He turned them both on full. In seconds, he was drifting back into oblivion. Good. He hoped that the nurses would be busy with other patients. They should be.

He did not know that the system was purposely designed so that the maximum rate allowed would be far below the lethal dosage. He entered an extended sleep that allowed his body and mind to begin the process of repair and restructuring that was necessary for his recovery.

During that same period, the complex machinery of inquiry, investigation, and recovery was set into motion by the company and the governments of Hong Kong and the USA. The Hong Kong Civil Aviation Department, CAD, had the primary responsibility, but they would request the aid of other agencies. The NTSB GO team was collected and sent on its way. The FAA principal operating inspector for Intercontinental and the Air Carrier District Office in Singapore was on his way. Intercontinental was sending a contingent including an accident investigating team, the chief pilot, the MD-11 section chief, a public affairs officer, and the vice president of operations.

Of course, the local and international press descended like a cloud of vultures, feeding on the carrion of disaster, attempting to get conclusions or statements from anyone they could contact. This was big news, and the reputation of each news organization and its reporters depended on getting there first with the best information they could obtain for their next issue or broadcast.

A police unit stationed at the hospital kept the reporters at bay, but the uninjured passengers were free to make statements of their own. A reporter managed to get a statement from one of the firefighters saying he knew the plane was in trouble when it went by the station. Other witnesses from around the airport stated that they heard an explosion and fire coming from the airplane while it was in the air. This led to immediate speculation that there was a bomb on board, and that it was a terrorist attack. The reporters knew from experience that no responsible official would conjecture on any theory at this point, so they were left to their own devices to deliver the most exciting version they could muster.

While this maelstrom of activity swirled about, Dan lay in a deep sleep. The few times he drifted upwards toward waking consciousness he could sense the nightmare awaiting him and he drifted back. The first person outside the hospital staff to reach him was the local aircrew representative of IFALPA, the International Federation of Air Line Pilots. The local investigator of the CAD soon joined him. Later, Bill Konig, the International Chief Pilot, and Feron Stewart, the MD-11 Chief Pilot, and someone from the NTSB GO team entered the room. When Dan finally gained consciousness, he was comforted by the knowledge that they were all professionals and sympathized with his situation, but he was alarmed because he knew that the protracted and exhaustive process of investigation was about to begin.

At some emotional level, he wanted no part of it, though it was necessary. He still couldn't accept Manalani's death and those of the other crewmembers, so a process of subtle denial had begun. If he didn't think about it, they could still be alive.

The team enacted the formal ritual of sympathy and condolence, but it washed over Dan without affecting him. He appreciated their efforts, but his shock and grief were so deep that they were on a completely different level. Bill Konig, with his silvery gray hair and fatherly manner, at least instilled confidence.

Konig spoke first. "Dan, we realize that in your present condition you are in no position to give your official statement that will be necessary later, but if you can remember at all the events or cause as you see it, it would save the investigation team hours or possibly days running down blind alleys. This would be held in the confidence of this room."

Dan gathered his energies to reply. "Before that, I need some information. The hospital staff doesn't seem to know or is waffling on casualties. What is the bad news?"

He could see concerned looks pass between the men in the room. Finally, Bill Konig replied, "I'm afraid only two flight attendants from the crew and twenty-two passengers survived."

"I'm sorry. I'm sorry. I can't believe this really happened. These are people I knew—my comrades, my wife. I feel like this is a combat zone."

Konig replied, "We feel the same way, Dan; though our hurt can't be as great as yours."

Dan shelved the numbers away in the back of his mind to deal with later. Then he searched his memory for images he did not want to recall and replied cautiously, "First there was a computer EAD message, overheat, I think. Then the number two engine failed. I don't know why. The overheat shouldn't have caused it to happen by itself. We were handling that okay. Then we hit windshear, and we just couldn't climb out. I kept bringing the nose up, and we used max power, but it didn't work. That's all I can say now."

The CAD representative answered, "That's okay. That's enough. That gets us started in the right direction. We are recovering the flight data recorder and voice recorder now, and that will give us the details. We appreciate your help. Get some more rest. You need it."

Dan replied, "I hope I can. I don't know what else to say. I feel responsible. I feel like I let everyone down. Manalani dead. It is unbelievable. I keep hoping it's a bad dream."

Feron Stewart broke in, "That's why we don't want you to make a statement. It may take some time for your mind to clear." His round tanned face, steel-rimmed glasses, with crow's feet at the corners of his eyes, gave him a confident but sympathetic appearance that Dan had learned not to trust.

Dan asked, "What now? What happens next?"

Bill Konig replied, "Once the hospital clears you, we will get you back to the states. We will fly you back on one of our flights. You can use the flight crew bunk room to travel in."

"What about my kids? Have they been notified? I want to talk to them. Can they be flown over here?"

Konig and Stewart glanced at each other before Konig replied, "They have been notified by our director of internal relations. You certainly can talk to them; we have installed a phone in your room. However, since you only should be here a few days, we think it would be best if they see you on your return to the states."

Dan wasn't sure he agreed with this. He really wanted to see them, but he was too tired and devastated to argue the point. Instead, he asked, "What have the doctors told you about me?"

"Your lung and ribs will repair themselves, though they

will be painful. The various cuts and bruises of course aren't a problem. Your ankle is pretty badly messed up. They can operate on it here, or it can wait until you get back to the states. There is a good orthopedic surgeon here who will give you more details."

Dan said, "I know I want to get back. Even if they are good here, I still want it done back home."

Stewart replied, "I can understand that. From what I can tell that shouldn't be a problem." Then he looked at each of the men in the room. It seemed to Dan that there was some agreement reached among them. "Dan, there is one more difficult decision we must bring up. What are your wishes about Manalani?"

Dan was stunned. For a few minutes, at least he had diverted his mind from that loss. Wishes, he wanted her back. But he knew what they meant. What was to be done with her body? Her body, an ugly word that he felt no one should ever have to say. What could he say? They had never talked about it seriously. The assumption was that he would die first at some distant point in the future. They had a trust agreement and wills made up, but Dan had never carefully considered Manalani's death. Once, while working in the garden, she had jokingly said that she would like to go into the compost pile so she could come back as a carrot or broccoli.

Finally, Dan said, "I just don't know. We never really talked about it. We don't have any burial plans. I can't decide now. I need some time."

Stewart reassured him, "Of course. We understand. I don't want to put any more pressure on you. We will support you any way we can."

Dan dutifully answered, "I appreciate that. I'm sorry I'm so indecisive. I just can't think. I feel like I'm drifting in a terrible dream, and that one of these times when I wake up, she will be here." Dan began choking up. Tears formed at the corners of his eyes. He had to get control of himself. He could see them looking away, uncomfortable, afraid he was going to break down in front of them.

The CAD man said, "Well, gentlemen, I think we have enough to work on. We had better get started. We appreciate your help Dan. You have my condolences."

With that, the group began slipping out of the room, mumbling their well wishes. Dan could sense their relief to be leaving. He wished he was one of them, able to walk out of this room, a whole person, going into a world that made sense.

The aircrew representative was the last to leave. He said, "There should be an Air Line Pilots Association lawyer from the states contacting you. Meanwhile, don't talk to anyone else. You have their sympathy now, but they all have jobs to do, and if you get ground up in the process, you would just be another casualty."

The next few days Dan felt like he was in a world of hurt. At one level, he still wanted to die, though he largely suppressed the image of a few days ago when he had turned on the morphine. The morphine dulled the physical pain and clouded his mind, but it also produced the effect of everything being a terrible dream. He kept thinking he would wake up to a new reality, but each time he did wake up, a sense of immense loss flooded over him that the morphine could not erase.

The only relief in this dark scenario was a chance to talk to his younger son and his daughter. He reassured Mark and Liz that he would recover, and they would not need to travel to Hong Kong. However, when he tried to speak about Manalani, he choked up and had to hang up. After a few minutes, he did call back. Each effort to string a logical series of thoughts and sentences together required great concentration. Often, he found himself mumbling half coherently, as his thoughts wandered away from the subject at hand. They finally decided to have Manalani's body cremated and the ashes sent back home. Probably, Manalani's folks would like to have them. The idea of having an urn around was unacceptable. During their conversation, he noticed that Liz did all of the talking, but he didn't attach any importance to it at the time.

A doctor came in and explained the splint they would use on his leg for transportation back to California and the likely procedure used to correct his fractured ankle. Dan listened but felt like it hardly mattered. Feron Stewart visited him, and told him that they had recovered the digital flight data recorder (DFDR) and voice recorder. The local CAD office agreed to send the tapes back to the states to be decoded by the manufacturer and the NTSB. They were recovering the aircraft hulk from the water and reconstructing it in a maintenance hangar. Though Dan knew this was all very important, he also felt that somehow it did not concern him personally.

The doctors gave permission to pull the tube from his chest, and they released him for the return trip. By now, he had lost track of time. Without the date on his watch, days would have been meaningless. He sometimes could not recall how long he had been in the hospital and would have to ask. At one point he woke up from his drugged sleep completely disoriented and started to panic thinking he might be losing his mind. A nurse reassured him that it was only the effect of the medication, and he would recover when he could function without it.

Three days later they rolled him out to an ambulance, and he began the trip back stateside. The ambulance drove directly out to the MD-11 on the ramp. It was strange to approach the airport this way—helpless, not in control.

They used a service truck to lift him up to the jetway, and then they rolled him on board in a wheelchair. All these years he had watched people trundled on board in wheel chairs and now he was one of them. At the back of first class, they helped him struggle through the door and into the lower crew bunk. The company had a nurse to attend to his needs and medication on the return trip. Everyone was very solicitous to him. The flight crew dropped back to say hello and give him words of encouragement. He thanked them all, but at another level, he hated the attention and the feeling of dependence. Now he knew why injured animals holed up in some dark quiet place until they either died or recovered.

CHAPTER 4

Dan found the flight back comforting in a strange way. Familiar vibration, motions, and air-rush sounds allowed him to relax, and his thoughts drifted back to days when his goals and future seemed simpler and more secure.

As a child, his father instilled in him a strong work ethic, but like so many Norwegian farmers, his father's emotional range was limited. Crises and hardships were endured with little complaining. His mother and father worked well as a team, both with their appointed tasks. They were unquestionably bonded for life and loyal to each other, but even as a child, Dan knew that part of the harmony of their relationship was that they tamped down their emotions to keep the farm running smoothly.

His father was a stern disciplinarian, and when Dan's older sister rebelled, they sent her to a strict girl's school. When she returned home at breaks, she still challenged and subverted her father any time she could. It set the whole family on edge and often ended up with her sent to her room as though she was a child. When this happened, Dan could see her eyes lock with her father, but she was afraid to cross him.

Dan also held a certain fear of his father, but for him, it was not so much of a problem. He enjoyed the physical labor of working in the fields and milking the cows. Over the years, he and his father learned how to complement each other to cover most of the tasks involved on a dairy farm. He was the only son. His mother required a hysterectomy not long after he was born. Normally, several sons would be required to keep the farm running, so his father used hired hands to fill out the work force.

His hand-eye coordination and solid physical endurance made him a halfback on the football team, but he missed both practice and games when his duties on the farm took precedence. To his classmates, he was a good, solid, dependable guy, maybe a little stuffy and reined in, but in a small farm community in the fifties, this was the norm for country boys. The cowboy-pioneer ethic and myth still cast its brooding and stoic dominance over this part of the country. Dan unquestionably absorbed its values through his community and his father.

Even college was an easy transition. Though he had greater freedom, the turbulence of the sixties had not yet arrived. He had built up some rigid patterns to deal with the world, mostly learned from his father. They seemed to work well for him, so he saw no reason to change them. His lack of flexibility and emotional limits had caused various girls to drift out of his life. If they pushed him too hard emotionally, he would withdraw. He began to recognize this pattern but couldn't see his way out of it, so he accepted it as just part of his life. He felt that somehow, if the right woman came along, the magic would be there, and he would change.

***

As Dan reviewed these events, the MD-11 covered the first part of its thirteen-hour flight. On arrival at LAX, after the other passengers deplaned, paramedics reversed the loading process, and the ambulance took him to the UCLA medical center. Several pilots and officials from Intercontinental met him at the airport during the transition and wished him well. He asked when he could see Mark and Liz. An attendant told him he thought they preceded him to UCLA.

At the hospital, they took x-rays of his ankle and ribs before they admitted him to his room. Tomorrow, a Dr. Thomas would explain in detail to him the procedure that they would use to restructure his ankle. Restructure, that word did not sound good to Dan. When at last they wheeled him into a sunny room on the fifth floor, and he saw his daughter standing on the far side of the room, he felt that he had made an immense journey. She was in many ways a larger version of her mother. She had lighter skin and hair, but with the same dark brown oval eyes.

Suddenly, the pain, which had been merely physical, engulfed him in waves. An immense sense of loss washed over him. He could barely breathe. It hit him with hammer-like intensity. She's gone. *She's gone. Will I ever be able to look at Liz again without her being a symbol of losing Manalani?*

"Oh honey. What have I done?" As he raised his arms, she rushed to his side. The aides stepped aside. When she pressed her face down on his, he could taste the salty wetness from her tears, or was it his; it didn't matter. He just wanted to hold her forever and let the world disappear.

At one point, she pressed on his ribs with her arm and an involuntary gasp shuddered through his body. She pulled back.

"Oh Dad. I didn't mean to hurt you."

"Don't worry about it. The physical pain is nothing. I may look like a mess, but I will recover."

They were rolling him off the gurney onto the bed. The pain in his ribs caused him to gasp again. As they settled him in, Liz said, "Dad, we are just glad to have you back in any condition."

Liz covered her mouth with her hand for a moment. She was trying to cover a yawn, which turned into a gulp. Dan saw it as a sign of nervousness. Her body shook, and he knew she was on the verge of tears again. Before she could speak, he said, "Come on over here. Let's just hold hands." As they made contact, he felt another tremor go through her. For all he knew it might have started in him. He squeezed a little tighter.

Liz finally spoke. "Dad, nothing I can think of to say seems right, except that it is so good to see you."

Dan replied, "You can't believe how good it is to see you, too. I never thought I would see this day." He paused. His mind had slid again. He lost his train of thought. He could see the concern in her face and fought for control.

"Don't worry. They have me on drugs. Makes me goofy. I'll be okay once they get my ankle taken care of and I can come off them."

"When are they going to do that, Dad?"

"Dr. Thomas will see me tomorrow and then operate the next morning."

Liz said, "How bad is it? Can they fix it? I mean will you be back one hundred percent?"

"Apparently, that is not easily determined. It is going to take some screws or pins, and the recovery takes months. I won't know the details until I talk to the doc tomorrow. He is supposed to be the best."

Liz asked, "How are your ribs doing?"

Dan was relieved. He thought that she might open up the subject of Manalani, and he wasn't ready to cross that bridge yet. He just wanted to relax with her for a few minutes. "They only hurt when I laugh, and I'm not laughing much."

Dan felt that his attempt at humor was misplaced and quickly followed up with, "Actually the ribs hurt more than the ankle at times, but they say the ribs will heal by themselves. Nothing much they can do about them. The good thing was they didn't puncture my lungs."

A few moments of awkward silence followed. Neither of them knew what to say next. Manalani's ghost was hanging around the edges of their conversation. They did not know how to deal with it. Finally, Dan edged toward that gulf. "I assume that Takeshi and Nona were notified. How did that happen?"

Liz hesitated and looked away briefly before replying. "Someone from the airlines called us, to let us know what happened. They asked us if we wanted them to notify anyone else. At first, I thought I should do it. But then…I don't know…It's hard to say. I mean my mind was just whirling. I couldn't think of how I would say it. I finally took the easy way out and let them do it. I don't feel good about it, but…"

Liz alternately looked at the floor and ceiling and shifted her weight from side to side. Her discomfort was obvious. Dan searched for the right words to comfort her. "Look Liz, that was probably the best way. If anybody should have made the call, it would be me, but I was so broken up and in shock that I could hardly even think. Facing something like this…well, it's just too much."

Liz squeezed Dan's hand to get his attention. When Dan looked at her, he almost lost control. Again, he could see Manalani in her eyes, her face, her hair, and her mannerisms. She choked a little, cleared her throat and said, "It's really weird, I feel like I, we, are in a bad dream. Somehow, I will wake up, and we can start over, before all this happened. It just doesn't seem right."

Dan looked back and forth between her and the window for a few seconds; he did not want to set off any outbursts. For a moment, he looked at the sun, the trees in the breeze, the grass and the flowers, and his breath caught. She would never see that again. No. He had to stop that. He couldn't think of her that way now. He brought his mind back into the present, into the room. When he looked at Liz, he could see that she sensed his absence and was worried. She spoke next. "I just keep getting the feeling that something is really wrong. I mean, what did Mom do to deserve this? Or us. I mean I know people die in accidents all the time, but somehow it shouldn't happen to us. It just feels wrong. It just does. It does."

She couldn't go on. Dan could feel her trembling. He had to help her. What could he say? "I know honey. I felt the same way in Hong Kong. I'm sure not going to say that it's God's will, and it's no better to say that it's fate, or bad luck, or karma, or some other bull shit answer. I don't have an answer. But I know one thing, Manalani would want us to stick together and help each other any way we can. And that's what we've got to do. We can do that, right?"

He received immediate agreement, but then she mumbled something about Mark that Dan couldn't hear clearly or understand. "Well, what about Mark? Is he parking the car? Shouldn't he be here by now? I want to talk to him, too."

Suddenly, she tensed; her eyes opened wide, and she averted her face.

In his body, he felt a sinking sensation; a cold dry shiver ran through him. Something was wrong. "What is it? What about Mark? Has something happened to him?"

Her shoulders had been hunched. Now she drew them back, took a deep breath, then another, and said, "Dad, Mark isn't here, not at the hospital."

"Well then, where is he? What's happening?"

"He isn't coming."

"What do you mean he isn't coming? He can't come, or what is it? What's wrong?"

"He isn't coming because he doesn't want to see you."

"What! What's this about? How could he do this?"

Now Dan's stomach was churning. His jaw clenched; his whole body stiffened as though he was preparing to receive a physical assault. His mind slid sideways and whirled, but through it all, he realized he had sensed trouble since the moment he saw she was in the room alone. He was retreating from words he knew were forthcoming, and he did not want to hear. What part of him knew this ahead of time? It was like deja vu, sensing what was going to happen next and yet being powerless to stop it.

Liz broke the terrible silence hanging between them. "Dad, this is really hard to say, but Mark was completely broken up when we got the word. He took it a lot harder than I did. We held onto each other for a while, and then he turned and went into his room. I could hear him in there almost sobbing, but when I opened the door, he told me to get out. He wouldn't talk to the McCartys when they came over. He didn't come out for hours. I was feeling terrible myself. I couldn't deal with him."

"Okay, I got all that, but what did he say when he came out?"

"This is the hard part. He said, 'He killed her. I know he didn't mean to, but he killed her, the only one that was on my side.' I didn't know what to say. I was too shocked."

Each time Dan heard the words, "He killed her," he flinched visibly; he tried to sink into the bed, to disappear. He heard it as a death sentence. Worse. He was not going to die. He was going to live with those words for the rest of his life.

"Oh, my God! Doesn't he realize I have said that to myself at least a hundred times since the accident? Does he think that I don't feel that? And it isn't just her, hundreds of people, passengers, crewmembers died back there. How does he think that feels, to carry that with you, to wake up every morning with a feeling of dread, having that thought as your constant companion?"

Liz moved closer and squeezed his hand so hard it hurt. "I know Dad. It must be a terrible burden. And Mark will get over it. I think he's just in shock now."

"We are all in shock honey. It's at least as tough for you two as it is for me. We are all hurting and want to lash out at somebody. I know that is what happened to Mark."

"I don't like to say this, Dad, but maybe he is getting back at you. Maybe there is a little revenge motive here. I'm just guessing of course."

"Revenge? Getting back at me? For what? What have I done to deserve this?"

"You remember when you two had the fight in the car coming back from when he was in detention?"

"Of course I do, but what did he expect, that I would approve of what happened?"

"No, but then he was scared and felt alone, and he felt like he wasn't getting anything from you but a lecture about morals."

"You're right. I was out of line there. But to bring it up now? Now, of all times, is when we need to hang tough together."

"I think this has built up for years. You have forgotten what it is like to be a kid, and always be under someone's thumb, and you were pretty heavy handed sometimes."

"Well, maybe I was. And I'm sorry for it, too. I'm not the perfect father. I know that. Lyle left home as soon as he could, probably because of that. I've lost him forever. And now I feel like I'm losing Mark."

Liz sat on the side of the bed, turning her body towards Dan. An awkward position, but they didn't want to break contact. "Dad, when he does come, you are going to have to listen to him without judging him. You know you are not a very good listener."

"What do you mean I'm not a good listener? I have listened to your stories all these years, and listened to your troubles, too."

"Sort of, but your idea of listening was to solve problems and give out advice or approval. See, we only came to you if we had a problem you could solve or had done something good and wanted a pat on the back. If we screwed up, or just needed to talk something out, we always went to Mom first. She would listen. We always felt she took our side or at least didn't judge us."

"Oh, Oh. I never thought of it that way." He realized that

what Liz said was often true.

"When Mark screwed up in Hawaii, and you came down on him, that just confirmed his idea of you. So when Mom died, he felt he had lost the only person that was on his side."

"Okay, now at least I can see it, even if I don't agree with it. Somehow, we've got to pull through this together. I'll make it up to Mark somehow. Let him know that."

His voice was getting hoarse, and the force with which he delivered his last statements made his ribs hurt. His breath came in shallow gasps trying to get more oxygen in without breathing deeply. Liz looked alarmed, afraid that something was wrong. He reassured her. "I'll be okay. I just can't take a full breath without it hurting."

She said, "Well, maybe you shouldn't be talking so much then. It probably tires you out."

"Doesn't matter. This is important. I will get plenty of rest later."

As he said this, he could see tears begin to form in Liz's eyes. She leaned down and put her face next to his. It felt so good to feel her here. He didn't know how long they stayed that way. He wanted it to last forever. Eventually they released, she said goodbye, and left the room.

After Liz left, Dan felt crushed by the thought that he still was facing a call to Manalani's parents. How could he handle that? He fell asleep as he was framing in his mind variations on how he could initiate a conversation that would bridge the gulf that must now separate them. No matter how sympathetic they might feel toward him, on another level, he was the man who killed their daughter, their only child.

He fell asleep and started dreaming, the classic fear dream for pilots. He was climbing out from an airport in a canyon without enough performance to clear the wires and other obstructions ahead. Then, he was dodging down city streets with skyscrapers looming above him on both sides. Each decision he made was wrong, leaving him in a more desperate situation. He woke up in a cold sweat, body shaking, the icy clutch of adrenaline coursing through his body. He felt drained of all energy. He couldn't take this. What was happening to him?

He rang for the nurse and told her what had happened. She said that this was not an uncommon reaction for people that had been subject to a traumatic incident or accident. For some reason the mind needed to rerun the same event in varying forms until the emotional content of the event became defused. Drugs were available that could suppress this dreaming, but they were not good in the long run. Usually the dreams would slowly decrease in frequency and intensity. She did say that talking it out with a therapist usually helped. One of the doctors might be able to make a recommendation.

All of this was only slight comfort. Dealing with the accident itself was bad enough, but to have it intrude, into his sleep and dreams created an unwarranted burden. He did think of the therapist who he had seen about Mark's problem, but he didn't know if this was in her area of work. Besides, he had more immediate concerns to take up his time. He would just have to live with it for a while.

When Doctor Thomas arrived the next morning for his consultation, he was in a jolly mood. Dan could hear his laughter down the hall before he entered. What was he laughing about? This was serious business. His whole future might depend on the outcome of this operation.

"How are you feeling today, Captain Swanton? I hope our accommodations suit you."

Who cares about the accommodations? My future lies in your hands. Let's talk about that. He restrained himself. "The room is fine, and it seems that hospital meals have improved over what I last remember."

"It's not the Ritz, but we are getting better. Now I suppose you would like to talk about your ankle procedure."

No, you fool. I'd just like to discuss the weather and politics. "Yes, of course. My whole future in flying depends on regaining strength and mobility in that ankle."

"That shouldn't be a problem, though your recovery will entail several months of therapy. You probably won't be back to 100%. For instance, you may not be able to play tennis for a year, and then maybe not at the same level as before."

"That's a disappointment, but I can live with it. How long before I can get back to flying?"

Doctor Thomas looked off to the side before replying. "That depends of course on how you respond to therapy, but it will be several months."

"Several months," replied Dan. "That could be three, six, nine. Give me something better."

"Well, it certainly should be less than a year. Quite possibly within six months. Each person's ability to repair and respond is highly variable. Your physical therapist will have a better feel for that, after he or she starts to work with you."

Dan didn't like this hedging, but he realized it was an innate part of the doctor's business. "You can at least tell me what the operation entails."

Doctor Thomas smiled. He was on his own territory now. "I

don't know how well you can read these x-rays, but what they reveal is that you have a bi-malleolar fracture of the ankle. That means that both the major bones of the leg have broken at the ankle. Our first concern is that we align the joint perfectly. This is to prevent post-traumatic arthritis later on. The ankle is subject to more pressure than any other joint in the body. That means we have to fix the joint so that the fracture doesn't move while the ankle repairs itself. We do that by attaching screws through the bones on the leg and the ankle. Usually a stabilizing plate is also inserted on one side."

"That sounds pretty major to me," Dan said. "What happens next?"

"You will have a cast to wear for four weeks, then a removable cast, somewhat like a ski boot, for six weeks. After about three months, you will be able to bear full weight on the ankle with the use of an air splint or taping. The screws and plate may come out in six months to a year."

"What do you mean, may come out?" Dan asked. "Do they or don't they?"

"Sometimes they are left in permanently. They have no deleterious effect."

"Do you think I can fly with a plate and screws in my ankle?" Dan didn't like the implication of that pronouncement.

"I don't see why not. You might have a small restriction and a slight limp. You will probably want to use a cane for a while."

"Oh, that's just great," Dan said. "Can you imagine getting on an airplane where your captain limps out using a cane? I can see it now. Here comes our captain, Dan Swanton, our token cripple. Welcome aboard."

Doctor Thomas shifted nervously before replying. Dan could

tell he was not happy with the way things were going. *Tough luck. It's my life that hangs in the balance here.*

"Well, you see Captain Swanton, that's why I can't be more precise on my estimate of your recovery. It is largely out of my control. In your case, appearance may be just as important as function. I can't help you there."

"I can see your problem," Dan replied. "I will just have to accept that it is going to take a long time. So when does the operation take place?"

"I have you scheduled for tomorrow at 9:30."

"Good, I want to get things rolling as soon as possible."

"I will see you tomorrow morning then, Captain Swanton. The nurses will prep you first thing in the morning. No breakfast. The anesthetic sometimes upsets people's stomachs and that could cause complications on the operating table."

"That's no problem," Dan said. "Get the ball rolling."

As Doctor Thomas left, Dan could see that he wasn't sorry to leave. *Too bad I wasn't your model patient, Doc, but I've got too much riding on this to be sensitive to your feelings. Besides, after tomorrow morning, you are history. I can see though that I had better develop a good working relationship with my therapist.*

By the time they rolled Dan into the operating theater, he was feeling no pain, literally. They had sedated him during the pre-op. The anesthesiologist was a good-looking redhead with a nice figure, but it hardly registered with him. As Doctor Thomas entered the room, he nodded to her when she looked questioningly at him. She turned a valve on a bottle on the tree above Dan's head and said with a smile, "Good night, Dan. Sweet dreams."

He felt a cold sensation rush up his arm. When it reached his neck, he was out. Without any sense of time passing, he was awake in the recovery room, blinking at the strong lights there, and feeling like a truck had run over him.

He felt helpless for a period after the operation. Sleeping with the cast was difficult. For a few days, he could only lie on his back. It made a big difference when he could roll onto his side. He could not stand up for more than a few minutes. Blood would pool in the ankle and it would begin to throb. Going to the bathroom was a major effort. His abilities improved slowly, but he hated his helpless, childlike, dependent situation. He noticed that most of the staff unconsciously responded to patients in a condescending manner. They equated a physical problem with mental impairment, and that a patient couldn't function normally on any level.

CHAPTER 5

One of Dan's visits in the hospital was by Feron Stewart and Bill Konig. They needed his official accident statement. While he realized that it would clear the air and allow him to think about other things, it would also force him to recall details he would rather forget. The gray layer of stratus outside fit his mood. When they entered the room, he couldn't tell if their forced camaraderie was to make him feel at ease or to cover their own nervousness. They brought a short stocky woman with them and introduced her to Dan as a stenographer to take his statement.

He decided to cut the chitchat and get on with it. "Has any info come out of the investigation yet?"

Stewart replied, "They do know that the tail-mounted engine shut down. Apparently, when the high-pressure bleed system failed at a joint, the hot air melted a bundle of wires that sent information to the FADEC system. Since the data given to the engine control system was either missing or wrong, the internal logic was programmed to shut the engine down. The flight recorder shows that you had full power on the other engines and a good pitch attitude, so that indicates wind shear. Of course, they are being careful not to make any conclusions yet."

"I should hope so," Dan said. "So, what you are telling me,

is that I had an engine that was physically perfectly capable of producing power, but because the computer that controls the engine couldn't figure out what was happening, it shut the engine down, and left me hung out to dry. How do you think that makes me feel?"

There was a pause as each man in the room evaluated the implications of Dan's statement. Finally, Bill Konig said, "I can sympathize with your feelings Dan, but the situation isn't really much different from the older airplanes, where in the case of a failure of a linkage to the fuel controller, you would be forced to shut the engine down. Besides, who knows what other damage that hot air might do?"

"But to me there is an important difference," Dan replied. "In that case, I get to make the decision, not some computer. But I realize I'm flailing a dead horse here. It's not going to change what happened, and they are not going to change the way engines are designed. So, let's get on with it. Now how do we go about making this statement?"

Konig replied, "There will be an official report to my office that will be forwarded to the NTSB, FAA, and the Hong Kong CAD."

Dan winced slightly, looked out the window, and said, "Oh, that's right. I forgot that the FAA gets a swipe at me too, don't they? That's two strikes already."

"I don't think you will need to look at it that way, Dan. There shouldn't be any concern about violations of Federal Air Regulations."

Dan cut in. "No matter. They will still go over my records with a fine tooth comb, won't they?"

"That's true," Konig replied, "But you shouldn't have any

problem there either. Your records are good."

"What about that proficiency check I busted about four or five years ago when I had the flu?"

"Sure, that will come up, but it shouldn't have any bearing on this case. That can happen to anybody."

Dan still didn't like it, but he realized there was nothing he could do about it.

Konig went on to explain, "All we need to do is get down the facts as you can remember them. No need to amplify them or offer opinions. As usual with any official statement, the less said the better."

"Yes, I get that for sure." Dan replied.

Feron Stewart motioned to the woman, "Mrs. Kettering, you can sit at the table here if you wish. We may engage in some unrecorded conversation, but when I want you to write it down, I will signal you. Then we will make sure that Dan agrees with every statement before you type it up for him to sign. Is that okay with you Dan?"

"I guess so. I never was a good typist anyway. I'll be glad to have someone else do it. Where shall I start?"

"Anywhere you like that you feel might be significant," Stewart said.

Dan stared out the window for a few seconds. Then he drummed his fingers on the table. He knew he had to do it, but he wasn't sure where to start. Finally, he said, "Everything seemed routine as we rolled out onto the runway. There was some rain, but nothing unusual. We tried to tilt the radar up to get a good scan of the cloud buildups and rain, but the ground clutter covered it up.

"Roll-out seemed normal but right after liftoff we got an

overheat warning. It seemed like only seconds later number two shut down. I figured we still had it handled, but then we ran into turbulence."

Stewart asked, "Can you describe the type of turbulence? Did it seem severe?"

"No, it wasn't severe, hardly moderate," Dan replied, "If I had all three engines running, I wouldn't have thought much about it. Then we began to get into sink, and I knew we were in trouble."

"Do you know how high you got before you ran into the sinking air?

"No, I can't say. Probably a couple of hundred feet."

"That's okay. We can get that from the DFDR. Go ahead."

"I was getting altitude call outs indicating we were slowly sinking, so besides firewall power I rotated up to an eighteen to twenty-degree pitch up. I still thought we were going to pull out of it. Then I began to get intermittent stick shaker. The airplane was also lurching around. I had a hard time holding pitch attitude and heading, but I didn't want to put in large control inputs that would make the spoilers rise and increase drag."

"At any point did you feel it was hopeless?"

"Not really. I kept thinking, this is not going to happen. Not on my airplane. Then at some point, maybe around fifty feet, instead of getting ground effect, the airplane just seemed to sag."

Dan realized that as he made this last statement with his jaw clenched, and his voice sounded thin and strained. He tried to relax by taking a couple of deep breaths. There was silence in the room. No one wanted to break into his train of thought. He forged ahead.

"I think there was an initial impact with the tail, which I felt. Then another tremendous impact. I suppose that was when the wing and engines dug in. I blacked out. The next thing I knew we were settling into the bay. Only the emergency cockpit lights were on. I looked over at Greg Allred and down at Dick Borman and somehow knew they were both dead. I couldn't see Tom Spanger at first. He was wedged behind my seat and the sidewall. He didn't respond to my voice or touch. Then, when the water started rising around me, I realized my left foot was jammed under the rudder pedal. It was unbelievable, but I was being dragged to my death after surviving the impact. I kept struggling to free my foot, but I finally blacked out again. Next thing I knew I was on the surface gasping for air and completely disoriented."

Stewart asked, "So, you don't really know how you got to the surface?"

"No, I don't," Dan replied, "But somehow there is a puzzle there. I can sense it, but I just can't recall it. Does this stuff have to go into the official report?"

Stewart and Konig looked at each other and at Mrs. Kettering. Konig replied, "No, I don't think so. I think we can just state that while in a semiconscious state you were freed from the wreckage and made your way to the surface."

Dan relaxed slightly. "I'm glad of that. It's all a mystery to me, and one I'd rather not contemplate. Too many lives lost. Too much damage done. I still can't believe it."

Konig said, "Dan, you did the best you could. That's all anyone can do. Don't blame yourself for anything. We will have Mrs. Kettering type this up. You can check it out. Make changes if you want, and we will submit it."

They stayed on for a few minutes of conversation to make Dan feel at ease, but he was glad when they left. The effort had made him feel wasted, and his ankle was throbbing again. He leaned back on the bed and rang for a nurse.

***

This was one of those times he just wished for oblivion. Instead, his thoughts drifted back to his family and oldest son, Lyle. He was an enigma for Dan. Physically he inherited most of Dan's genes, the narrow frame, outsize hands and feet, and hawk-like face, but ever since he could talk, he and Dan didn't get along. Whatever Dan wanted him to do, he would turn a different direction. He had no interest in sports. He did have musical talent, piano and composition, but his obsession with rock music was something Dan couldn't begin to understand. He was always running off to concerts and forming groups with his friends.

Dan couldn't stand the noise, so he let him out of the house whenever he was with the band. Then he wished he hadn't when Lyle got into trouble with drugs. Luckily, as a student, Lyle received probation, and the experience scared him enough that he seemed to be straight since then. All of this just about drove Dan around the bend. Nothing seemed to work except that Manalani was able to talk with Lyle.

Lyle had been such a problem that, for a while, Dan gave up on having any more children. Manalani convinced him that this wasn't a mold that each child would follow. She read books on psychology that Dan couldn't absorb. She also seemed to have an intuitive sense about these things that Dan didn't share. She told him that it wasn't his fault; parents can't always keep a child on the right path, but Dan never could fully accept that. Often he reviewed what he had tried to do with Lyle, and how he might have changed it.

When Lyle moved out of the house after high school, Dan gave up on him. Their relationship improved, at least to the point that they could talk without being at each other's throats. Manalani said now that Lyle was on his own, he did not need to feel threatened by Dan. Dan felt that the only time he ever threatened Lyle was when he was way out of line. What else could he do when a kid wouldn't listen and was headed for trouble? Anyway, he was relieved that the load was off his back and that their relationship was smoothing out.

Then fate intervened. Lyle was out joyriding with some of his friends from the recording industry in New York—raining, wet pavement, heavy traffic. The car in front of them swerved and hit its brakes. Their car hit it a glancing blow, but the impact lifted them up and they rolled over the guardrail, crashing down onto the docks below. One of the passengers survived with disabling injuries, but not Lyle. When the word came through, Dan was more than stunned and devastated. A wave of guilt swept through him, that he had failed Lyle at every turn of his life. He had sensed that Lyle was headed for trouble, and he felt he had failed in a parent's basic responsibility, to safeguard his family. After long talks with Manalani, he was able to reconcile the loss, and rationalize his guilt. But now, he faced it again, combined with Manalani's death, coming back to haunt him.

***

Dan anticipated leaving the hospital with mixed feelings. Of course, he was glad to be going home. Besides leaving the hospital environment, he was also glad to be done with visitors, with their mumbled words of condolence and attempts to cheer him up. The effect achieved was usually the reverse. A few, like some of his old flying buddies, did rouse him out of his dark ruminations, but mostly he wanted to be left alone. At home he would be faced directly with the loss of Manalani. So far, her death had been an abstraction. His surroundings were so alien, that part of him could believe that she would still be there when he got home. He knew that seeing all her things there would be a shock. Though their good friends the McCartys had offered to pack away Manalani's personal effects before he arrived, he decided that this was something he had to do himself. He didn't want to make a shrine out of their bedroom, and the act of putting her things away might help the process of closure. When a staff psychologist had stopped by for an interview with him, they had discussed this subject, and it made sense to Dan.

The hospital wanted to use an ambulance to transfer Dan, but he stood his ground and insisted on going home in the Cherokee. Mark would drive him. When he called home, he asked Mark specifically if he would do this. Mark agreed. Dan took this as a good sign. Perhaps on the drive home he could begin to close the gulf that had opened between them. The orderlies did insist on taking him out in a wheelchair. Though Dan resisted that idea, he had to admit they were right. By the time they reached the car he was sweating with effort and pain. When they rolled through the doors of the hospital, traffic noise and fumes assaulted Dan's senses, and he welcomed them. He felt like he had been in a sterile cocoon since the accident, and he wanted out to regain his sense of autonomy.

His meeting with Mark filled the car with the detritus of unexpressed emotion on both sides. They were on guard and unable to cross the barrier between them. As Mark started the car, Dan looked across at him. A sense of immense loss opened a hollow pit of anxiety in Dan's stomach. His only remaining son was turning into a stranger. He wanted to reach across to him, to have some physical contact and reassurance, but the distance was too great with this barrier between them.

Once they were rolling, Dan was content to let sights and sensations flood his body and brain. But after a brief interlude, he decided it was his job to open the subject of their separation. "Mark, it seems like we have some difficult things to discuss."

Mark glanced at him briefly and said, "You're right Dad, but I don't want to right now."

"What could be a better time? This is the first time we have had any time together."

Mark leaned back and exhaled. "Look, I just don't want to yet. I'm still too wound up, or something. I would think you have enough on your plate right now anyway, just dealing with going back home. Our stuff can hang fire for a while."

"Well, if you don't want to talk, I still have something to say."

"You always do."

"Come on, Mark. Give me a break. Do you think this is easy for me?"

"No, it isn't easy for either of us. I'm sorry. Go ahead."

"As a result of what happened, the crash I mean, it seems

that a big gulf has opened up between us."

"Wrong, Dad, it's always been there. You are just finding out about it now."

"You won't let up, will you."

"Hey, who's the one not letting up here? I told you I didn't want to talk about it. Look, I'm sorry again."

Dan realized that maybe Mark was right. Maybe this wasn't the right time. He still had one thing that he wanted Mark to know. "Look, I really haven't been the father to you that I should have been. What I'm saying is that I realize that Manalani was the one that really held us together as a family. She made it easy for all of us. She was the one who brought us together as a family. But now, now that she isn't here, well, we have to do it ourselves. There are tough times ahead. Somehow, there will be good ones too. Right now, it's just hard to see when they will be coming. I just want you to know that I will be there for you, whatever happens."

There was a long pause before Mark looked over and replied, "Dad, I really appreciate that, but I still don't want to talk about it. Anyway, we'll be home in a few minutes."

Dan nodded in agreement. His pulse raced as the familiar surroundings of the neighborhood swept into view. Dan looked out the window. Eucalyptus trees and red tile roofs formed a reassuring sight.

As they turned up Via Dolores, above the golf course, his level of excitement rose. His face flushed, his skin tingled, his thoughts flashed rapidly in a discontinuous stream. He wondered why all this was happening. The McCartys' had parked their car in front of the house, and they were coming down the drive to meet him.

Dan turned to Mark and said, "Stop by the curb. I want to walk up to the house."

"Okay Dad, if that's what you want."

Mac stooped over to open the door and said, "Welcome home, soldier. Your troops await your orders."

"Thanks for coming Mac. I guess you can help me get this stupid leg out. Hi Ruth, thanks for coming over. Liz, honey, hand Ruth the crutches. Once I get upright, I should be okay."

With the crutches under his arms, he hobbled up the driveway. Each impact was painful, but he leaned into the pain, deriving a sense of satisfaction from it.

"Liz, please open the garage door. I want to go through to the back patio."

Liz rushed ahead to comply. As he stood waiting, Dan took in the smell of the trees and cut grass, of paint and asphalt. A suppressed part of him was returning to life. The creaking and grinding of the garage door lift were comforting sounds.

As he swung by Manalani's Mustang, a small lump formed in his throat, but he forced it down. When they reached the patio, Dan handed his crutches to Ruth and lowered himself into a chair, with his left leg stuck awkwardly in front of him. He was facing the woodpile set under the eaves of the house. During the cold winter months, Dan loved to build fires. He always had the wood, well-seasoned oak and madrone, delivered in unsplit logs. He insisted on splitting it himself, his favorite form of exercise. The right tools, a Mackinaw eight-pound splitter, wedges, and a double-bitted ax for light work, rested next to a log cradle he had built himself. His proficiency was a legacy from his days on the farm. Manalani and he shared some of their most relaxed and intimate times sitting in front of the fire. Now, even the woodpile represented a sense of loss.

Dan fought that feeling. He felt that he had to say something positive. "It feels good to be back, but I can see my damn leg is going to give me problems." Dan wasn't sure where this conversation was going to take them.

Mac said, "It looks good to see you sitting there. You've been through a lot."

"And I've got more coming up," Dan said, as a continuation of Mac's line of thought.

There was a long pause. Nobody wanted to break into that dark area of discussion that would logically follow.

For the moment, Dan was satisfied to let the late afternoon sun penetrate his body and mind. But then he could sense the quiet pattering of the little feet of fear running behind all the thoughts he collected to protect himself. He grew tense as he gathered up his energies to cross the line into the dark domain of the world he and Manalani shared, a world, which for years had been a shelter, and now represented everything he did not want to face.

The conversation skittered around, treading lightly on the thin ice of Manalani's absence. Dan's attention turned inward. Years ago, his father taught him to face his fears, and when he could identify them, to walk into them. It had been a long time since he had found it necessary to call up that advice, but it seemed like the time had come again.

During a pause in the conversation, Dan spoke, "Let's go ahead and move into the house. Ruth, can you hand me my crutches again."

As if in a play, he watched as everyone moved into appointed positions, Ruth by his side, Liz and Mark moving ahead to open the door, Mac to the rear guard position.

As soon as he crossed over the threshold, Dan was acutely aware of Manalani's imprint. The kitchen table, plants and flower arrangements, the furniture, artwork and crafts, all of these things were choices made by her with his agreement. He sensed that everyone was studying him with covert glances to see how he held up.

He turned right, down the hallway toward their bedroom. A surreal clarity began to envelop his consciousness. The pain pulsed up his leg with each heartbeat. The pressure of the crutches under his arm reflected the sound of their tapping on the tiles. His breath rasped slightly, and his feet scraped unevenly on the tiles. The smell of basil from the kitchen gave way to eucalyptus in the bedrooms.

He considered this strange psychological state. Why this acute awareness, and what was there to fear from it?

When he turned through the door and entered the bedroom, like a predator waiting its chance, the fear charged him. He had made a big mistake. Her clothes were hanging in the closet, her books on the table on her side of the bed. He could see into the bathroom, her perfume, brushes, and makeup were still in place. The entire room was suffused with her presence, and he couldn't face it.

He staggered. The pain of her absence hit him in the chest, as though he had broken his ribs again. He gasped, trying to control his breath. Abruptly he turned to leave the room, but he was clumsy with the crutches. One tip caught in the carpet. He was off balance, twisting, falling down. This couldn't be happening. A feeling of unreality arose, like that during the crash. Hands reached out for him, but they were already too late.

He kept his bad leg free by rotating his body, but he was tangled up in the crutches. A searing pain flooded his right elbow as he hit it. He heard clattering sounds from the crutches at the same instant his head hit the carpet.

An instant of silence, then a sudden babble of voices. He was rolling back and forth on the carpet clutching his right elbow. Mark's face swept into his vision. "Dad! Dad! What's wrong? Are you okay?"

Through clenched teeth, Dan said, "No. No, damn it. My elbow."

"Did you hit it?"

"Of course I did."

"Can I help?"

"No, just give me a minute." The pain was rapidly subsiding.

"What about your leg?"

"I think it's okay. Can't really tell. It hurts all the time. I just feel stupid lying here tangled up with the crutches."

Both Mark and Mac leaned down to disentangle him and help him up. Ruth was crying and said, "Oh, you poor dear."

"I'm not a poor dear, damn it. I'm just clumsy. Damn crutches anyway."

The anger gave Dan energy. He also hoped that it would distract the others from what had just happened. Maybe they hadn't picked up on it. No, that wouldn't work. He was going to have to talk about it. The effort and complication of getting him upright and back to the kitchen area kept everyone busy for a few minutes. That gave him time to collect himself.

He directed everyone to the little breakfast nook overlooking the pool and yard, where the family had always held their conferences. He seated himself looking out with his back to the kitchen. There would be fewer distractive reminders that way. The tablecloth, the salt and pepper shakers, the window curtains, how was he ever going to live here without her? He approached the matter of her loss in his usual direct and straight-out way. "Look, I made a major mistake back there."

Mac said, "You mean falling?"

Dan looked at him sharply. Was he being dense?

"No, I mean thinking that I should shoulder the burden of, ah, cleaning out…Oh no." He could feel his voice trembling. The lump was coming up in his throat again. He couldn't shake it. He tried to continue, "Letting go of Manalani's things." His body started trembling. He was choking up, breaking up. He couldn't let this happen.

Simultaneously, they all moved toward him. He felt Mark's arms around his shoulders. Liz took both his hands in hers. Mac put one hand on his shoulder. Ruth looked imploring and sad.

Dan rocked back and forth slightly. All he could say was, "Oh God, Oh God. It's not right." He pulled one hand free and wiped the corner of his eyes. Then he said, "We all share in the loss. All of us. She was so important to us. Mac and Ruth, thank you. Thank you for being with us in this, this hour of our distress. You are true friends."

Ruth said, "That's what we're here for. We're not just fair-weather friends."

Liz replied, "Dad's right. We really appreciate everything you've done."

"Well, there's more that we can do," Mac said. "I think that Ruth and I can put away most of Manalani's things. That would be a tough task for any of you. Your only decision would be to decide what things you would like left out."

Everyone looked at Dan. He realized that he was to make some decision. "Well, pack away her clothing and I guess the cosmetics, unless Liz wants them."

"No, Dad, she and I don't have the same coloring. I'd feel weird about it anyway."

"What about jewelry?" Ruth asked.

Dan looked up at the ceiling, then at Liz. She shrugged. Then he said, "That's a tough one. We'll have to think about it. Just get it together, and Liz and I will go over it later."

The conversation moved on to other areas, and the level of tension in the room lessened. Dan started feeling better now that there was a plan of action, and he didn't feel so adrift.

Dan spent that night on the couch. Then he moved to the guest bedroom. He would wake up several times during the night with vague memories of disturbing dreams. After a week, he slept in their bedroom, and then only because he had consumed some wine along with the pain pills he had taken, and he was in a stupor.

On his first night in their bedroom, he made a disturbing discovery. Manalani's slippers were hidden under the bed. He picked them up and brought them to his face. The scent of her body still existed in them. Immediately, he was consumed by intense memories of her. Her feet were always large for her size with a noticeable space between the big toe and the next one. When he massaged her feet, which she loved to have him do, he would slip a finger into the space and stroke it. There was a slight sexual suggestion to it, and it formed a regular part of their foreplay. Her soles were always callused because she enjoyed going barefoot. He softened them with oil. Her foot had a pronounced arch and he remembered stroking from there over the ankles and on up to the skin and muscle of her calf. With the slippers against his face, lying there, she was in the room with him. He went to sleep with the slippers in his hands.

In the morning, when he realized what he had done, he felt an embarrassed childlike guilt rising up in him. Was there something wrong with him, that these slippers would be so important? Was he entering a world of demented fantasy? He was adrift on a psychological sea where he had no bearings, no course that he could steer. He told nobody about it, and kept the slippers with him at night for over a month, before he let them go.

CHAPTER 6

His life was unraveling. Looking back, he decided that things started to go wrong about the time he decided to transition to the MD-11 over a year ago. He remembered coming in from his company pre-rating ride late that night. Manalani was shocked when he stormed into the bedroom. Usually he quietly slipped into bed next to her. She asked what was wrong.

"I just finished the check ride from hell. I got a clue when I handed over my packet of papers to the weasel who asked for my license and medical. This guy even looked like a weasel, narrow pointed face, tiny ears, beady eyes, little narrow shoulders. That didn't help any. I kept some other documents in that packet, radio-telephone license, engineer's card, ALPA membership. He handed it back to me and said, 'What is all this shit, I just want your license and medical' Things went down hill from there.

"I missed one of the performance problems because I misinterpreted his question. Then he wouldn't let me do it over or give me another one.

"When we got to the flying part, things went okay until climb out. Bill, the other pilot, got his check first, and he was working on a navigation problem using the FMS computer. He was having trouble and I leaned over to help. The check pilot told me, 'No. He's got to do this part himself. This isn't crew concept. You just sit over there and be the dummy. Leave the FMS to him'

"So I'm sitting there with nothing to do, and I notice that the power settings are wrong. They are still at take-off instead of climb power. I figure that either we, or the computer, had screwed up, so I started making a correction on the keyboard. Later, I realized that he had set this up as the next problem to be solved, but he hadn't given me any sign of that.

"So he turns to me and says, 'What are you doing?'

"Just fixing the power. It's set wrong."

'Well, how are you doing that?'

"At first I didn't understand what he was getting at, so I replied, 'Using the keyboard, of course.'

"Then he says, 'And is that part of the FMS?'

"Suddenly I see where we are headed, and I'm already mad. All he needed to do is just look at me and shake his head or finger, and I would have realized what was happening. So I grudgingly reply, 'Yes, of course.'

"Then here comes the kicker; he says, 'I thought I told you to keep your hands off the FMS.'

"Well, it's a good thing I was strapped into the seat, because I wanted to hit him so bad I was shaking. Bill told me he could see my ears turn red, and the blood pulse in my forehead.

"It wasn't just that I felt insulted. He struck a sensitive nerve from the past. My father used to say to me when I was a kid, 'Didn't I tell you to keep your hands off that?' and it made me mad back then.

"I was so furious that when my turn came, it affected my performance. I couldn't concentrate. Up until then, I didn't think anyone could get to me that way. So anyway, I'm stumbling through the rest of the check. At one point, the simulator breaks down, and we get held up for about an hour. It's already 01:30. We are all tired and want to get the hell out of there. I'm doing what should be my last approach, an engine-out, hand-flown, ILS down to one hundred feet. I figure it will be to a landing since I had done a go-around earlier.

"Just as we get to minimums, I'm looking out and see nothing, so I call 'TOGA', that's short for take-off or go-around; we start going around. At the same instant, Bill says, 'Runway in sight,' but it's too late. Once I give the command, TOGA, we are committed to going around. We level off at our missed approach altitude, and I know there is going to be trouble.

"The check pilot says, 'You know why you missed the approach?'

"I know I'm being led down the path to slaughter, but what else can I say besides, 'I didn't see the runway, of course.'

'Why didn't you see the runway?'

"Now I am pissed. I don't want to play this game anymore, so I reply, 'You tell me.'

'Your seat was set too low,' he says in his most caustic tone of voice.

"Now, I've been in that simulator for many hours. I've shot numerous low-vis approaches in it. I know where my seat needs to be positioned. I also know that in that simulator, independent views are flashed onto each pilot's window by the projectors that are supposed to be locked in sync with each other by a master clock. Sometimes they get a little out of sync, and it only takes a second to screw up a low-vis approach. I told him that. He wasn't buying it and said, 'Do it again with your seat higher.'

"Well, at this point, I should have said, 'This check ride stops right now until this is sorted out between you and me.' But it's the last maneuver; then we can go home, so I grit my teeth and do it.

"When we get to the debrief room, I'm seething. If he busts me on this ride, I'm going to deck him. I've got my fist cocked and my shoulder's twitching. It might be the end of my career, but I don't care. I think that maybe he sensed he crossed the line into dangerous territory, because his only real comment as he signed my check ride sheet was, 'It wasn't a pretty ride, but it was satisfactory.' I almost started in on him, but I realized I was treading on thin ice too, so I snatched the papers from him, glared at him, and walked out without saying a word. Even now, when I start in on it, I can feel my blood pressure rising."

Manalani said, "I can feel it rising too. You better come over here where I can give you a back rub. I haven't seen you this worked up in a long while."

"I guess I'm mostly mad at myself for letting it happen. Mmm-that feels good. The one good thing I can think about this is that it will make the FAA rating ride seem like a piece of cake." Dan started to relax under her hands. Within minutes, his complaints were reduced to mumbles, and he was drifting off to sleep.

The following morning, when she touched him, he awoke with a start and had that disoriented feeling that often comes from falling asleep at odd times. Her presence and the familiar surroundings of the house brought him out of it quickly. Sometimes, when this happened on a trip in a hotel, he would have to lie quietly for several seconds until he could recall which hotel, which city, and which trip this was. Sometimes the hotels seemed too much the same, and the days and nights blurred together, particularly when too many time zones were involved.

At breakfast, they discussed their upcoming trip to Hawaii. Dan asked, "How are the kids taking to the idea?"

"Liz thinks it's great. She's all for it and thinks she would like to stay on after we come back. Mark wants to go, but he doesn't want to miss out on water polo. There are several guys gunning for his position. On the other hand, he has been looking forward to surfing in the islands."

As Dan considered these decisions, Manalani broke in on his thoughts. "What about Liz? What do you think about her staying on?"

"Well, she's got a good head on her shoulders. I trust her, but there would be a lot of temptation over there, without us to watch over her."

Manalani realized how difficult this subject was for him. Even though it was unrealistic, Dan expected Liz to be a virgin until she married or at least was planning the event. "Look dear, it's going to happen someday. I've talked to her about it. She knows the dangers and how to protect herself. At sixteen, she's a lot more mature in some ways than you realize. She's not going to lose her heart on a fling with some young stud."

"It's not her heart I'm worried about. These days it's a gamble with her life."

Manalani set down her drink, put a hand on his, and replied, "She knows all that. Kids today are a lot more savvy and sophisticated than you were at their age. They have to be. It's both a blessing and a curse, but it is definitely a fact. She can stay with my folks. She has friends to hang out with. She will be okay. But I can't guarantee she will come back a virgin."

When she said that, his knuckles whitened on the chair arms. Though they had talked about this before, he still couldn't accept it. He would agree with her verbally, but at another deeper level, Liz was still his little girl. That day of reckoning was going to be hard on him. He also knew he was dense and inflexible about some things.

At another deeper level, he had a fear of losing her. For a while, after Lyle's death, he would hardly let Mark and Liz out of his sight. They were young enough that they rebounded quickly from the shock; Lyle was older, and they weren't close emotionally. He had always been a loner and took little interest in their lives.

The combination of remorse and guilt in Dan caused him to lose his self-confidence and sense of assurance. He began to wait up for them and ask them to call home if they were delayed. Mark and Liz chafed at his constant hovering over them. As his anxiety gradually lessened, their relationship normalized, but anytime they were out and the phone rang unexpectedly, he would feel the sharp chill of dread for a few moments. More than once his friends heard him say, "No parent should ever have to face burying one of their children. It's a task with no redeeming qualities."

Dan shifted the subject. "Did you send in the deposit for the Strane's house?"

"Yes, that was no problem," Manalani replied. "Later in the summer it's rented out, but the summer rush hasn't started. Of course, my folks made an offer for us to stay with them. I told them that we would be better off at the Stranes."

"I guess we had better give up on my plan for Kauai," Dan said. "With only about ten days I don't want to break the trip up after all. Besides, I would like to do some glider flying out at Dillingham. There should be time for you and the kids to go up if you want to."

"That would be fun," Manalani replied. "I really enjoyed it the last time we went up. Now that I think of it though, Mark may want to be on the south shore in Honolulu. It will be mostly south swell at this time of year. The north shore will probably be flat."

Dan thought about that. "You are probably right. He will have to make a choice. I know he's been looking forward to having another shot at surfing. He was shocked last time that he couldn't jump on a board and be out there like a pro. He got in more time swimming after his board than he had planned."

Manalani chuckled. "Yes, but now he has been challenged, and you know he is going to have to rise to that."

Dan thought about that comment. He and Mark were certainly alike. Once they took something up, they were like bulldogs. They wouldn't let it go. "Well, it will be vacation time; he will just have to decide what he wants to do the most."

"I'll bet he'll choose to go to Hawaii."

"Have you talked to your folks again so they know for sure when we are arriving? And how is your dad's diabetes? I sure wish he would come over here and take some tests at U.C.L.A."

"They know we will be there Tuesday, and they will be glad to see all of us. Pops hasn't changed his mind. As far as he is concerned, he wants to live and die on the island. He doesn't want any strangers poking around at him. It was hard enough to get him to change his diet and do the shots. You know his saying, 'You have to die of something some day anyway.'"

"He sure is a stubborn old guy. I like him and I think he likes me, but I certainly can't influence him, even when I know what's best for him, and I think he knows it too."

Manalani quickly replied, "Hey look, you can be just as stubborn as he is in your own way. Besides, you may not really know what's best for him. You may know what is best for his health, but not for his peace of mind. His Hawaiian side gives him a strong sense of ohana, of family and home. His Japanese side demands a sense of peace and fitness. As long as he can work in his garden, have his family around him, and go out fishing in the boat with his buddies, he is happy. If he can't do these things, then I think he would fade fast. He doesn't ask much from life, but the things that he does ask are very important to him."

Listening to her, Dan realized how lucky he was that their relationship had lasted. She seemed to know his shortcomings and could take them in stride. She was the one who slowed him down and made him loosen up when he was being manic or uptight about something. When he sometimes was like a locomotive barreling down the wrong track, she could deflect him.

His first marriage had gone on the rocks in just a few years. She was a hometown girl from Delavan, plain looking and plain spoken, with no desire to move to Los Angeles. The glitz and glamour of the L.A. mode had no attraction for her. Once there, like so many young couples, their interests drifted apart. Dan was totally committed to his progression up the ladder of the airline seniority list. During his off days, he played tennis whenever possible and on weekends often played his sax in jazz clubs around the area. Left alone, she often took advantage of their passes to return to Wisconsin. When he bought the new airplane, instead of buying a new car for them, it formed the catalyst to increasing conflict that resulted in their separation. Though Dan considered this a failure on his part, he also tried to lay the blame on her. Only after he married Manalani did he begin to admit to himself that he was not an easy person to live with.

With their Hawaii plans set, Dan was eager to fly his Christen Eagle at Torrance Airport. In the car, on the way to the airport and to drop off Mark, he offered to change his routine so that Mark could also fly. "Look, I could come and get you after water polo practice."

"No Dad. After practice, Stan and I are going to the cove to catch some waves. He has a new board for me to try. I don't want to look like some sort of kook when I get to Hawaii. Then I have a date with Ellen. We'll get something to eat, and then we're planning to go to the Catalyst to pick up on a reggae group that is playing there."

Dan knew he was defeated. "I suppose you would want to spend sometime with her before we leave for the islands. Just be packed and ready to go tomorrow. Are you planning on taking a board there?"

"Not for just a week. I should be able to borrow one there. Though, if I'm lucky, I may find one to buy. There are a lot of good backyard shapers over there, or if I have the money, I might buy one of B.K's boards. I don't know though. I don't have much time to surf over here, and the waves aren't good that often. Thanks for the offer on the ride though."

After Mark got out and they continued toward the airport, Liz said to Dan, "Dad, you never give up, do you. You know he gets airsick really easy."

"Yes, I know that. But a lot of good pilots got airsick when they first started out. Hell, Bob Hoover did, and he's one of the best pilots in the world. It's something that can be overcome. Besides they have those patches you can wear these days."

"Look, Dad, he just doesn't have the desire. He's an ace jock, class officer, good student, popular; be happy with that. If you want a pilot in the family, you're stuck with me."

Dan realized she was looking for approval and reassurance. "You are right honey; you are the one. You have the talent and the desire, and I'm glad you do. I'm proud of you. Besides, in this day and age a woman has an advantage once she has the qualifications."

When they arrived at the airport, the hangar doors were open. A small thrill coursed through Dan each time he saw the Eagle glistening in the hangar. He bought a two-place aerobatic airplane, instead of a more conventional four-place utility airplane, because he believed that spins and the ability to handle an airplane in any attitude were important parts of a pilot's primary skills. He could rent an airplane from one of several operators on the field if he wanted to go cross-country with the family. He also admitted to himself that he loved its sleek lines and the precise way it handled. He liked the comparison between an ordinary sedan and a highly refined sports car. Of course, he didn't appreciate the bus analogy that some pilots drew when they talked about the airline jets.

They flew an hour of aerobatics in the designated air space south of Palos Verdes. After their session, Dan talked excitedly, his hands flashing about describing maneuvers. A part of his normal reticence was temporarily dissolved, and he was years younger. In these moments, he felt closer to Liz than he did to either of his sons. They shared the joy of mutual skills and adventure. His conventional viewpoint made him expect to share this with his sons, but somehow it hadn't happened. It puzzled him that it worked out that way, but he had no choice but to accept it. He was glad that he had someone with whom to share his love of flying and to pass down his skills and knowledge.

CHAPTER 7

The next day, they were on their way to the islands. After the usual rush to get organized and on to the airplane, Dan felt he could relax. They were lucky that they were ahead of the jam that started later in the month. The privilege of flying free on their own airline was somewhat balanced by being last in the boarding priority. During holiday periods, that could mean waiting for several flights, or even several days. For this reason, they took most of their vacations in the spring and the fall.

On board the airplane, Dan was asleep in a matter of minutes. Unlike some pilots, he had no problem with worrying about what was going on up front. The exception to this was if some event occurred that resulted in an unusual sound or motion. Then he would wake up, alert and analyzing.

After landing and collecting their baggage, they rented a car from Tropical, and they were on their way to the north shore. Passing through Wahiawa, they reached the crest of the saddle and started down the long slope toward Haleiwa. From this point, most of the north shore spread out in front of them. On the left were the bluffs of Kaena Point, the western-most tip of the island. From here, the Hawaiians believed that after death their spirits departed for the land of Po. To the right the view extended to the heiau above Waimea Bay, a site that was sacred in ancient days, and even today held an aura of mystery.

Dan glanced at Manalani as they started down the slope. For years, she had tried to talk Dan into buying a retirement place in the islands, but he never would commit himself. He enjoyed visiting but was worried that he would get "rock fever" if he lived there on a full time basis. He had never quite been able to hang loose in the Hawaiian way and sometimes felt awkward around her father and mother.

Dan knew he wasn't the most congenial of men; he was at his best when he was in familiar surroundings. They traveled abroad to exotic destinations other than layovers, most often at Manalani's urging. Dan would study the geography and history of the country where they would travel. He loved maps and the background preparation. Once they arrived at their destination, and people who were foreign in their language and manners confronted them, Dan would clam up. Manalani would often have to take the lead. Manalani told him it had to do with his desire to be in command of any situation as he was when he was flying. Since she had grown up surrounded by different cultures and the languages of the islands, she felt little hesitation when thrust into a new unknown situation.

When they reached Haleiwa, they stopped off at the Fujioka store to buy supplies. Then they continued up Kam Highway past Waimea Bay, to the Strane's cottage they rented each time they were on the north shore. It faced the ocean, off the highway, on Ke Iki road. The beach from there on up to Rocky Point was wide and flat in the summer. The lake-like appearance in summer made it hard to believe that some of the biggest rideable waves in the world hit there in the winter.

They picked the key off its hiding place above the door,

opened up the windows to the trade-wind breeze, and began settling in. Manalani cut flowers outside, and soon the scent of plumeria and ginger wafted through the rooms. "There," she said, "Now I really feel like I'm back." They emptied suitcases, made phone calls to friends, stocked the refrigerator, and there was still time to hit the water before they went to Manalani's folk's house for dinner. Mark had heard that a south swell was going to hit town in a day or two so he was eager to get a board and head out the next day. He would stay with friends in town.

The sun was setting as they drove up the hill through tasseled cane fields, the horizon filled with a golden and peach colored light. Puffy cumulus clouds floated westward on the trade winds. Green mountains rose up into the clouds, and the ocean spread to infinity, shimmering and turquoise. The combination provided an ambiance lifted from a tourist picture postcard. A cliché, but when encountered in reality, it was still a thrill to behold.

Manalani's parents lived in a small plantation cottage, surrounded by other sugar mill workers in the hills behind Haleiwa. Most of the houses were little more than shacks to Dan's eyes, but they certainly had a fine location overlooking the entire north shore. As Manalani explained, they enjoyed being around their lifetime friends, the rent was dirt cheap, and it was just a short drive down to Haleiwa Harbor where her dad spent much of his time these days.

The beat-up old jeep with its fishing racks and the rusty Subaru station wagon were under the mango tree. Like nearly all the other houses, a picnic table, storage shed, and fishing gear filled the carport area. Most of the year, this served as the outdoor living room and workspace. About the only time they were found inside, was when they watched television or went to bed. The usual junk cars, boats, and machinery parts did not fill up the yard. Instead, the house was hedged with carefully trimmed hibiscus, ti, and mock orange. Croaton, ginger, and lawaii fern bordered the house. The space not taken up by their orchid and vegetable garden was a blanket of zoysia grass. When the jacaranda and shower trees out back were blooming, Dan thought it looked like someone's dream of Hawaii living.

There wasn't room to park directly in front, so Dan pulled over on a wide spot in the road next door. As they were getting out of the car, the neighbor, a small but rough looking oriental guy, gave Dan a hard stare, and without saying anything, stalked off into his backyard.

Dan couldn't figure what the problem was, but thought he would ask Takeshi about it. When they had settled down at the table with a couple of beers, he asked if he should move his car into Takeshi's driveway. Takeshi replied, "What for? You no like walk? I move my car. But you look like you got two legs."

Dan said, "No, that it isn't it. It just looked like your neighbor didn't like me parking there."

Takeshi replied, "Oh him. You no mind. He one pake wit nose in air. By'm by I going broke his face."

Oh no, Dan thought, *there he goes again with the pidgin. I can't be sure what he is saying.* When he was alone in conversation with Takeshi, he always felt slightly uneasy. Half the time he couldn't understand him. Then there was Takeshi's sly sense of humor that slipped out at odd times, so that Dan never could tell when to take him seriously.

He would never forget the time, years ago, when in an attempt to be friendly, he asked Takeshi what kind of fish he was after when he saw him packing up the jeep. Takeshi gave him a sudden fierce look and said, "Ain't going nowhere fishing." Then he immediately began unpacking the jeep. Dan knew he had committed some blunder but could not figure what it possibly could be.

That same night Manalani laughed when he told her of the event. She explained that it was an old island belief that the fish could hear you coming if you were asked that question. You would have no luck on that trip so you might as well pack it up.

Dan said, "Oh come on. Do you think he really believes that?"

"I think Pops would have a hard time answering that. He probably doesn't believe it in a literal sense, but he has lived with the tradition all his life, so he's not about to lose it. Like me. I wouldn't say I believe the Pele legends literally, but you wouldn't catch me with pork in the car traveling the saddle road at night or taking rocks from a heiau. There is a certain mana here, a spiritual power that haoles don't understand. But, if you live here all your life, and hear the stories and legends, there are certain lines you don't cross."

The evening though was a warm and cordial event. Takeshi and Nona were obviously happy to see them all back in the islands. Liz and Mark received special attention of the kind that grandparents can so willingly give. By the time they left, everyone was in a mellow mood and anticipating the days to come.

As they were going to bed that night, Dan brought up the incident with the car to Manalani. "Takeshi said something about the guy next door being a bocky or pocky with his nose in the air, and how he was going to broke his face. What was that all about?"

Manalani tried to stifle a giggle, but couldn't, "Oh, he got you going again didn't he. Sometimes I think he does that on purpose. The word was 'Pake' meaning a Chinese. One who has his nose in air means he is stuck-up, won't talk story with Pops. And you can guess 'broke his face' means punch him out. But that is just talking stink. He doesn't really mean it. Too bad, but he and that Pake have never been able to hit it off together. Not to worry."

"But why does he say "broke his face' instead break his face. That doesn't make any sense. He's using past tense for something in the future."

"Well dear, that's just pidgin. It has nothing to do with grammar; that's just the way you say it. The other way, the way you would say it, would be faking it."

Dan was still bothered. "It sure makes it difficult to learn if there are no rules to depend on."

Manalani replied, "Not if you live with it all your life. People usually don't learn pidgin, they grow up with it. It started in the fields so the workers could understand each other. But there are still differences. I have a hard time understanding a group of Portuguese if they are talking together. Don't worry about it. Nobody expects you to talk pidgin. I think you would sound silly doing it anyway."

That satisfied Dan, but as he was falling asleep, he still could feel a small twinge of dislocation. It seemed that the islands always held some mysterious element that he could never quite master. It would crop up in small ways just out of his reach, intimating an existence out there that he could not quite grasp. It bothered him, but also fascinated him, that there was this side to Manalani that always belonged to the islands, that he saw rarely, and he could only partly fathom.

The next few days fell into an easy rhythm, sleep late, tennis in the morning, swim, read, and trips to Dillingham to fly the gliders. The outfit out there, Soar Hawaii, had two Grob-103's, German built two-place ships that were approved for aerobatics.

After the flights Manalani joined them for drinks and dinner on the terrace at Jamesons in Haleiwa. They were all in an ebullient mood, the perfect way to end the day.

***

That good feeling disappeared the next morning when Dan received a phone call from the Honolulu Police Department. "Mr. Swanton, this is Sergeant Webber, booking desk, downtown. We are holding your son, Mark, for you to pick up. Actually he is at Halekipa on McKinley Avenue, where we retain minors."

Dan was shocked. "Hold it. Did I hear you right? You are holding Mark? There must be some mistake."

"No, sir. There's not likely to be a mistake in these matters. You do have a son named Mark, right."

"Of course. But why would you be holding him? What do you think he has done?"

"It says here the code violation is number 232, open indecency."

Dan couldn't believe what he was hearing. "What the hell

does that mean?"

"According to the arresting officer's report, your son and another boy were nude on the beach below Diamond Head."

Dan exploded. "What? That's ridiculous. That's impossible. There has got to be a mistake."

The Sergeant replied in an even tone, "No, sir. We don't make mistakes when it comes to these things. Unless, of course, someone is impersonating your son."

Dan didn't like the insinuated humor. "Look, you don't know my son. If you did, you would know that this charge is ridiculous."

The Sergeant replied, "I might suggest, sir, that you may not know your son as well as you think. In any case I would suggest that you go to Halekipa to pick him up. You can find out more details there."

Dan was so mad he found himself stuttering slightly. "Where is this place? I'll be down. I'll come down there to straighten things out."

The Sergeant replied. "It's at 2007 McKinley, sir. You can park right in front."

Manalani had entered the room catching part of the conversation. She stared wide-eyed at Dan as he hung up the phone. "What is it dear? Did I hear the police are holding Mark?"

"Yes, that's right."

"What for?"

"It's some trumped up charge. There has to be a mistake."

"But what is it."

"We need to get going. I'll tell you about it in the car."

On their way to Halekipa, they went over the phone conversation several times. Dan kept up his consistent denial.

Manalani sat quietly. Dan twisted in his seat; his grip on the steering wheel clenched so the cords stood out on the backs of his hands. Manalani turned to Dan and then hesitated. His intense stern attitude showed that he was focused on one point, proving the police were wrong. This wasn't going to be easy. "Look honey, what if the police are right?"

He shuddered, then turned toward her, his face a hostile grimace, his tone flat and metallic. "What do you mean right? Whose side are you on?"

"I'm on Mark's side, honey, and so are you, I hope. No matter what has happened."

"What has happened is obvious. There has been some kind of screw up. We'll straighten it out. Then we will bring Mark home. It's very simple."

"It may not be that simple. What do we really know about Mark's sexual desires?"

Dan cut her off. "Get off it Manalani. He's our son. We should know that much about him. Look at him. Look at his life. There's no indication that he would be, ah, different."

"Dan, that's just it. We have hardly ever talked to him about sex. Obviously, we didn't think it was necessary. And if he is different, do you think he would show it? Of course not. He would stay in the closet, as they say."

Dan scowled at her, his forehead wrinkled until his eyebrows almost touched. "I can't believe we are having this conversation. Do you honestly think that Mark, our son, who we have lived with and loved all these years, could be queer?"

Manalani took a big breath. "Yes, it is possible. We really don't know, and you had better be prepared to accept that possibility, and if you really love Mark, you had better be prepared to accept him like he is, whatever his sexual life is like."

Dan received this in stunned silence. He made no immediate reply. The remaining ride into town was conducted in almost complete silence. They found the house on McKinley. There were only two small signs to separate it from the other residences on the street. Dan strode up the stairs ahead of Manalani, hardly looking back, intent on his mission. Sandals and tennis shoes were piled in front of the screen door that marked one entrance. As they opened the door, they could see boys of various ages lounging around several interior rooms. They were met by a young woman who introduced herself as Dorothy Robinson, a guidance counselor.

Dan spoke immediately. "We came to pick up our son, Mark. I assume he is here."

Dan's posture and tone with her were aggressive, but she didn't react. "Yes, he is here."

"Well, where is he? We would like to see him now."

"He is upstairs now. Before we release him to your custody, there are some papers you will need to sign."

"I expected that. Let's get it done."

Dorothy turned to a file on her desk and gave Dan some documents to sign. While he was doing this, she questioned him. "Do you know why your son is here?"

"I know what the police told me, and I intend to straighten that matter out next."

A small smile crossed Dorothy's face. "And how do you propose to do that?"

Dan peered up at her with his sternest look and replied, "I will get Mark's story, go down to the station house, confront the arresting officer, and then find out what went wrong."

Without flinching Dorothy replied to Dan, "And what if Mark's story agrees with that of the arresting officer? What then?"

Dan was then the one to flinch noticeably. "Young lady, that is preposterous. I know my son. He has done no such thing."

A shape appeared in the shadowed doorway to the kitchen on Dan's right; Mark was standing there.

"Think again Dad. The facts are there in front of you. The arrest report is right."

Dan swiveled around in the chair so rapidly he almost fell over. At first, he started to rise. Then he hunched over. He clenched his jaw, but his body began to crumble. He almost collapsed. "What? What are you doing here? Do you know what you just said? Why would you say that?"

"Because it's true, Dad. And you are going to have to live with it. We all are. Don't think I chose this. Don't think I wanted to do this to you. It should never have happened. It's like a bad dream or something. I wish I could take it all back, but I can't."

Dan sat for a few seconds in stunned silence. Then he recovered. "All right. All right. We'll handle it. It will be okay. We'll work it out. I don't understand it, but we'll work it out. Damn it, I thought," and then his voice trailed off. There was nothing more he wanted to say.

Mark stepped into the room. Manalani went to him and hugged him. As Dan looked over his shoulder past the doorway, he could see a huge Hawaiian man who had been standing in the kitchen behind Mark. With a shock, he realized the man was there for protection. Probably some fathers became abusive or violent. He was there to make sure no threats were carried out. He also guessed they had the legal power to hold Mark if they felt they needed to protect him.

The tension in the room subsided noticeably when Dan rose, placed his hands on Mark's shoulders, and said, "Let's get you out of here now. We can talk about this on the way home."

In a few minutes, the processing was finished and they were allowed to leave. As they did, Mark thanked Dorothy profusely, and on the steps outside said, "You know, she's really a cool lady."

Manalani replied, "That's nice, that you could relate to her. Dan, what did you think of her?"

There was no response from Dan. Storm clouds were gathering about him.

During the ride from the police station, the mood was as though a conversational package bomb had been placed in the car, and nobody wanted to open it. Dan could not get his mind to work in a useful channel. Gay, fruit, homo, fag, queer—all the forbidden words seemed entrained in his stream of consciousness. The jokes, told over the years in the cockpit, somehow they could not apply to his son. His choked mind would not cross the bridge to acceptance of the evidence he had just heard.

Mark spoke first. "I guess I screwed up big time, huh?"

Dan replied, "Yes, you did, Mark. I don't see how you could have been so far off base."

Mark's jaw clenched and unclenched. "Look Dad, it was a screw up that should never have happened. If things had gone right, you would never have known anything."

Dan said, "But that's what really hurts, that we had to find out this way. How do you think that makes us feel? Didn't I tell you, you could always come to us with your problems?"

Anger replaced the contrition that had been Mark's emotional surface. "You said that Dad, but you didn't really mean it. The message I got over the years was that I could come to you with my ordinary little problems, things you could handle with fatherly advice. But this is beyond that. This is something you don't know anything about. This is something you don't want to hear about. That maybe your son is gay."

Dan broke in, "We could have helped somehow."

"What advice do you have about that? It is something you thought you would never hear. And if things had worked out, you never would have heard about it. Life for you could go on in the same smooth vein it's been flowing in."

Then Dan exploded. "You sound like you don't think we care. What do you think we have been doing for you all these years? Haven't I backed you in whatever you wanted to do? Have I tried to force you down any certain path? "

Mark's bitterness was still showing through. "That's right. You didn't push me, but that's because you didn't need to. You thought you were getting what you really wanted, a new improved version of yourself. A continuation of the gene stream, but this time with a twist on it that no one would have guessed at. Do you think I wanted this? I didn't choose the way I feel."

Manalani broke in. "Look, both of you are taking positions and trying to defend them, and it is about something that's emotionally charged, and neither of you knows anything about it. This isn't about who is right or wrong, or who screwed up the most, or who is expecting what. I think we need to do two things. One, Mark is in trouble with the law, so we need to get him out of that any way we can."

"What do you mean by that?"

In a firm voice Manalani replied, "Just what I said. Hire the best attorney we can. See about getting the charges dropped."

Dan couldn't believe what he was hearing. "You can't be serious about that."

"You're damn right I'm serious. This isn't some abstract principle of law we are talking about here. We're talking about our son, his life, which could be devastated if this goes too far. I know how the law works around here. There is an old boy network that can do a lot of good, particularly if things haven't gotten too far into the system. So we do what we need to do to minimize the damage."

Dan said, "I can't believe I am hearing you say this."

"Honey, I know you are a really ethical straight shooter, but if you get caught in the judicial system and go to court, there are only winners and losers, and as the accused, it's pretty damn hard to win. I can make some phone calls to start."

Dan, though shocked again, could see the sense she was making. At least it replaced the confusion in his mind with a sense of purpose. "Okay, I will buy your idea about the law, but what was the second thing you had in mind?"

"The second thing is that Mark and you and I are dealing with something we know next to nothing about. If you agree with that, it means we need to find someone who does know something, who can act like a referee, or at least be neutral. You know, take some of the emotional weight off of it so both of you guys can ease up on each other."

Mark replied first. "Ah, no Mom. It sounds like you're talking about a shrink. They just get you screwed up more from what I've heard."

"No, I don't mean a shrink. I'm talking about a family matters counselor. There are people who specialize in this kind of stuff and they can really help you get your head on straight."

"See! There you go. 'Get your head on straight.' Everything has to be one way or the other, straight or gay. Like you have to go one way or the other. Remember what Woody Allen said, "If you are AC/DC you get twice as many chances to get laid'"

Mark's attempt at humor did relieve some of the tension, but Dan couldn't stop himself from moralizing. "Yeah, except in this day and age it also gives you twice as many chances to die."

Manalani said, "Look, can we agree that we need help in this area, that none of us really knows what we are talking about? Besides, when it comes to dealing with the authorities, I'm sure it will look good if we can say we are getting counseling or therapy."

Both Dan and Mark agreed with that, and the rest of the drive was devoted to a strategy for dealing with the legal system.

Manalani gave Liz a brief outline of what happened before dinner. She also was initially shocked but recovered quickly. She said she knew some boys at school that were gay and got along with them just fine. After a further moment's consideration she said, "The statistic I remember from our sex education class was that seven percent of the population is outwardly gay, and the real percentage is definitely higher than that. It's just that you always figure its going to be somebody you don't know very well. Besides, whose business is it who you want to do it with? I think it's the churches and the military that are so paranoid about it. I think it's screwed that somebody's life could be ruined by his sexual preference, and Mark is a good example. He still is the same great guy as far as I'm concerned."

Liz was building up a real head of steam rising to her brother's defense. Manalani told Liz to cool it with Mark. That subject was closed unless he brought it up. Dinner that night was a tense and subdued affair since the subject was hanging around the edges of their desultory conversation. They watched television for a short while and everyone headed for bed.

After they showered, Dan was still distracted and needed to talk some more, but he didn't know how to start. Manalani broke the ice. "Okay big boy, come on out with it; you still can't accept all of this, can you?"

Dan sighed and leaned back against the pillow. "How could this be happening to us? I mean, I know it sounds selfish, but I feel like we are being punished for something we don't know about, and for Mark it has to be tough. I know it isn't something he would choose."

Manalani said, "He was trying to keep it from us so we wouldn't have to deal with it."

"But now that it has happened, I feel like we have plunged into some strange kind of soap opera. It makes me afraid that something will happen to Liz next. Am I getting paranoid?"

"Yeah, but it's probably only natural," Manalani replied. "You know, compared to a lot of families, what we are going through is no big deal. We will work our way through this. I'll bet we can get the charges dismissed or reduced, and the therapy will be good for us all."

"Yeah, what about this therapy or counseling? Do you think I need to go? Mark is the one who needs help."

"Oh, do I catch just a little edge of apprehension here, just a little nudge of fear? Look, this really is a family matter; it might be that even Liz should come to one session. The object is to clear the air out for everybody, not just to try and straighten Mark out. I don't know the details, but I would be willing to bet that we should be there for some sessions."

"You know I have got to go into training on the MD-11 when we get back. I don't want that broken up. It is the most difficult transition we have to do. You know how I am about going into training."

Manalani hadn't considered that. "You're right. I just hope the first session or two can be before you start, and then any others scheduled during a big break."

"I don't like that. You know that I don't want to think about anything but the airplane during that period. I just become an airplane monk. Hell, though, I guess in this case there is no other way out."

Manalani replied, "This is a tough one because I know you need total concentration, and yet Mark will need your backing on this now more than anything else that has happened in his life. You know how we've talked about how you become Mechanical Man when your flying time approaches. How you can split your mind off and drop everything else. Well, this time you will need to do it in both directions. Come off training, and get totally into Mark's world, and then go back. Think you can do that?"

"I really don't know. I haven't had to try it before, but I think I can. As we've said though, it usually takes at least twenty-four hours or more after a long flight before I'm fully grounded."

Eventually, Dan agreed to Manalani's wishes. He knew she was right, but the whole business left him with a sour taste in his mouth as he went to sleep.

Manalani found that since Mark was a minor, and they were from out of state, there would be no problem with them not showing up at the hearing. The attorney would explain that they were obtaining counseling in California. The case would remain open but not be pursued. He advised them to drop the matter and quietly leave the state, which they did immediately.

She also obtained the name of a highly recommended family therapist through a friend and arranged for an appointment when they returned to the mainland. Since they had cut their vacation short, and Dan did not have to go to training yet, he was committed. He and Mark managed to almost completely avoid each other in the interim.

CHAPTER 8

On the way to the therapist's office, the mood in the car was understandably tense. In the waiting room, there was almost complete silence. Mark appeared to be interested in the diplomas on the wall. Liz read a magazine that was months old. Manalani looked at Dan, but he couldn't return her gaze for more than a few seconds. He could hardly think of anything to say that would not be either inane or loaded with possible implied meaning.

Dan was rather surprised that the therapist was a woman. He guessed she was in her mid thirties, heavy set, black hair, olive skin, dark eyes, with an almost offhand casual manner that seemed inappropriate at first contact. Dan realized that he was influenced by the stereotype of the Viennese Freudian analyst with his attendant couch. He could see that she had the requisite certificates on her wall. At least her name, Lydia Skoros, resonating with the weight of Greek culture, gave her standing in Dan's mind.

After an introduction, she asked her first leading question, "I would like to ask each of you what results you expect to come out of our sessions?"

There was a quick frantic exchange of looks among the four of them followed by an awkward pause as they each hesitated to speak what was on their mind. Dan decided that he should take the lead. "Well, Mark has this, uh, problem, and as a family, we really don't know how to handle it. We don't have the skills in this area. So, by coming to you we hope you can, ahh, straighten it out."

"By that, you really mean straighten him out, don't you?" was the therapist's reply.

"Well, yes, I guess so. Though that's not the way I think I would express it." Dan could feel the color rise in his cheeks. He was distinctly uncomfortable, feeling like a schoolboy corrected in class.

"Liz, what are your feelings about this?"

Liz looked startled, as though she was jolted out of reverie. "I guess I don't have any expectations myself. I mean, I accept Mark whatever way he wants to be. I guess I just want him to be happy."

"And you, Manalani, what are your expectations?"

As Dan looked at Manalani, he realized that she appeared to be the most composed of all of them. He thought that must be because she had devoted a good bit of thought to this moment.

"Since I have never been in this position before, I don't really think I have any expectations as such. I do know what I hope for though. I hope that Mark can see himself clearly, and come to terms with whatever his feelings are. That he can be happy with those feelings, and know that we will support him in whatever he feels. And that we as a family will not be divided or lose our closeness over this. My hope is that if we approach this correctly, that we will have a stronger bond at the end, that it will produce a greater closeness and more love between us than before."

Dan felt a twinge of envy as Manalani was speaking. *Why couldn't I have expressed myself that well?* He also noticed that she looked at Mark as she was talking, not at the therapist.

The therapist turned to Mark, "Well, Mark, you are unavoidably the center of attention here, and I know you are feeling uncomfortable. I don't want you to feel pressured. If you do have expectations you can express at this point, or a feeling for what you think we can accomplish, let us hear what that is."

Mark's face flushed. He opened and closed his hands, but they remained clenched. He opened his mouth twice before any words came out, and his voice was unnaturally thin. "Well, I guess like what Mom said, I want to find out who I really am. Sometimes I have so many different feelings, I can't sort them out. Then I feel different ways at different times. It's like I see myself as different people at different times, but I've learned to always put out one type of person out front, the one that is okay for everybody. So I guess I want to feel like just one person, the person I want to be, and still have that be someone acceptable to everyone else. I mean, I know I'm popular in school, and I like that. I like being liked by other people, and I don't want to blow all that away by being some sort of weirdo. Does that make any sense to you?"

The therapist smiled benevolently at Mark and said, "It makes very good sense Mark. Between what you and Manalani have said, you have expressed what I hope we can accomplish together."

There was a rather long pause as she wrote down some notes on her tablet. When she looked up at them again and smiled, Dan realized that her smile reminded him of the Mona Lisa, the

Gioconda smile, as if she held some secret knowledge inside. He found it unsettling.

Then she spoke, "Actually today's session will be a rather short one, an introduction so to speak. I will want to speak to Mark alone for a few minutes before you leave, and my next session will also be for him, as you might expect. It is a very good sign that you showed up today as a family unit and expressed support for Mark. This is important. You might be surprised how often I see only the principal, who is expected to go it all alone. So, we are off to a good start. These kinds of revelations are painful for the whole family, especially for the father in most cases." She said this looking directly at Dan, who recoiled slightly in his seat.

"Each family member has adjustments to make in their thinking and attitudes, but fathers usually have the most set and rigid expectation for their sons, and also daughters if it comes to that. When these expectations are violated, if the father is completely inflexible, a complete disruption of relationship can occur. Just by showing up here Dan, you have taken a big step that many fathers would not take.

"Now there are certain ground rules that exist here that you need to know. First, this is a safe place. By that, I mean anything can be said in here, and it never goes outside these walls. I want you to feel free to say anything, secure in the knowledge that it will never travel, and you will never be censured by me. I'm not here to pass judgment, cast aspersions, or give approval. Probably, nothing you can say will shock me. I may not look old, but in the last twelve years, I have heard enough so that there isn't much new under the sun. You may think that your problem is particularly terrible, or tragic, or unique, but in the human condition, the odds are that it has happened before.

She glanced at her notes and then looked back and forth between Dan and Mark before she continued. "I also want you not to hold anything back. Whatever feelings come up, I want you to express them without reservation. What I am interested in here are feelings and emotions. I'm not interested in rationalizations, or demonstrations of cleverness. IQ's don't count here. Honesty does. This brings up the next point, a sticky one for many people. I want to hear the truth in here. You have heard the expression, 'The truth will set you free.' In this room that is a given. If you don't speak your truth in here, the whole process will grind to a halt. This is not an easy thing to do. We are not trained to tell the truth in our society, particularly when it comes to matters of the heart. In here, I want to hear your microscopic personal truth. That means your feelings, unadorned, uncovered, not altered for approval or effect. I know from experience that you won't be one-hundred-percent on this but the closer you can come, the faster we will move. Now do you have any questions?"

A stunned silence pervaded the room. Dan was shocked and at the same time impressed. It seemed that he might have underestimated this young woman. She certainly appeared to have a clear idea of the direction they needed to take. Quite a few questions had formed in his mind, but he felt they could all wait. He was interested in what would happen next.

"I hope I didn't shock you all into a form of speechlessness," was her next comment, accompanied by a more open smile.

This was met by a chorus of denials mixed with nervous laughter.

"Then as a demonstration, I would like to have your feelings, of homosexuality, gay people if you prefer. I don't want to hear what you have read, or what some expert has said, or what you think is socially correct. I want to know what you feel in your heart of hearts. Your gut level feeling. Dan, you are on the hot seat; you're first."

Dan was shocked. Temporarily he was speechless. His mind raced over several possibilities. Then he thought, *She wants the truth. I'll give it to her.*

"I don't think this is fair. I have not had time to clear my thoughts about this. Unfortunately, I've had very little chance to think about this in any organized manner."

"There we go, Dan. You gave me one feeling, not fair, followed by two rationalizations. Remember, I'm not interested in your organized thoughts or your considered opinion. I want your gut level feeling. You've got a gut level feeling, don't you?"

Dan knew she was goading him, but he still rose to the bait. If she wanted gut level he would give it to her and damn the consequences. "Yes, my gut level feeling is there is something wrong with homosexuality. I don't think it's sick, like some people do, but my god, if we were all homosexual, there wouldn't be any procreation. It's got to be wrong at some level."

"Good Dan, that's what I wanted to hear. That's gut level honesty. That is your truth. Mark, what you need to realize is, that this is not about you. This is about what Dan feels. How you react to that is part of your truth. How the two of you relate to each other and these feelings we will get into later. For now, we just want to get the feelings out in the open. Now, Manalani what are your thoughts?"

In his agitated state, when Dan looked over at Manalani, he

wondered how she could seem so composed. Then he thought, *Of course, she has had a chance to think this through.*

Her reply surprised him. "People are different in different ways. This just seems to be one more way we are different. I don't really understand how it can happen that there can be a sexual attraction, so in that sense I guess I feel personally that it is unnatural, but it doesn't threaten me. I just think of it as an oddity, like someone who likes strange food combinations. As long as they don't push their oddity on me, it is okay. Maybe growing up in the islands with so many different and strange customs makes me more tolerant of different life styles."

Dan watched the therapist, who was regarding Manalani very intently as she talked. Dan guessed that she was looking for outward signs that Manalani was really being open about her feelings. She must have been satisfied because she then turned to Liz.

Liz stumbled a bit at first. "I don't know if I really had any opinions about gay people, at least until we had our sexuality class in school. If the information they gave us is correct, nobody really knows why anyone is gay or straight, and that in all cultures a certain percentage are gay, even in some of the animals. So I feel like it's just luck of the draw. If you draw the short straw, then you've got problems. And it hasn't changed my thoughts about Mark. I still think he is a great brother, and I'd defend him to the death."

"That's a very nice testimonial Liz," was the therapist's comment, "But it really isn't necessary. I'm sure it makes Mark feel good to hear your support, but I want him to know that his self-worth is independent of anyone else's opinions of him. That is not an easy thing to do at any age, and is particularly difficult when you are in the process of forming your characteristics that you present to the world. At this point, it would be unfair of me to ask Mark the same question I have asked of you. I would like to speak to both Dan and Mark separately before you leave today, and I would like to have a session with Mark whenever he can return.

As the rest of the family filed out of the room, Dan felt particularly uncomfortable. Though he had been honest, he felt that he should have joined Mark's cheering section. The therapist was busy writing up her notes. Then she looked up at Dan and smiled in that Gioconda way again. "Dan, I know this is hard for you. In some respects, it is a father's worst dream come true, but you have to come to terms with it. There is an important question to answer here. Can you still love your son if he is homosexually oriented?"

Dan was shocked at the question, but the answer came easily to him. "Yes, I can. I have no doubt of that. But it seems like there is an assumption being made here, that Mark is definitely bent that way. From what Mark has said to me, I don't think he knows for sure how he feels. If he is telling the truth, and I think he is, this was his first experience. So where does that leave us? I'm in muddy waters here. I don't know what to think or do. That is why we have come to you."

Dan basked in her smile of approval. Then he asked himself, *Why are you looking for approval from her?*

"Dan, those are good observations. I'm glad to know that Mark has your support. That doesn't always happen. Some men just can't deal with it. You are also right that this isn't an all or nothing situation. In our society, we tend to categorize people in that manner, but the truth is that there is a whole range of sexual expression. Mark is really going to need your support and approval no matter how this works out. If he knows he has your unconditional approval, it will make a big difference to him."

Dan mulled this over. This wasn't going to be easy for him. He still loved Mark, but to give him unconditional approval, that was a new subject. How could he approve of something in Mark that he had never approved of in anyone else? He also had another important question. "How did Mark get this way? I mean, what went wrong? Is there anything we could have done?"

"In a sense, Dan, you are asking the wrong question. Nothing went wrong. There isn't anything wrong with homosexuality except the cloud we place over it in our society. Homosexuality is part of the human condition, and always has been. A certain small percentage of the population is always going to be oriented that way. How this happens is still somewhat of a mystery. I will want to talk to you about this in another session. In the meantime, don't go blaming yourself or anyone else. Blame has no place in this situation." She leaned back in her chair, pushed her hair back, and leveled her gaze at Dan.

"That does make me feel better, but there is no denying that this whole situation makes me really uncomfortable."

"That's okay, Dan. I wouldn't expect you to feel any other way. You need to be very honest about your feelings. Mark will be able to sense any insincerity on your part, and that will break down communication between the two of you. Don't worry, you are more than halfway there if you can just be honest with yourself and him and keep on talking. Now, if you don't mind, I would like him to come in."

As they both rose and shook hands, Dan felt disoriented. Things were not moving as he thought they should. The bedrock, on which he believed his family relationships were founded, had suddenly cracked. The tectonic plates were shifting; he was adrift in a world that had suddenly turned strange.

As he walked into the waiting room and told Mark to go into the office, their eyes met. Dan was acutely aware that a part of his son was a stranger to him, a side that was entirely unknown. Even more than unease, it caused a mental shudder that quickly turned to one in his body. He hoped that Mark's attention was elsewhere so that it passed unnoticed. During the next few days Dan and Mark avoided each other as much as possible. The tension between them was like the grating of unlubricated gears.

During a break in Dan's training, Manalani scheduled his second appointment with the therapist. Her office was located in Long Beach near the airport. He needed to stop by operations anyway to clean out his mailbox. As he moved out onto Palos Verdes Drive North, he was on the first stage of a voyage of transition. He quickly traded the well-tended homes and eucalyptus and palm groves of Palos Verdes for the Latino and Indonesian enclaves that coexisted with the industrial underbelly of Los Angeles and its harbor.

If he did not close off his mind to it, he was very conscious of the vacant stares, the vacant shops, and broken and vacant windows that lined Anaheim Blvd. However, there was a gritty tenaciousness to these people, and a sense of liveliness showed in their windowsill flowers, their backyard gardens, and their weekend fiestas. Oil fields and refineries - giant cracking towers, condenser towers, serpentine pipelines, and acres of massive steel reservoirs, dominated the surrounding landscape. The sky was bronze to slate gray depending on the cloud cover. Even with the air-conditioning on, the odors of benzene, gasoline, sulfur, old rubber tires, steel, and rust seeped through.

Ah yes, the air-conditioning system. He had time to stop off at Miguel's Service Station and ask him about that. As Dan pulled to a stop next to the pumps, he could see Miguel wave one of his boys off, and he came toward the car smiling while wiping his hands on a shop rag.

"Buena dias, Señor Swanton. You need gas today?"

"Si, si, Miguel, leno por favor."

After all these years, Miguel insisted on the 'Señor Swanton' formality at the station. Dan could never get him to change that. Dan and Manalani had been invited to the christening party of the Allende's second son. When they had consumed enough beers, Dan broke the barrier, so that Miguel had finally called Dan by his first name and had continued to do so away from the business. Dan still remembered that night fondly. At first, he had been nervous that cultural and economic differences might make things awkward. Manalani bridged that beautifully. The present she chose was perfect. With Dan accompanying her on harmonica, she traded Mexican and Hawaiian songs on guitar with all the guests.

That night was one of the few times they both drank too much to drive, and the Allendes insisted that Manalani and Dan sleep in the guest bedroom. The following morning they had a breakfast of chorizo, huevos, frijoles, and Spanish rice, and Dan became "mi amigo" and "mi compadre" from then on. Dan realized that the event, and sharing of food, drink, and home, had created a bond, that though limited in scope, was rock solid and important to them all. When Dan had suggested to Manalani that they reciprocate, she had wisely said that the Allende's would feel uncomfortable in Palos Verdes at their house, and they had settled on a picnic at the beach in Seal Beach.

As the tank filled, Dan broached the subject of the expensive air-conditioning repair he was facing at the dealership. "Miguel, at first the parts were going to be about a thousand dollars, but now they say the condenser also needs to be replaced to the tune of three hundred dollars, and labor is going to be about another three hundred."

Miguel briefly frowned, then smiled and said, "No, no, amigo, no necessario. I, Miguel, will take care of this. Es no problema. I will get parts for you at less than half what they charge, and my shop rates are thirty dollars per hour; theirs are fifty-five."

Dan could see a possible flaw. "Miguel, I want to use new parts. They have a guarantee."

"Again, no problema, mi amigo. I will guarantee everything for six months—for a year. You are my friend. You can trust me."

Dan felt relieved. "Of course, Miguel, I trust you. I just wasn't sure you did this kind of work."

"I have many years of experience. I do all kinds of work. You give me a list of parts and one week, maybe two. I pull out old parts, replace with new parts. Put in new Freon charge. Simple. Anyone can do it. No problema."

"Good, we have a deal. Do you need a deposit?"

Miguel smiled slightly and said, "Five hundred dollars would be a help."

Dan wrote him out a check, and Miguel waved him on his

way saying, "Hasta la vista."

Dan pulled out of the station, waiting for the left turn light onto Alameda, feeling quite satisfied with their deal, when the thought suddenly hit him. *Parts at half-price or less. That means he's going to be getting them through the steal-to-order market.* Dan learned a long time ago about this custom stealing operation when a friend of his ordered a transaxle for his Porsche through some guys operating out of a panel truck in a Safeway parking lot. Dan never was tempted to participate. Besides the ethical implications, it just encouraged auto theft and jacked up everyone's insurance rates across the board.

Now he was almost sure he was about to be implicated in a similar operation. What could he do? If he tried to back out now, Miguel would be offended, and it would put their relationship on the rocks. Dan was sure of that. Miguel's code of friendship and honor didn't revolve around the niceties of stolen goods. Earlier conversations together had hinted at what a Mexican-American had to do to get by in a gringo's world in El Norte. The comment wasn't directed at Dan, but it let him know there were certain lines that could not be crossed in their friendship. Dan was not the happy man that had just pulled out of the station minutes ago. His mood was a good match for the heart of industrial darkness he was about to traverse.

As he turned left onto Alameda, along the railroad tracks, the landscape ahead shimmered in heat waves augmented by the gas flares from refineries and the occasional illegal junkyard fire. On his right rested the detritus of the industrial revolution. Not just cars and trucks, but cement mixers, oil tankers, buses, derricks, railroad cars, steam shovels, and bridge structures. The flicker of arc welders and the glow of acetylene torches illuminated these dismantling lots day and night. In the corners were dredges and barges so massive that they seemed to be impervious to all attempts at their destruction. The black drifts of cinders and dirt that built up alongside and under them attested to their age.

After he turned up the onramp to the freeway, he was plunged into the streaming vehicular capillary system of the Long Beach Freeway. He always found it hard to believe that all these brightly colored cars were spawned in part by the Dantesque underworld he had just exited.

At the airport, he encountered another quintessential experience of the industrial age as he rode the shuttle bus to flight operations. Within the airport boundaries, there might be a hundred fan jet engines gulping thousands of cubic feet of air per minute at idle, spewing out the same air with the addition of hundreds of pounds of burnt kerosene. Within the same area, there could easily be a thousand cars, buses, and trucks adding to the mix. Considering that oxygen only makes up twenty-one-percent of the atmosphere, Dan sometimes wondered how there was any left for humans to breathe. Though he had been through this routine hundreds of times before, he always experienced a sense of relief when he closed the steel outer door and stepped into the quiet, air-conditioned, rational, world contained inside. Today he was in a hurry since he had to be in Lydia Skoros's office in less than an hour. He quickly picked up his mail and revisions and returned to his car.

When he arrived at her office, he felt distinctly uneasy sitting in the waiting room. He felt like he was about to take a check ride for which there was no possible preparation. He disliked her attitude. She seemed more interested in his thoughts and feelings than in Mark's. He realized this was relevant, since it obviously affected Mark, but he still didn't like it. The whole affair was also tinged with guilt for Dan. He felt that he should have sensed and taken control of matters before they got out of hand. Of course, Manalani had not sensed anything wrong, so maybe that let him off the hook.

Dan looked up from the magazine he had in his hands. She stood in the doorway to her office. She greeted him, beckoned with her finger for him to follow, turned and strode into the office ahead of him. For a large framed woman, she certainly moved quietly and quickly. When she turned to face him, he again noted her dark hair and olive skin, accompanied by deep-set ebony eyes divided by a prominent nose. Definitely a Greek visage that fitted her name. For Dan it produced a sense of mystery that added to his unease, since he did not know anyone from that part of the world. Rather than sit behind her desk, she motioned to a table with two chairs off to the side, a more informal arrangement.

When they were seated, her first question, quite ordinary under other circumstances, seemed loaded with implications. "Well, how are you today, Captain Swanton?"

Dan replied, "I think we can drop the Captain title, unless you would prefer to be known as Doctor Skoros."

"No, that is not necessary. Technically, I'm not a doctor anyway. In fact first names are fine with me. But I do usually allow my visitors to choose the level of formality that makes them comfortable."

"That's fine with me, too. I do not wear my stripes when I'm away from the job."

"Well then, Dan, how do you feel today."

Dan had no doubt that this was not a casual question. Her delivery and look were serious and probing. Dan decided not to dodge around with platitudes. "I suppose I could say I feel fine, but that would hardly be the truth. The truth is that this entire process makes me nervous."

"Do you know why?"

"It should be obvious. Mark's situation has me and the rest of the family upset. I feel like somehow we should have been able to head this off or resolve it in some way."

"And how could you have done that?"

"I really don't know. But somehow, as a father, I feel I have failed. You have to realize that all my career I have been trained not to fail. That is a cornerstone of my profession."

Lydia leaned forward, her eyes unblinking and intent. "In your profession, Dan, you receive many hours of training to accomplish a specific task. How much training have you had in the psychology of family matters?"

"None, of course."

"There you have it. No reason for guilt. You have much to learn if you wish. That is why I am here."

Her confidence startled Dan. "That is almost the same thing that Manalani said."

Lydia leaned back, relaxing slightly and smiled. "Well, she was right. Unlike with an airplane, I may not be able to give you a specific set of procedures, but I certainly can help you see the situation more clearly."

"I'll admit that would be relief, but how does it work?"

"Well, first I need to know your feelings and knowledge about sexual orientation."

"I can tell you I don't know much. It's a subject that never interested me much, and one that I thought I would never get involved with. Even the term sexual orientation seems strange to me."

"It is a term that now is widely used because it is not emotionally loaded and is rather accurate. You see, this is not an either-or situation. Like a compass, a person can point in various directions that contain components of each extreme."

"But does anyone know what makes somebody pick a particular orientation?"

Lydia paused slightly and looked down at her notebook. Dan could see that she was giving her reply careful consideration. "The answer to that question, Dan, is strewn with a number of discarded theories. We know it isn't the role of a domineering father or an overly protective mother, or a single parent situation, or an artistic temperament, or the result of an incident in childhood, or the influence of another gay oriented person. The latest studies and theories revolve around the hypothalamus, particularly the interstitial nuclei called INAH3."

Dan felt simultaneously relieved and disturbed at these remarks. "How sure are you of this stuff? You said most of the earlier theories are out the window. Will the same thing happen here?"

"We are on firmer ground now. The prejudice of the past has hopefully been dropped, and these new studies have a good scientific basis. However, they are still very preliminary. Human behavior is a very complex phenomenon, that's why scientists and psychologists prefer to work with rats when they can."

This humor on her part relieved some of Dan's tension, and they both had a small laugh from its benefit.

Lydia continued. "What we can be fairly sure of at this point is that the determinants of **sexual orientation** take place very early on, probably in utero. The main point of my little presentation is that you are off the hook. You may have influenced Mark in other ways but you did not determine his sexual orientation. Does that make you feel better?"

"Of course, but where does that leave us?"

"To a large extent that depends on you, Dan. I can help Mark find his way through the maze that he is in, but the more support you can give him the easier it will be. He may not admit it to you, but he probably needs your understanding and backing more than any time since he was a baby."

"I'm willing to do that, but I'm still bothered by a couple of things."

"Good, Dan, I really want the air to be cleared so there is no confusion or mixed message between you and Mark."

Dan hesitated. He felt distinctly uncomfortable talking to a stranger about sexual matters that he had never discussed with anyone. To help Mark though, he needed to plunge ahead. He looked out the window past her head and said, "It seems to me that Mark could still be influenced in his, ah, preferences. And, if that's true, I think he should be pushed, even leaned on to go the straight route. Let's face it. It's just a lot easier road. I mean how many men end up gay anyway? It's a lifestyle that is something I certainly wouldn't want to deal with and could get Mark in a lot of trouble."

Lydia paused before answering him, and Dan decided to tell her what was really bothering him. "It seems to me that you don't care what route Mark takes. I realize you should maybe be professionally neutral on this subject, but I have to live with Mark; my God, he's my son. I want the best for him." Dan found himself twisting in his seat. He clenched his fists and then opened them. Lydia was watching him closely.

"Dan, this again is a subject that is open to interpretation. As far as percentages go, surveys have come up with numbers from two to seven percent, but we know that surveys on emotionally loaded subjects are unreliable. Mark could probably continue to live as he has, but this will leave him with internal conflict that will express itself in any of a number of negative channels. I'm not suggesting that he flaunt or express his orientation to his peers, but he has to come to terms with it, within himself."

She paused, and Dan launched a question. "Where does that leave us? What can I do, or Manalani? I still think he can be influenced to go straight. Wouldn't that be best for him?"

Dan could tell she was impatient or unsatisfied with his questions. She frowned and raised her hand to cut him off. "Dan, what I'm driving at is that it is already too late to influence Mark's orientation. That was set a long time ago. We can influence his outward behavior, and he can control that of course, but he must be free to find his own way. Any attempt by you to influence him will probably be met with resistance and possibly antagonism."

"Well, that doesn't leave me with much to go on."

"What he needs from you is your support and acceptance of him the way he is."

"What if I don't like the way he is?"

"You don't have to like it, Dan. You just have to accept it. I know this is tough for you. You may feel like you are giving up on him. But I can't overemphasize, what he needs from you are approval and acceptance."

"It's damn hard for me to approve of something I couldn't accept in myself."

"I don't expect it to be easy for you. This is hard for any father. But, I hope you can find it in yourself to do it. This is a turning point in your relationship with your son, and it is up to you how it turns out."

"Okay, Okay. I got that. I don't like it, but I can do it."

Dan looked into her eyes, and she stared back unwaveringly. Then she stood up, and as he rose, she took his hand. "Dan, you may find this hard to believe now, but I can assure you this is the best path." Next, she gave Dan a book detailing some of this information. Then he was out on the street, in the blinding sun. He looked down at the book in his hands and felt nervous, a little guilty, like a high school boy with a porno book that he wants to hide. This is ridiculous, he thought, but the feeling would not go away.

CHAPTER 9

Those memories of the past intruded into Dan's life. The whole issue of Mark's sexuality and the visit to the therapist was bad enough, but Dan also had present concerns. Now he wasn't sure he could ever fly the Eagle again. The ankle gave Dan as much trouble as the doctor said it would. He had to elevate it repeatedly, as the blood pooling inside the cast would throb painfully. Learning to maneuver in tight situations was more difficult than Dan could have imagined. The pain of his broken ribs forced him to rise from bed like an old man, rolling over onto his side and then pushing up slowly with his arms.

The days did begin to settle into a routine punctuated primarily by two visits each week to physical therapy. His condition and mood improved considerably when the cast came off. Some days involved reports that were necessary for the company, FAA, or accident investigators. There were visits by Airline Pilots Association (ALPA) lawyers, insurance adjusters, and friends. He felt duty bound to contact the families of the dead crewmembers. Before he contacted anyone, he had to go through several layers of company protocol. On one level he resented this, but he also realized that the process was necessary. His presence could be emotionally explosive.

In the case of Ann, the lead flight attendant, a dramatic confrontation ensued with one of her brothers at a large family gathering. Apparently, he did not know about Dan's presence. When he found out Dan's identity, he rushed him. "What are you doing here? Who let you in? Ann is dead. Why aren't you?"

Unprepared for the outburst, Dan hardly knew what to say. The best he could come up with was, "Don't you think I have already asked myself that same question, over and over? I'm sorry; I thought I could help."

The brother was stocky and well muscled. His pent-up grief and frustration had found an outlet. Dan could see that they were on the thin edge of a physical confrontation, probably only stayed by his own obvious injuries. He found himself backing up step-by-step. Other family members, obviously upset by the outburst, were frightened into passiveness. Dan looked from side-to-side, hoping someone would intercede.

"What are you looking for? Nobody's coming to your rescue. Get out of here! We don't need you. Go question yourself somewhere else."

Mac stepped in; "Look we are sorry. We didn't realize the affect this would have on you. We will leave immediately."

When they reached the car, Dan found himself shaking and hardly able to speak. A family member came up to apologize, and Dan mumbled his thanks. Now he just wanted to get away. His skin felt clammy, the shaking increased, and he felt lightheaded. He turned to Mac and said, "This is crazy; I feel like I'm going to pass out. Won't this nightmare ever end?" Mac reassured Dan as best he could. Dan finally reached a state where he felt like an empty shell, drained of all emotion.

***

On his return home, he dreaded making the phone call to Manalani's parents, but when he did, it took a great load off his mind. His apology was not needed. They knew that he had done everything he possibly could. He felt they were holding back, but maybe that was best. They accepted his offer to bring Manalani's ashes to them, though it might be several months before he could visit. They had no desire to come to the mainland.

He hired a gardener and a housekeeper to take care of chores. When the flowers that Manalani had planted began to die, part of her presence was withering away, and he would become depressed. Sometimes he would gather a few into a vase in the kitchen. Then he would sit and stare at them for long periods, his mind spinning with memories or strangely blank. Some days when the stratus moved in off the ocean, and the atmosphere turned ominous and cold, he felt like the sky was pressing down on him. He would look out the bedroom window in the morning at the steel gray clouds and feel like they were sucking the energy from his body and mind. Getting out of bed would be an invitation to a dissonant dirge of a day. But a classic azure Southern California day with puffy clouds scudding by wasn't much better. It produced memories of the days with Manalani, an intense loneliness, a separation that he could not disperse by any of his ordinary activities.

They had held a small memorial service for Manalani not long after he was released from the hospital. For a while, he was comforted by the number of people at the ceremony and by those who called afterward, but eventually they moved on with their own lives. Dan felt he also should be moving on, but he couldn't find the energy to do it. He would reach in the cupboard for a coffee cup and see hers. Immediately, a series of visions would flash into his mind; the cup at her lips, in her hands at the breakfast table, the light shining off it on the deck when she put it down to dive in the pool. He would walk by her chair near the fireplace, his hand drifting across it, and he imagined he could feel her hair on its back cushion. In the garage, her gloves and grass clippers produced the image of glistening drops of sweat on her tanned back, and the way she would brush the sweat and hair from her face.

The whole house was invested with the presence of a ghost who he did not want to exorcise. Yet, in an attempt to do this, Dan and the kids decided to have their own private ceremony with the McCartys. They invited Mac and Ruth over late in the afternoon. Dan made sundowners, and they sat around telling stories about Manalani.

What they were trying to do, Mac said, was to evoke a sense of Manalani's presence, not just to recall her, but also to get a feel of what she would want them to do in their present situation. He expanded on this thought. "Dan, somehow you need to get a feeling of closure. That one chapter, or a whole book of your life has ended, and now there is a new one opening up."

"I know that's what should happen," Dan replied, "But I just can't get to the point where I want to open a new chapter or book."

Liz suggested, "What about doing something with her ashes, Dad?"

"I've been thinking about that. You know she joked about coming up as a carrot or broccoli in the garden, but maybe it wasn't just a joke. I think that would make her happy. The garden was mostly her creation, except for the corn, which was my baby."

"Well, should we do it?"

"I think so. It somehow would make me happy too, knowing that part of her was still in one of her favorite places, regenerating each year."

From the urn, inside its box, they each spread a little of her ashes over the garden. Each of them said a few words to her spirit. Dan found the event strangely anticlimactic. He couldn't rise to what he thought should be a significant occasion. No way could six pounds of substance, resembling gray kitty litter, represent the woman he loved. Any attempt to force his emotions into what he thought was an appropriate mode met with an internal resistance from a source he could not locate. If he let this mood run free, he knew it would turn bitter and self-destructive.

Dan had hoped that their little ceremony would lessen the intensity of his mood swings, but that night he had one of his falling in the chasm nightmares and had to take a pain pill and sleeping pill to go back to sleep.

Later, he did perform his own ceremony. One night, when the kids were gone, he went to the library and music room where he kept his horn. When he took it out of the case and twisted on the mouthpiece, he found the reed was dry. He soaked it in a glass of water then kept it in his mouth to lubricate it. He never liked the new plastic reeds. Though they didn't crack or dry out, they just didn't have the right tone and resonance.

While he was doing this, he wondered, *Is this right? Can I make it through this? I've got to.*

He fingered the horn. Good, the keys were still lubed, and the pads were soft. A few scales, some chords, and a couple of riffs. Yes, feeling was coming back, and it felt good.

He made it through the first few bars, but when he hit the rising phrase, where the melody floated over the top, he flashed back to that night. He could see her in all her loveliness, and his breath caught; the lump in his throat choked him off.

"Honey—I can't do this."

But from somewhere the reply came, "Yes, you can."

He took two deep breaths and went back.

This time it flowed, and he flowed with it, back to that time and that feeling. He and his sax became one, lost in the music and the scene. When he finished the long extended last phrase, he felt empty. But it was the emptiness of peace and resolution. He gently placed the horn back in its case and collapsed onto the couch. His mind had stopped in a place of extraordinary calm and stayed there until sleep replaced it, utterly entranced and feeling whole for the first time.

***

As the weeks went by, Feron Stewart kept Dan aware of progress on the investigation in Hong Kong. They had reconstructed the airplane in a maintenance hanger, and checked all the systems. The technical part of the process was finished. At one point Dan and a clerk sent the Civil Air Department his logs and recent aircraft experience. The day finally came when a date was set for his appearance.

The flight to Hong Kong was a strange experience for Dan. The flight crew knew why he was on board and tried in a not very subtle way to keep his spirits up. In spite of assurances from all those concerned in ops and safety at Intercontinental, he was aware that none of them had any vested interest in the outcome except to keep the company's name in the clear.

They told him that although he could have a lawyer with him, this was not a legal proceeding; it was a technical investigation. Only those with a proven need to know would be there. The ALPA view was that the company's and Dan's interest might not coincide, if things came to a crunch. The union rep encouraged Dan to have a staff lawyer accompany him, but Dan felt that would indicate a defensive attitude, so he declined the offer. A company officer from the legal department could be there that Dan could use for consultation.

During the night, the crew invited him up to the cockpit jump seat. At first, Dan hesitated. He would have a hard time making it up the aisle using his cane, and he wasn't sure about how the conversation would go once he got there. When the captain came back personally and said, "C'mon old buddy, you need a break from sitting back here," that broke down any reservations he had.

Once there, he fought with two conflicting feelings. It was comforting to be back in that environment which had been his life for so many years, but when would he be able to sit in that seat again, watching the night sky revolve overhead?

Ahead and to their right, a line of huge buildups showed on the radar. Outside, they were illuminated by lightning and the moon behind them. The outlines of the cauliflower shaped clouds glowed as lightning flashed like a series of flashbulbs along their interiors. Occasionally, lightning would strike out at the ocean or leap from cloud to cloud, fireworks of the sky gone berserk. The tops of the massive columns of rising air spread out into huge anvil heads up at altitudes far above them.

This display of nature's power they only appreciated at a distance. No pilot ever penetrated a line like this purposely.

Dan remarked on this, and the captain replied, "Yeah, we had to divert about a hundred miles left of course to avoid those beauties. One of the great things about being out in this empty ocean is we can go just about anywhere we want."

Dan looked out the side window. He could see the first light of dawn rising in the sky behind them. How many times had he seen the sun rise or set? Sometimes the sun would descend into the horizon as a red disk and they might see the green flash. More commonly, there were clouds that would produce a different effect each time, from brilliant yellow and salmon through the spectrum to pink and violet. Now he wondered if he would ever see this display again, to know the earth as a vast blue marble, to see its veins and arteries, its connectedness, its displays of energy and calmness.

From his viewpoint he saw how fragile and yet destructive was man's hold on the planet. Only small areas were open to colonization by humans, and yet those areas were eroded and overrun. Sometimes at night, the city corridors looked like cancerous cells spreading over the land. On the other hand, he could see long rift zones formed by shifting tectonic plates, huge pits where giant meteorites struck, chains of volcanoes, all indicating forces beyond man's control.

He was also aware that transportation in general, and airplanes in particular, contributed to the process of pollution on the earth. When confronted about this at one gathering his reply was, "You are right. I won't argue that. But, unless you are willing to go back to bicycles and sailboats, there is no way around it. Besides, I am just your servant. If it bothers you enough don't fly. But don't drive either; collectively that's worse. Eventually we will go to hydrogen fuel, and that will be non-polluting, except for water vapor."

As all those thoughts spun through his head, the crew was quietly attending to position reports. When they were done, the first officer leaned back in his seat and said, "Well, you are on your way to the inquisition, right?"

"You got it," Dan replied, "And that's the way I feel about it right now."

"Yeah. They sit back there for months, consulting with the experts, running through the tapes for hours, and then second-guess us on a decision we made in seconds."

"Well, I guess that's the way it's always been, but believe me, when it's you on that hot seat, it doesn't feel good."

"We've already heard that you lost an engine and then hit a sinker. Is that right?"

"Yes, that's the gist of it. You know, I think Ernie Gann said, 'The emergencies you train for almost never happen. It's the one you can't train for that kills you.' And there sure as hell isn't an emergency procedure for windshear with an engine out at heavy weight."

"That should let you off the hook, shouldn't it?"

"In theory you're right, but you know they are always looking for a fall guy."

The captain added, "You know they say that 70% of accidents are pilot error. That's because unless the wing falls off, or the plane blows up, there usually is something the pilot could do to save the day, even if nobody thought of it before."

"That's what I'm afraid of. For most of the industry it's better if the pilot can be found at fault rather than have to look at any system-wide changes."

The captain said, "Good luck on this, Dan. Here's my card. I would really like to hear your view on this, after it's all over. I can well imagine it may be different from what we read in the papers or see in one of our ops bulletins."

"I'll do that," Dan replied, "And thanks for calling me up front. I almost didn't do it, but it meant more to me than I thought it would. Believe me, you never want to be in the position of even considering you may never sit on the left seat again. I've got a long ways to go to come back to flying status."

"Well, stay there as long as you want. You deserve it, and we're in no hurry."

Dan did that for a while, his thoughts idling over other trips he had made out to the orient, avoiding the thought that this could be his last one.

***

Dan was disturbed by his return to Hong Kong. He never loved the city the way Manalani did. The smell of garlic and ginger cooking would create a lump in his throat. He would see the path by the church they had walked and a shudder would run up his back. The Hilton was full, so they stayed at the Islander Hotel. Dan was glad of that.

At dinner that night, Dan met the rest of the Intercontinental contingent. He had spoken to most of them at one point or another, but Feron Stewart and Dennis Silver, from the Safety Department, were the only two he knew well.

The next morning, when they arrived at the building set for the hearing, the granite structure and Greek columns made it appear impressive from the outside. As they went through the doors into the hearing room, Dan was surprised. The style was what he thought of as the Swedish mode, all clean lines with very little decoration. The physical layout disturbed Dan. The separated witness seat, and the tables and chairs facing it, reminded him of a courtroom. The only missing piece was the raised dais of the judge's bench.

Dan was introduced to a number of people, technicians and officers from the airplane and engine manufacturers, weather forecasters, tower personnel, crash and rescue firefighters, airport operations people, someone from the United Kingdom Air Accident Investigations Branch who was there as technical liaison. An FAA Air Carrier Inspector from Honolulu was present, not a good sign for Dan. The one man who held his attention was the chief investigator for the Hong Kong CAD, a Mr. Harold Dunsett. He would ask Dan most of the required questions.

Dan tried to size him up in the brief introductory period. Physically he was not imposing, medium build, a perfunctory handshake, thinning dark hair, very white skin, fleshy cheeks, dark brown eyes, set in a perpetual squint behind metal-rimmed glasses. The only aspect that Dan found remarkable was his voice. It had a resonance that came from deep in his chest and projected outward with no seeming effort. Dan imagined that he could use it for dramatic effect if he chose to. Though nothing yet warranted it, Dan could not help but think of him as an adversary.

The presentation of many technical details, most of which had almost no bearing on the actual event, took a good part of the day, through the lunch recess, and into the afternoon. This demonstrated that the investigation had left no stone unturned in their search for the cause.

Dan did pay close attention when they revealed that the weather radar had picked up the image of a big rain cell approaching the runway. This information had not reached the tower operator by the time of Dan's take-off. He wanted to make sure that they understood that he and the other pilots had no warning of the situation they were about to encounter.

When his turn came to take the hot seat, as he thought of it, he saw people throughout the room began to shift in their chairs, sitting upright. A pulse of anticipation ran through the room. He could see everyone was waiting for this event.

The cane made Dan feel clumsy, and as he took his place in the seat facing them, a wave of nervousness swept over him. His ankle throbbed, and he could feel his legs shaking slightly. He was glad that they not visible. As he adjusted the microphone to his height, there was a slight tremor in his hand. Why was this happening he wondered? He had nothing to fear, nothing to hide. He shrugged his shoulders and pressed his legs together to compose himself.

The preliminary questions were easy to answer and dealt with his background and flying experience. This put Dan more at ease. His voice lost its edginess and deepened as he gained confidence. In part, he was trying to match the stentorian tones of Mr. Dunsett. It seemed to Dan that Mr. Dunsett used his voice to inject drama into a dry proceeding that held little interest except to those who had a vested stake in some technical details. Dan distrusted him for this.

Dan recounted the events leading up to the take-off. When he reached the point of describing their attempts to get clear radar returns, Mr. Dunsett interrupted him for the first time. "Captain Swanton, could you please give us some more details on how you set the radar in your attempt to clear up the ground clutter?"

"I'm not sure what details you are interested in," Dan replied.

"Oh, angle of tilt, range, gain, that sort of thing."

"We tilted the dish up to ten degrees. We tried twenty-five and ten-mile ranges. The gain we always leave on automatic."

"And how long did this process take?"

"It's hard for me to say, I wasn't timing it."

"Just an approximation will be fine."

"Well, certainly less than a minute, probably around thirty seconds."

Dan was disturbed. What was going on here? What point was Mr. Dunsett trying to make?

"Are you aware that we were able to obtain another MD-11 with identical radar and ran some tests on the end of runway 13?"

"No, certainly not. What did you expect to find out?"

"We had no expectations, but we wanted to determine if it is possible to separate cloud returns from the ground clutter the mountains produce."

"So, what did you find?" Dan didn't like this. Mr. Dunsett had no reason to pursue this line unless he had some dramatic revelation to produce.

"We found that if you raise the tilt up to the twelve to fifteen-degree range and reduce the gain somewhat, it is possible to separate cloud and ground clutter returns."

Dan now saw where this was leading and replied, "That's

not a procedure we have ever used at Intercontinental. A twelve-degree or more tilt is far above the flight path we can achieve."

"I realize that, Captain Swanton, but I want you to know that it is possible."

Dan had a flash of inspiration. "How long did you take?" Dan could see that this challenge startled Mr. Dunsett.

"I don't quite understand your question."

"How long did you spend on the runway making your determination?"

"I would say somewhere between three and five minutes. We did it during a slack traffic period."

"I would like to remind you then that we had less than a minute on the end of that runway. Traffic was already turning in on final. We had to clear the runaway." Dan could see that he had dampened some of the impact of Mr. Dunsett's revelation.

"I was simply pointing out to you, Captain Swanton, that this was possible. Did you know that Dragon Air has a similar procedure that they use at Kai Tak Airport?"

"No. I was not aware of it. Never heard of it until you brought it up now."

"That is a pity."

"Of course it is, but you can't expect us to use a procedure that we are unaware of."

"That is not the point I am trying to make. It is unfortunate that airlines are not aware of each other's procedures. Sometimes a little local knowledge can be quite valuable."

"I won't argue that point," Dan replied.

Mr. Dunsett continued, "Many of us involved in accident

investigation—air, sea, or land—adhere to the principle of attempting to determine where in the chain of events lies the last clear chance to avoid this accident. If this determination can be made, then the chain of events can be broken, and such an accident prevented. Many of us hold the philosophy of last clear chance to be an important doctrine. It appears to me that the last clear chance in this case occurred on the end of the runway. If you had been able to see the return from the rain cell, which was approaching the runway, would you have made the take-off?"

"No, of course not. But in the thirty or so seconds we had, there was no way to make that assessment given our knowledge at the time."

Sensing Dan's rising anger and frustration, Mr. Dunsett smiled for the first time and said, "Captain Swanton, we are not placing blame here. This is not a legal proceeding or an adversary situation as you sometimes face in the United States. This is simply a technical investigation that attempts to determine cause and provide a means of prevention in the future."

Though Dan didn't like it, he felt there was little more to be said on the subject. He could not help but also feel that his leadership was being called into question, that somehow he should have known of this radar procedure. He admitted to himself that had he known of it, they probably would have refused the take-off clearance and the crash would not have happened. He stuffed that thought into the recesses of his mind for later consideration. He replied to Mr. Dunsett by saying, "I'm glad to hear that."

Mr. Dunsett shuffled some of his papers and said, "I think we can move on now. Continue, Captain Swanton."

Dan moved through the rest of his narrative to the actual moment of contact with the water and came to a stop. Silence prevailed for several seconds. Then a representative from McDonnell-Douglas stepped up to an available microphone and introduced himself. "I am Robert Chapin, from engineering flight test, and there is one point I would like to clarify."

"Go ahead."

"I believe you stated that at contact you were about eighteen degrees pitch attitude with two engines at maximum thrust."

"That's correct, to the best of my recollection. Of course, the airplane was not in a steady state condition. So what is your point, Mr. Chapin?"

"The Digital Flight Data Recorder concurs with your estimate."

"So, what is your point?"

"I think you should know that there is no transport category aircraft constructed in the world that is designed to withstand contact with the water in that configuration."

"That does not surprise me." Dan could not stop the sarcasm slipping out from his voice.

Mr. Chapin continued, "I'm sure you know that the proper ditching configuration is a five to eight degree pitch attitude with engines close to idle."

"Of course, but we were not performing a ditching then. We were trying to keep the airplane in the air."

"I realize that, but at any point did you consider going to the ditching configuration. In other words, did you at some point realize that you were going in, in spite of your best efforts?"

Dan now sensed where this line of questioning was going, and he didn't like it. He replied, "We were probably within fifty feet

140

of the water before any thought of that entered my mind."

Mr. Chapin pressed on. "You do realize that if you had ditched in a normal configuration, that the airplane would have remained structurally intact, and the loss of life would have been minimal."

Dan was furious. Who was this imperious bastard, and who did he think he was talking to? Dan leaned forward scowling. His knuckles were white where he gripped the witness box. "I'm sure YOU are aware that besides the loss of passengers, eight flight attendants, and three pilots, my wife died in this crash, and I was doing my utmost to save their lives."

Mr. Chapin started to speak, but Dan waved him off and pointed his finger at him. "You talk about a ditching procedure. Where would you have us decide—at fifty feet, one hundred, two hundred? It would take at least two-hundred feet to convert to a ditching mode and the highest point in our flight was barely that high. Your question has no basis in reality, in the situation that we faced."

Although he was across the room, Mr. Chapin recoiled at Dan's pointed finger and anger. In a conciliatory tone of voice he replied, "I did not mean to criticize your actions, Captain Swanton. I merely wanted to make the point that the airframe could not be expected to survive water contact in the flight configuration that was present."

Dan relaxed slightly. He realized that this questioning was all a posture for the lawsuits that would eventually follow.

Mr. Dunsett called for a recess. When they reconvened, Dan was asked no further questions. When he realized that the proceedings were winding down with only a few details remaining, he exited quietly. Unlike the United States, there was no mass of reporters and camera operators outside the doors.

He reached his hotel room in a state of exhaustion and agitation. When he lay down on the bed, exhaustion won out, and he slept for two hours. When the phone rang, his mental state was such that he could not recall where he was, or the time. For a few seconds he thought he was at home. The call was from Feron Stewart. He and Dennis were ready for dinner. Would Dan like to join them? Dan accepted, though part of him just wanted to stay in bed and disappear. At dinner, they reassured Dan that things had gone well. He did not need to worry about an assault on his character or flying skills.

However, a few weeks after Dan returned from Hong Kong he received a letter from the Federal Aviation Agency. As he opened it, he had a premonition that it was not routine mailing. He paused a few moments to calm himself before reading it. Just as he suspected, it was a Notice of Proposed Certificate Action requiring him to respond within fifteen days. Immediately, anger rose to the surface, but simultaneously he felt his stomach churn. The FAA seldom backed down once they started this process. Unless they were completely off base, the best a pilot could hope for was some form of compromise.

At first he thought they would be going after him for "careless and reckless operation," the catch-all regulation they used any time a pilot made a mistake. To his surprise the regulation in question had nothing to do with the accident; it was FAR 61.57, failure to report a visit/consultation with a health professional.

Dan was relieved in part. He knew it must have been about his visit to Lydia Skoros concerning Mark's problems. He immediately phoned Dennis. He was an old friend of Dan's, a classmate, with whom Dan had always felt a bond. In the Air Force, Dennis had been a safety officer and accident investigator. He was a good listener and a keen observer of human behavior, a combination that instilled trust in his peers. Though his office was outside the direct chain of command, he held a position of influence.

After giving him a summary of the letter, he couldn't help complaining. "See, Dennis, I told you they would get a swat at me, and now it has happened."

Dennis replied, "I guess you are right, but at least it doesn't have to do with operational matters."

"Yeah, but what business is it of theirs if I saw a shrink about a problem my son was having."

"I don't think that is much of a concern," Dennis replied, "but the fact you didn't report it gives them an open and shut case if they want to push it."

"I didn't report it because it wasn't about me."

"But they don't know that, do they. All they know is you had a consultation. The way to handle this is to send them a letter asking for an informal hearing as they call it. Go to it with an ALPA attorney. Don't get in an uproar over something that will probably come out in the wash."

"Easy for you to say. It's not your license that is on the line."

"Hey, they're not going to yank your license over something like this. It is a hassle, but just go through the process. Okay?"

Dan agreed. He knew there was no other course. He contacted ALPA legal services and they drafted a letter in reply requesting an informal hearing and admitting nothing.

***

When the letter reached the office of the FAA Air Carrier Inspector who originated the case, he leaned around his cubicle to comment to his neighbor, "Looks like we're going to have a hearing with that Intercontinental pilot who crashed in Hong Kong."

"Well, that's what you expected, Jack. So what sort of compromise are you going to propose?"

"Compromise! Hell, I'll propose that he never flies again. You can't tell me that someone can recover from an accident like that without Post Traumatic Stress Disorder. He'll be a walking time bomb. Besides, he probably shouldn't have been making that flight anyway. He was seeing a shrink just shortly before."

"Yeah, but you don't know what it was about."

"Who cares what it was about. He didn't report it, so he must have something to hide. He busted a proficiency check a few years before. Report says he had the flu. What the hell was he doing taking a proficiency check if he had the flu? I think what we have here is a guy who doesn't know when to quit. A hero complex. Mr. Superiority."

"Well, I've got a feeling that he won't feel so superior when you are done with him."

"It's nothing personal, but I think here is a guy who should ride off into the sunset; take advantage of his medical retirement; go fly a chair, or a glider, or an ultralight where all he can do if he screws up is kill himself."

"Sure, I can see your point, but try and convince him."

"I'll make a bet with you. Whether or not I convince him, I'll bet you he never gets back into the left seat again."

"Hell no, Jack. I wouldn't take that bet. Not when I see that crusading gleam in your eye."

When the appointed time arrived, Dan and his ALPA attorney, Phil Durskin, faced the inspector, Jack Rulley, and an FAA attorney, James Schiffer, across a large table in a conference room big enough for a dozen participants. Dan was glad this was not a physical confrontation, since both of the men across the table looked like they were ex-linebackers cut from the same mold. Schiffer, behind his glasses, exuded a predatory power that was imposing. He hoped that Phil wasn't cowed by their presence. The FAA held most of the cards in this proceeding. Phil's relaxed manner and his almost college boy good looks seemed out of place here.

After the preliminaries were over, the FAA attorney said, "As you know, when we were going through your records after your accident, we discovered that you had made two visits last year to a therapist, Ms. Lydia Skoros. Would you like to comment on this matter, and why it wasn't reported."

Dan glowered at him and said in a contentious voice,"I thought you would already have that information, Mr. Schiffer."

As he said that he felt the impact of Phil's foot against his leg. When he turned slightly to look at him, Phil's eyes held a warning that obviously implied, back off, be cool, don't get things stirred up.

Mr. Schiffer calmly replied, "The dates are a matter of record. The subject matter is privileged information. It is your choice if you wish to divulge it."

Dan had to choke down his desired reply, which was that he didn't think any information was privileged if the FAA or the

IRS wanted it. Phil replied for him, probably fearing another retort. "Captain Swanton was seeing Ms. Skoros about a matter that concerned family problems with his son. It had nothing to do with his state of mind."

"Yes, it appears to have involved a code violation in Honolulu, 232 I believe," replied the attorney.

Dan couldn't help himself. "How did you get that information?"

"The police blotter is a matter of public record."

Dan looked at the slight smile on the attorney's face as he said that. Smug bastard. I can't let this get through to me. Just pretend that it is happening to someone else.

For the first time Jack Rulley spoke, "Would you care to tell us why you didn't report this, Captain Swanton?"

"Of course. It wasn't a matter that concerned me directly. It was about my son. I felt that it had no bearing on my career, my ability to fly."

"Yet this must have been upsetting to you; serious enough to involve the entire family and at least two visits to the therapist on your part."

"Certainly. But a lot of things in family life are upsetting. Certainly, you don't think that pilots should go on sick leave every time a family crisis comes up. I don't think the company would look kindly on that event."

The inspector tilted back in his chair, rotated his pen in his hand, and glanced up at the ceiling as if addressing an unknown audience of angels. "Yes, but most family problems don't result in visits to psychiatrists for family counseling."

"Look. Like most pilots, I have the ability to shut out my family life when it comes to flying. When I fly, I have a job to do, and I do it. Everything else gets put on hold. In my judgment, my son's problems were not going to affect my performance. As a captain, making judgment calls are part of why I'm sitting in the left seat. It goes with the territory."

"Your point is well taken," replied the inspector. "If you don't mind, I would like to move to another related subject."

Dan looked at Phil who gave a slight shrug of his shoulders. "All right, go ahead, Mr. Rulley."

"Four years ago, on February fourteenth, you failed to pass a proficiency check. I believe our records show that you were sick with the flu at the time."

Phil jumped in at this point with an objection. "I don't see, Mr. Rulley, where this has any relationship to the matter at hand. Unless it does, I would have to object to including it in this discussion."

"Just bear with me for a few moments please. Captain Swanton has raised an interesting point here about making judgment calls, and I would like to expand on it a little."

"All right, I will withdraw my objection for now," Phil replied.

Dan didn't like this turn of events, but if Phil didn't object, he felt he had better play along.

The inspector continued. "Now Captain Swanton, if you had the flu, why did you decide to go for your proficiency check. Surely you could have called in sick."

Dan was prepared for this. "If it had been a revenue flight, I would have called in sick. But a simulator check presents a different problem. I just started feeling sick the night before. In the morning, when I woke up, I didn't feel that bad, so I decided to go on with it. You have to realize that if you cancel at the last minute for a check, it really fouls things up. The sims are on a really tight schedule, and of course no one can take my place as on a revenue flight."

Rulley broke in, "Yes, Captain Swanton, I am familiar with the problems of simulator scheduling. I have to deal with them more than you do."

Dan shrugged off this rebuke and continued. "As the day and the period progressed, I obviously became more sick, headache, shakes, joint pain. I couldn't hold that intense concentration that is required for several hours to get through a check, so I called it quits."

"An understandable decision," the inspector replied. "However, earlier in your judgment, your condition wasn't such that you thought it would affect your performance."

"Of course, but the situation changed as the day progressed, and I had to change my mind. I am not inflexible."

"Yes, that decision was forced upon you by your condition. The point I am making here is that judgment calls are a difficult matter, especially when they involve psychological matters. Your ability to judge when your performance is affected is not an easy one to make."

Dan was furious at the inferences that the inspector was making. He knew it was showing but he couldn't stop it. Luckily, Phil stepped in. "Your point is very interesting Mr. Rulley, but I think in the matter at hand, it is quite obvious that the failure to disclose on Captain Swanton's part was inadvertent. There was no purposeful attempt to conceal, and that should weigh heavily in your findings."

The FAA attorney replied, "Of course we will take that into account, Mr. Durskin."

After a few closing comments by both attorneys, they were finished and out the door. In the parking lot Phil said to Dan, "Hey, you are off the hook, pretty much. Go home and relax. You look furious. Have a drink or something."

"Of course I'm furious," replied Dan. "What was all that crap he was throwing in there at the end, about me busting the checkride?"

"Oh, that was just a fishing expedition. Won't have any bearing on the outcome. As long as your failure to disclose was inadvertent, they only have a technical violation. They will give you a slap on the wrist. It will probably be a warning notice. Anything more, and they know we would take it on appeal, and they would lose in court if it got that far.

Dan still wasn't happy. "But Phil, you know that letter stays in my file for two years. Combine that with my accident, and that is a big cloud over my head."

Phil replied, "There is no procedure to appeal that decision. That's why I think they will take that route."

As he drove home, Dan thought it would take a long time before he regained his old confidence. It was bad enough having to deal with the aftermath of his accident without having the FAA impugning his judgment.

***

When Phil reached his office he placed a call to a friend of his in the Intercontinental legal department. "Hello, Kay. This is Phil. It went just as I expected. He will get off with a slap on the wrist. They don't have much of a case. So how is it on your end?"

"Phil, this is something off the record. For your ears only. Okay?"

"Yeah, go ahead. I'm all ears and discretion."

"There are a number of people here in the company, fairly high up, that wish the FAA would have shot Captain Swanton down. It would have resolved a problem for them."

"Oh, I get it. Appearances, image and all that stuff. What about from your end?"

"No problem here. We just deal in facts, or what passes for them. But in marketing and personnel, appearances are everything."

"I can see that. Sure wouldn't look good if it got out that a captain with a big accident on his record is out there flying people through the sky again. Especially if something else should happen."

"You got it. At least it's not on my shoulders."

"Keep your nose clean over there. With your brains and charisma you should go far. See you this Saturday night at the party?"

"I'll be there, but late. I have a dinner engagement earlier."

"Don't worry; I'll wait up. Bye now."

Kay was attractive in an athletic way. With her trim body, dark brown hair, and emerald eyes, she was accustomed to being hit on by her professional single colleagues. She reflected back to a meeting earlier that day. She had not told Phil about it. She probably wouldn't. It was too dangerous a topic to disclose to anyone, outside the small group within the company that was involved.

At the end of the weekly operations meeting the Vice President of Operations held back Kay and the heads of the marketing, cabin service, flight operations, and Bill Konig for a private conference. His imposing frame and stern manner made even his peers nervous in his presence, and they usually deferred to his decisions.

"Well, where are we on this subject of Captain Swanton's possible return to the line?"

Kay responded, "He's at an informal hearing with FAA today."

"So, can you hazard a guess at the outcome?"

"His ALPA attorney thinks they don't have enough to shoot him down. I agree. From a legal standpoint there is probably nothing to stop him from coming back."

"Bill, what about the possibility of you influencing him to just ease into retirement? We certainly wouldn't mind paying him off in this case."

"I couldn't even begin that line with him. He would feel like it was a betrayal of trust. You know how the pilots are. They love to piss and moan about getting another job if they knew how. But if you actually suggest anything like that to them seriously, they will fight you tooth and nail. It's a matter of pride, and peer pressure too. There might be two percent that would walk away, but Swanton isn't one of them."

"Well then, Larry, what are the implications in marketing if he comes back?"

"On the surface at least, it should have no effect. Nobody should even know about it. He's just another guy sitting up front. But the implications aren't good. What if the crews start talking, or some reporter hears about it, or God forbid, there should be some future incident. I hate to think about the results if some program like Hard Copy decided to run with it."

"If it happens, then we will deal with it then, though you

might devote some time and energy to a contingency plan to mitigate the results. Now, what about the cabin service? Did you get a sounding or survey there?"

It was obvious to Kay that the representative from cabin service was not happy with her part. She kept pulling at her ear and brushing back her blond hair as she talked. "I'm not sure how to break this down but it seems that we have three groups. The majority of flight attendants have not given it much thought and probably would go along with the program. A small group knows Captain Swanton personally, and nearly all of them would back him in his attempt to return. Another larger group knew the flight attendants involved.

"As you know, even the two that survived will probably never work again, at least in flight. There is a strong feeling among their friends, and among the friends of those who died. Why should the captain be allowed back on the line? Wouldn't everybody be better off if he just stayed away? These feelings might not be expressed very openly or often, but they are definitely there. I suppose if he did come back, they would just try and bid off from his flights, but that won't always be possible."

"Okay. It looks like we have a definite problem there. Could you make some allowances in your line bidding procedures to compensate?"

"We never have before. It would set a bad precedent. I will look into it. Probably something more informal would be better."

"Do that, because my impression is that this guy may be coming back. Am I right about that, Bill?"

"He has two big steps to go yet. He has to get his medical

certificate back, and he is still a long way from that. Then he has to requalify in the airplane. That won't be easy. It's a long way from a sure thing."

"All right then. Frankly, we would be better off if he just faded away. He only has six years to go. If he chooses the hard route back, no one will take it upon himself to actively thwart his return. Don't give him any assistance beyond normal channels, but if he makes it, then we will deal with it at that time. Bill, I obviously will want you to keep me posted at each step along the way. None of this goes outside the group here. I don't even want to hear a rumor. Got that?"

Assents were given all around. Kay knew though that this kind of subject matter eventually would find its way into the vast rumor mill that pervaded the organization. She thought, *I wouldn't want to be in Captain Swanton's shoes from here on out.*

When the FAA inspector returned to his office, he reported to his chief. "It doesn't look like we have enough on him to directly stop his return. I recommend a letter of warning. However, he still needs to get his medical back and then go through a requal. It's a long road, and I'll be on his case all the way."

"You do that. Just don't get out of line in your zeal to protect the public."

"I won't have to. He will shoot himself in the foot somewhere along the way."

CHAPTER 10

Dan resumed his program to regain his flying status in the left seat. The effects of physical therapy were finally paying off for him. He walked with a noticeable limp when he wasn't using his cane, but that would smooth out with time.

His first flight in his Christen Eagle left him flushed with excitement and confidence. His enthusiasm only slightly dampened when on his return to operations, he received a lukewarm reception from the Vice President of Operations. Fortunately, Dennis Silver had warned him that some people in operations felt that he should just stay out on medical retirement. Dan shrugged off the warning and reception. He was determined to forge ahead with his plan to return to the left seat. He regained his first class medical certificate, a process that was surprisingly simple once he showed that he could press and move the rudder pedals normally.

He received notification of his requal class. Now he felt that things were moving his way. He had a brief phone consultation with Lydia Skoros reinforcing the necessity of talking things out with Mark. When Mark came home early from practice one afternoon, Dan decided the time had come.

"Look, Mark, I think this is a good time for us to have a talk."

"Yeah, I know, it's just that I'm not sure what we are going to talk about."

"You're right in a way. I never was much good about talking about this kind of stuff, but if we don't clear the air around us, it's going to be lurking around the edges of every conversation we have."

"So what's wrong with a little lurking?"

Dan wasn't sure how to take this. "I hope you're joking about that."

"Of course I am, Dad, but lighten up a little. It's not as though we're talking about the end of world civilization."

For the first time Dan smiled and looked Mark directly in the eyes. "You're right. I can be pretty heavy-handed sometimes."

"That's better. Why don't we have some of your wine and cheese and crackers while we decide the fate of our father-son relationship."

Dan looked shocked again. To make sure Dan knew he was joking, Mark threw two left jabs at Dan that he fended off easily.

"See, your old man can still defend himself, though I don't think I could whip you any more."

"Yeah, you lost that opportunity a few years ago. Missed your chance."

They rummaged through the kitchen as Dan replied, "You know, I never thought of that before. In a way, father-son relationships do change when the old man can't beat up his son if he has to. It doesn't have to actually happen; just the knowledge is enough to change things."

"You're right," Mark replied. "I have read some good stories where the turning point is when the son pushes the father too soon, or the father too late tries to dominate the son and loses."

They sat at the table out on the deck. Long afternoon shadows mingled with light reflected off the pool. Dan poured two glasses of Fonseca port to go with the Stilton cheese. Dan knew that they were sidling up to the main event and were nervous about how to bridge the gap. Plunging in might break the rapport they had established.

He opened with, "As far as I can remember, I hardly ever used physical force to control you."

"But you sure were good at laying on the guilt trip if I didn't do what you wanted."

"Well there has to be some way of controlling you kids. Maybe guilt is as good as any."

Mark took a second sip of port before replying, "Hey, this is good stuff. How come I hardly ever get any?"

"Pearls before swine, you know. Though you have developed a taste for good wine. When I kick the bucket, whatever is left goes to you two kids. But you better drink it. If you sell it to some wine shop, I'll come back from the grave to haunt you."

"Don't worry; we will drink it all, though I feel like there is some responsibility involved to keep up the tradition."

Dan realized he had never thought of it that way. "No. Don't worry about it. You don't have to become a collector, just enjoy what's there."

Mark decided to use this as an opening. "Dad, I don't want you to get defensive. This is a compliment. Do you realize that this is one of the few times you have offered me something, no strings attached?"

"Oh come on, are you serious?"

"Sort of. See, one of the ways you controlled me was through incentive and reward. Pretty subtle but it works. At least in my case it did. There were always expectations, sometimes unstated, that if I performed or acted in the way you wanted, I would get a reward. Maybe something tangible, or sometimes just your approval."

"I'll bet all parents do that; it's the old stick and carrot idea."

"You're probably right, but then it means I always have to evaluate anything you offer. What's in the hidden requirement if I accept this?"

"You know, I guess you are right. Never thought of it that way. I wonder if I can stop doing that?"

"You don't have to, Dad. Just getting it out in the open means I can call you on it if I think it's happening."

"What if I don't agree? What if there are no strings attached in my mind?"

"Then we can talk about it. Clear the air."

"You are right again. I feel good about this. Don't know why we haven't talked this way before."

"I think it's because we always used Mom as a go-between or message carrier. I know I usually checked things out with her before I proposed anything to you."

They sipped their wine. Dan started to tense, and then he released it with a big breath and an audible sigh. "And now she's gone. Why does it take a tragedy to bring us together?"

"I don't know, Dad. Except that now we don't have her to depend on. We've got to do it ourselves."

"Yes, it ain't easy is it? And I haven't been easy to live with either. Sometimes I get despondent and just want to quit. Never thought I'd feel that way. And then there is the feeling of guilt; I caused it all."

Mark broke into Dan's thought. "Hey Dad, I wasn't much

help there when I didn't show up at the hospital. Hope you can forgive me for that. I mean, I was just going crazy, and I didn't know what to do. I wanted to lash out at somebody and took it out on you."

"Well, it hurt, but it's also understandable, and now that we are talking it out, I can get over it."

"Boy, I'm glad that's out in the open. I've felt bad about it ever since."

Dan used this expression as an opening to express a feeling he had never brought up before. "Feeling bad; I hope you never get to the depths I've reached sometimes. It's not just about Manalani. A hundred-ninety-three passengers died back there, and eleven crew members. Some of them were good friends of mine. Talk about guilt. When I have talked to their families, God, that's hard. None of them have made any open accusations, but I always feel that I have failed them, no matter what the official accident findings are. What are they thinking about me? Here I am walking around, and their loved ones are gone—dead."

Dan's voice was thin and raspy. His hand began to tighten around the wine glass. The cords on the back of his hand stood out.

"Dad, loosen up. You're going to shatter the glass and get blood all over the kitchen."

Dan laughed as the tension broke. "Sorry, Mark, but you can see what I am going through, can't you?"

"I can now. It's funny, but I guess I always thought in terms of us. I hardly ever think in terms of the wider tragedy, that in a sense there are hundreds of families out there going through some version of what we are. You know, because Mom died, I think they probably feel more sympathetic to you."

"But what a price to pay. Sometimes I think I'm just going around in circles of grief and guilt. I suppose someday I will get over this." Dan looked off towards the reddish sun sinking into a layer of haze and stratus over the ocean. He stretched his arm out, sweeping the horizon, and said, "I'd give all of this up just to be back to square one. We live all our lives next to the gulf of death and pretend that it isn't even there. If it reaches out and swallows us up, or our loved ones, you'd give up everything just to have another chance. It's like Ernie Gann said in one of his books, 'Fate is a hunter that strikes from the skies.'"

"That's scary, and sort of profound," Mark said. "I guess most of us don't like to think in those terms. I know I think of death as something that happens off in the vague future. At least I thought that way until Lyle died. And now with Mom…"

A long pause followed as they sipped their wine. The heat of the day decayed rapidly as the marine layer of air moved in off the ocean.

Finally, Dan said, "I feel guilty about another thing."

"What's that, Dad?"

"Not accepting you the way you are."

"Well, I can see how you might have trouble with it. In a way it's every father's bad dream."

"I guess so, but it's even more than that. In the generation I've grown up in, being gay was always the subject of bad jokes. Now I got a whole different take on them. They came from a standpoint of fear; homophobia I guess is the term."

"But in a way, that's natural, Dad. Don't beat yourself up about it."

"But that doesn't make it right. I went along with all of that stuff. Never thought much about it. How does that make you feel about me?"

"Not any different. I wouldn't have expected you to react any differently. Even now. I don't expect you to become a crusader."

"Well, I certainly have changed my views. My time with Lydia Skoros and the book she gave me did a lot of that."

"The more you know, the less you have to fear. Now you know you didn't make me the way I am."

"Yes, I'm off the hook on that one. But do you know when you first felt you were different?"

"Not for sure, but I remember when we first started getting interested in girls. Some other guys and I would be looking in a magazine, or at girls on the street, commenting on what turned us on. I noticed that the guys turned me on as much as the girls, but I wasn't dumb enough to say anything about it."

Dan decided that gave him an opening. "Now that's something I don't understand at all. How can you have sexual feelings both ways? AC/DC I guess they call it. You like girls too, right?"

"Of course I do. I've never gotten sexually involved with one, or a guy for that matter, but if the right girl came along, that wouldn't be a problem."

Dan suspected that wasn't the whole truth, but he let it slide and said, "I still don't get it. It seems like you would have to be one way or the other."

"I don't expect you to get it, Dad. It's like I'm wired up differently than you, or most people. Somehow, I sensed this even when I was a little kid. I just knew I was different, but didn't quite know how. When I got old enough to know, I also knew I'd better keep quiet about it."

Dan used this as an opening. "That's something that bothered me. It seems like all these years you were putting on an act for us."

"It wasn't an act, Dad. I just wasn't letting you know part of me that wasn't acceptable to you. What else could you expect?"

"I guess that is one thing I have trouble with. How can I approve something in you that I wouldn't in myself?"

"I'm just different, Dad. If you place value judgments on that, then it's your problem. I don't need your approval on this, just your acceptance of me as I am. Of course that is a quote straight from Lydia."

"You're right," Dan said. "She and I covered some of this same ground. The important question is, can I still love you just the way you are? I asked myself that and found it was no problem. My desires for the perfect son aside, I'll take you just the way you are. Don't change a hair for me."

They laughed at the reference to the song. As Dan made his last comments, he rose from his chair and put his hand on Mark's shoulder. Mark stood up, and after a moment's hesitation, they threw their arms around each other. They rocked back and forth, and as they broke apart, they both wiped at the corner of their eyes.

Dan spoke first. "Whew! I'm glad we got all that stuff out. Now we can move on to other things."

Mark replied, "Now at least I feel we are a team. I feel like I've got a monkey off my back."

They moved on into the house and prepared dinner together.

When Mark went out that evening, Dan was suddenly feeling lonely. He called up the McCartys; they sensed this, and invited him over. He gladly accepted.

CHAPTER 11

Too many loose ends at home set Dan in an anxious frame of mind when he left for requalification training. It was an intensive process lasting six weeks to two months. Ground school generally took fifteen days and flight training involved nine simulator periods.

Dan did not like any distractions during this period. He was serious enough about this to move out of the house to Rochelle's Motel during the week, even though the company was giving the training at Long Beach within a half-hour drive of home. The McCartys volunteered to ride herd on the kids. That way he could study nights with the rest of the group, immersing himself in the realm of airplane systems and procedures. Because he had been through the course before, he had an advantage, but he knew they would look at him closely, so he wanted to turn in a superior performance. Though he had regained his first class medical, he wasn't satisfied with the progress of healing with his ankle. Twinges of pain came at unpredictable moments, and a definite stiffness still plagued him. The combination left him with an occasional limp. Depending on his mood it was alternately annoying or devastating.

The challenge of learning wasn't as welcome as it was at an earlier age. He was not looking forward to moving into the motel and making the required monastic commitment. Entering the first morning's class did not raise the usual enthusiasm that he felt in his other transitions. The class was small, only two other captains and three first officers who would make three pairs later in the simulator. He hoped they would find each other simpatico since they would be like a small family in close contact for the next weeks. One first officer, Glen Miyashiro, from Hawaii, was a friend. Glen had been to Dan's house, and he and Manalani had connected from their common background.

The instructor, Bob Davis, with his beard, moustache, and sparse spiky hair, looked like a character from a Chekov play. He gave them handouts, and started a short introduction to the airplane and the course. "McDonnell-Douglas has designed their airplane to be flown long distances in a straight line with all the automatic equipment operating. From time to time you may actually be called upon to hand-fly this machine. Be assured it is possible, though I won't say it's a lot of fun. You will find, unlike the Airbus, that it has an old-fashioned yoke in front of you, just like a real airplane."

Dan could tell right away that he was going to like this instructor. His dry sense of humor would set the style and relieve the boredom of long hours in class. Some perfectly knowledgeable instructors seemed to leave their sense of humor at home. Others tried to be standup comedians, which seldom was wholly successful.

"You will now be introduced to the brave new world of computer-based trainers. These CBT's are the latest thing in training methodology. However, I'm sure that the company is disappointed they have not been able to completely do away with us instructors. In addition to having to reboot the little bastards when they go belly up, they don't seem to be quite as flexible in their output as the human machine.

"One thing I might as well caution you on now, unless you fall asleep during a whole section, you may not want to use the review button. That is unless you found the presentation so delightful that you want to get it verbatim again."

Another pilot asked, "What about a script? Don't we get a written copy that we can review?"

"No. Unfortunately, those at the head shed in consultation with the highest mucky mucks in the field of aviation psychology, have decided that a script is an unnecessary anachronism. You will notice that you still do have the Pilots Reference Manual (PRM) in your possession. This weighty little tome can and will be used for review. You will however find it written in its usual dense and impenetrable manner. I will be available at night and on weekends if necessary for review.

"I would suggest that each of you just pick yourself a little cubicle and get right into the introductory lesson and I will answer your individual questions as they come up. Of course if the interactive screen fails to react to your caress, don't bang on it. The glass will break, an expensive replacement will be charged to your card, and you will be up for a trip to the hospital for stitches. Following that you will be demoted back to an iron bird where you can flail away with impunity."

So, the process began. Each man sat in front of his touch-active computer screen. He could take breaks, and each pilot proceeded at his own desired speed, though the entire course had a daily schedule to meet.

They all finished their morning session at the same time, so they had a lunch break in the cafeteria downstairs. This was their first chance to get acquainted. Though they had exchanged names in class, the real process began now. Typically, most of the pilots were transitioning from the Boeing 737, 767, or Douglas DC-9 series of airplanes. The young first officers usually identified themselves with their previous careers as military, business, or commuter airline pilots.

The first subject of discussion was the base and airplane from which they had transferred. A captain from Denver, Mike Tomlinson, led off. "I've been flying the 767, so at least the glass cockpit and the FMS are familiar to me. However, I have heard that though the keyboard is the same, the interior logic is different. Just enough to drive you crazy sometimes."

The other captain, John Kovac, was a veteran of seventeen years on the 727. His comment was, "This is my first automatic airplane, so it's a big change for me. I'm trying to keep an open mind, but I can tell you right now that I don't buy the idea of the two-man crew. I don't care how automatic they make things; that doesn't replace the extra man when things get tight. Did you notice that they can dispatch us with one of the four major systems in manual? Then if another should fail enroute you have one guy turning into a defacto engineer. That leaves the pilot flying also handling communications, and the cross-check breaks down. But, what the hell, I have spent all my life in three-crew cockpits so I'm not about to like this change now."

To Dan, John Kovac was physically a classic type of pilot. Big bodied, big arms, wide faced, florid, with expansive expressions and a booming confident voice. He seemed to typify a breed that was getting more rare, the old Navy or Marine carrier pilot from WWII or Korea. The classic hard driving, hard drinking, womanizing guy, who would in the movies, and often in real life, bend all the rules, but when the shit hit the fan, always come through. The question in Dan's mind was if those instinctive types of qualities would still pay off as the world of aviation became more technically complex and cerebral.

Dan realized that it was his turn since it seemed that captains were first in this conversation. He was aware that everyone in the class knew about his crash, so he might as well get it out in the open. "My last experience in the MD-11 wasn't a happy one, as you all must know. So this time I just want to get through this course and back out on the line. I can tell you from experience that it's a ball buster."

Kovac looked surprised and said, "Didn't I see you coming out of Rochelle's Motel this morning? If you are based here, you don't need to suffer through the period in limited detention."

Dan explained his philosophy, "I just want to separate myself from all the family stuff while I'm in training. I can just barely absorb all this airplane stuff without outside distractions." He hoped that would satisfy everyone's curiosity.

Typically, they spent mornings in front of their computers studying a system or two. Afternoons, a fixed-base simulator provided all the dials, bells, and switches to practice normal, abnormal, and emergency procedures. The information began to pile up. Sixteen systems had to be covered: powerplant, fuel, electrical, hydraulics, flight controls, landing gear and brakes, pneumatics, pressurization and air-conditioning, anti-ice, warning systems, autoflight, navigation, communications, emergency equipment, oxygen, and auxiliary power unit. Sometimes, the list seemed endless, but there was a logical progression for each airplane. At night they would get together to study the day's system and quiz each other. It was at this time that Dan attempted to distill everything he needed into his 3x5 cards that he referred to constantly for his review.

One night they all got a little loose sitting around the pool drinking. To Dan's surprise John Kovac stopped after two beers. He offered an explanation without prodding. "I've had trouble hitting the booze in past years, so I have learned to put a clamp on it early. I used to love to get to that fuck-dinner stage, or maybe on to bulletproof. Then I got a couple of DUI's, and my doc told me to cut it off. Of course, my wife had been on my case for years. So, I guess I finally saw the light. After I retire though, I might hire a chauffeur and a masseuse and get back into drinking."

Glen Miyashiro asked, "I can figure out the bulletproof stage, but what is 'fuck-dinner?'"

"Well, you know, you're sitting at the bar with a friend you just met by chance, and you are really getting into a conversation about whatever. Earlier, you told him you had to leave at six o'clock because the wife is going to have dinner ready. At about ten after six he turns to you and says, "Didn't you say you had to head home for dinner at six?' Of course, at this point, feeling good and involved and defiant, your reply is "Fuck dinner." Now you are in for a ration of shit when you get home. Sometimes I wouldn't go home at all."

They all laughed over that but Dan wondered if the younger guys caught the inferred warning message. In the past, the hard driving, hard drinking, macho man image created problems for many pilots. There were a lot of late night parties, a lot of smoking of cigars in the cockpit, an old Navy tradition. Over the years though, those types dropped by the wayside, failing physicals left and right. These days almost nobody smoked, and the parties cut way back. Loss of pay due to a failed medical was serious. If you wanted to get a pilot's attention, all you had to do was hit him in the pocketbook. This night was typical of the new regime. Though they loosened up, no one got out of line, and they all turned in early because another full week was coming up.

During the second week, the routine was the same, but the pressure mounted; not because the material was more difficult, but there was more of it, and they all faced the oral at the end of it. A lot of material needed to be dug out of their reference manuals. This took extra time for both the instructors and pilots.

At the end of the third week, a company-designated examiner gave the FAA oral. That he was a company man made no difference. The exam would be the same as if he were the FAA inspector. Dan had heard his name but knew nothing about him. As it turned out, it was an anticlimax. He only stumbled at two places. When they filled out the mandatory paper work, he felt as though a big load was off his back.

***

Next came nine simulator sessions. Though they practiced procedures in the fixed base trainer, the realism of the simulator forced them into real-time load-sharing situations.

On their first day, after doing steep turns, stalls, and an emergency descent, they each shot several approaches. The instructor told them that the problems they experienced were typical of anyone making the transition to a glass cockpit airplane. That night, Dan expressed his doubts to Glen. "You know, if I was just learning a new airplane, I would feel better about this compressed learning. But, I have been through this program before, and I still keep screwing up."

Glen agreed with him and added, "If all I had to do was learn the airplane I could do that, but I spend half my time just trying to figure out how to run the computers."

Dan replied, "The only difference between an old hand and a newbie on this airplane is that the newbie says, 'What is it doing now?' and the old hand says, 'Oh, it's doing it again'"

Glen laughed and replied, "Well, you know they told us that the first day is a success if you can just make it do what you want."

Dan appreciated the comment, but he felt that at least in part it was said to make him feel good. He didn't like to admit it, but maybe he wasn't as fast on the pickup as he used to be. Hopefully years of experience would weigh in as they moved on.

On the two-day break during the simulator sessions, he invited Glen to the house. Glen was glad to get away from the motel, and the kids` had been interested in meeting him. Dan felt it was a good time to take a break. It was possible to get wound up too tight and start on a downward spiral. As they pulled into the driveway, Dan had to admit it was good to be home again. He was interested in seeing how Glen and the kids interacted.

Glen was a big man, taller and heavier than Mark. His dark skin and hair and rectangular face revealed his Hawaiian side. Only the tilt of his eyes pointed to his Japanese background.

Dan said, "Glen, do you want a beer? Liz will show you to your room and give you the tour if you want."

"Sure, whatever you've got. I'd take some water too."

Dan got the beers out and took them outside, settling into a lounge chair. It felt good to just lean back and know that he didn't have to get up the next morning at 0500 for a 0600 show at the sim. In a few minutes Glen and Liz returned preceded by the sounds of laughter. Dan had thought they would hit it off well.

Liz spoke first, before they had settled into their chairs. "Dad, did you know that Glen's family came from the Halepio Valley on Molokai? His dad grew taro over there. They have been there for several generations."

"No, I knew Glen's family was from Hawaii, but I didn't find out where," Dan replied. "Glen, did your father ever meet Manalani's dad?"

"I doubt it. Most of the plantation workers didn't like to travel, unless it's a flight to Honolulu or Las Vegas to gamble. In all these years my dad only flew to Honolulu twice for some special occasions."

This surprised Dan, though he remembered that Manalani had said the same thing about Pops. "Don't they get bored and get rock fever?"

"Not really. They were happy with their lifestyle. Back in the old days, the plantation in each town supplied everything they wanted. When they did travel, they didn't like what's going on in the cities. They were always glad to get back. Eventually, I plan to end up there. That is if it isn't over run by tourists. It's hard to explain to outsiders how the islands keep a hold on you if you grew up there."

Dan said, "It seems like I never was destined to remain in Wisconsin where I was born. It was almost like it was a mistake. When I learned about California, I knew that was where I wanted to be. Only problem is that too many other people figured out the same thing."

Mark had a question for Glen. "How long or how strong are your Hawaiian roots."

"I'm almost half Hawaiian," Glen replied. "My mother's side is almost pure Hawaiian going back several generations. In my father's family, the men kept marrying Hawaiian women. The women seemed to control the home life, so that though I have a Japanese name, I feel I was raised much more Hawaiian than Japanese. When I went to school, I would get in fights when other kids would call me a Jap or Nip."

Dan selected ahi to grill, with tako poki as an appetizer, in honor of Glen's presence. He chose a Mondavi Fume Blanc to go with it. He was pleased that Glen appreciated the wine, which he had not tried before.

Near the end, Liz brought up the question of how the training was going. There was a slight pause, and Dan could see that Glen was going to defer to him. "Damn, I almost don't want to talk about it. We are both having trouble with the FMS and doing go-arounds from missed approaches. The son of a bitch is just not designed to fly around the patch. It really is built to be flown for long distances in a straight line with the autopilot hooked up."

Liz asked, "Why do they build airplanes like this now days? Or maybe more to the point, why do the airlines buy them?"

Glen jumped right on that point. "Because they make money. Nobody cares anymore how well an airplane flies. They all look at it as a machine to make money. See, I have this theory about what is happening to the airlines and the builders."

Glen leaned back in his chair, took another sip of wine, and eagerly forged ahead. "It used to be that aviation pioneers ran these companies. Look at the names, Bill Boeing, Donald Douglas, Juan Trippe. If they weren't pilots, they at least had spent their whole careers involved in aviation. They hired accountants to give them advice on the money end of things. Now the tables have been turned. The MBA's are running these companies. Now the aviation experts are their advisors. We are getting what I call bottom-line aviation, where all that counts is the balance sheet. These guys don't care if they are running a storm door company, an airline, or a grocery store chain."

"What about safety, dispatch, maintenance, and all that?" Liz asked.

"Well, nobody knowingly crosses that line," Glen replied. "But it's not usually a line; there almost always is a gray area. Management invokes the magic phrase, 'Safety will not be compromised,' but it's empty rhetoric. Safety is always compromised by economics."

Glen arched his eyebrows and gave Liz an ironic smile. He leaned toward her and lowered his voice as though talking to a conspirator. "The people in the head shed aren't dummies. They know all about the accident odds, but they are counting on two things. First, it won't happen to them. And second, if it does, they have sat down with their actuaries and lawyers, and insurance policies, and balance sheets, and figured that they can still make a profit in the long run. That's bottom line aviation for you, but I can't prove it. Nobody can. And the Federal Aviation Agency, which is supposed to watch-dog this stuff, is right in bed with them. Everyone has jumped on the bandwagon until the shit hits the fan."

Liz said, "Wow, that's at least a little shocking. Aren't you exaggerating?"

Glen attempted to downplay it. "Sometimes I get a little carried away and start ranting and raving about this stuff. But as you can see, I think the industry is headed for trouble with this change in philosophy."

Mark asked, "What about you guys passing the rating ride. Think there is going to be any trouble there?" Dan replied,…

"No, never fear. I've passed too many to bust one now, and Glen is doing better than I am. At least he's catching on faster. Glen, would you like to shoot some pool to round the evening off?"

"Yeah, that would be a good idea, though I'm rusty."

Mark laughed and said, "Don't let him sucker you into any money games. The table isn't dead level anymore. He's the only one who knows all its little secrets."

That evening, when Liz and Dan were straightening up the room, she was still concerned about what Glen had said. "Dad, do you think he is right about what's happening with the airlines?"

"Well, he's got some good points, but one thing you have to realize about Glen is that he is a conspiracy buff. He's like a bloodhound on that stuff. He thinks that Kennedy was killed on orders from the Trilateral Commission. That the Council on Foreign Relations controls the U.S. government. That the CIA was running guns to the Contras and smuggling cocaine back into the country to pay for it. That there are hundreds of MIAs left in Laos and Cambodia."

Liz said, "Well, what about it? We've talked about those things. You told me yourself, after reviewing the evidence, that only a fool would believe Oswald was the only shooter."

"Of course there is a core of truth to each one of those theories or ideas. The problem is that it can become an obsession, and you are at the mercy of the media, so no way you will ever get the straight story. Some of these people are convinced that Hitler is alive and well in Argentina, and the government is hiding saucer people. There is no end to it. But, I do think he has a good point with what is happening in aviation, though he may overstate it. This MD-11 program is a good example, where they are taking our most complex airplane and rating two guys in the same number of hours as they used to do one."

"Can't you speak to somebody about it who will listen?" asked Liz.

"I did that the first time I went through this course, and nothing came of it. Right now, I just want to take full advantage of this little break."

As he was going to bed, Dan recalled the futility of that attempt to alert their management of what he thought were shortcomings in the MD-11 program. At the end of his first MD-11 qualification, he had made a special trip to the operations offices to make his pitch. Once inside, he wound his way through the stairways and corridors until he arrived at Feron Stewart's fourth floor office. Though they weren't close friends, they had started with Intercontinental at about the same time and had moved up the ranks together. Feron had chosen to go into the administrative end of the airline and, their paths had diverged. Unlike an outsider's assumption, the best pilots did not necessarily become chief pilots. The ability to work with people, administer policy, and attend incessant meetings, seemed to be the main requirements. Dan wanted no part of it.

He certainly did not hold those above him in awe. However, he did feel slightly uncomfortable in the tan and gray offices with their mandatory airplane models and pictures and airline logos as the main decorations. In the cubicles of the staff members, a great deal of effort went into personalizing their drab surroundings. At Feron's level though, except for a family photo on the desk, formality reigned supreme. When Feron waved Dan into his office, he bypassed the usual banal chitchat and asked him how he felt about the MD-11 and the course. This was the opening that Dan wanted, and he jumped at it. "Well, maybe I'm getting to be an old dog, but I feel like I just squeaked through."

Feron raised his eyebrows and replied, "How's that? According to what I've seen you were average or better in all respects."

It didn't surprise Dan that Feron had checked his progress records. He knew Dan wasn't coming in for a social visit. The failure rate on the MD-11 was known to be high. In talking to other MD-11 pilots Dan had sensed that they were relieved to have scraped by. The attitude of most of them was to drop their concerns and just get on with the business of flying the line. This was what he wanted to convey to Feron.

"Well, Feron, always before in making a transition, I felt I had it knocked. On this one, I think if I had to take the oral or rating ride one day earlier, I would have busted it. Every session, every ride was a cram course. We were studying every night and weekends. Even the instructors were out at night or weekends helping us. It was only through an all out-effort by everyone that we got by. Even the younger guys had to cram."

Feron raised his hands and smiled. "That indicates to me that we have designed the perfect course, no slack, very efficient."

Dan didn't let that go by unchallenged. "Hold it. If I'm average or above, that means that half the guys were in more trouble than I was. You are trying to rate two pilots in our most complex airplane, in the same time we used to rate one captain and just check out the first officer in his seat. For the first time, I felt like I was being trained just to pass the checkride, not to really learn the machine."

Feron rocked back in his chair, folded his hands and assumed a more thoughtful posture. "Dan, I'm not going to try and fool an old head like you. We are under the gun. When we committed to this airplane, we sold ourselves on this program. We did it on the 737, and of course there was a lot of pressure from the bean counters in the head shed. We did a lot of research, and got the latest teaching aids, consulted with NASA, and all that. Everyone agreed we should be able to do it. We got off to a shaky start, but things are looking okay now. Our pass rate is better than the industry average."

"But you can't base your evaluation on pass rates. In order to pass I had to cram so much that I'm sure a lot of it will drop out."

"Ah Dan, that is where experience comes in. This is not an initial entry airplane for anyone. All you guys, captains and first officers, have years of experience to bring in. If you feel weak in some area you will continue to study and pursue it."

"Yeah, but what about the guys that don't make it through? There must be a lot of them."

Feron smiled again and said, "I wouldn't want you to spread this around. We have purposely left open time in both ground school and the simulator for guys to get extra sessions if either they or the instructors feel they need it. All they have to do is ask."

"But of course that will sting their pride, so they will dig in to avoid it."

"Of course, let's face it. As a group, pilots are competitive and achievement oriented. Our whole purpose in life is not to fail. So, you might say we are just taking advantage of that trait."

Dan thought, *I'm getting nowhere here. Well, at least I spoke my piece.*

In reply, he said, "Well, you guys are sure cutting it close to the bone. I still don't feel good about it."

Feron said, "Dan, I'm glad you came in. I do value your observations and concerns. After you spend some time out on the line, I would like to talk to you again. See what you think then."

Feron got up to shake hands. He walked Dan to the door and asked the obligatory questions about the wife and kids, to which Dan made all the appropriate mundane responses.

On the way down to his car, he felt disappointed. He'd had his say, but he knew it would have almost no effect. On impulse, he stopped in the safety director's office. When Dan told his experience and opinions to Dennis Silver, he received quite a different response. Dennis suggested that if he felt strongly about it, he should write up a report and submit it to Feron, to Dennis, and keep a copy for himself. He also said that he was aware of the problem, but since it was a judgment call, his opinions held very little weight.

When he left the safety office, Dan felt discouraged. He knew that a single letter would have no influence and might mark him as a malcontent. He also knew that he would not be able to enlist other pilots in his effort, unless the situation was considered to be a clear and present danger. Dan knew he wasn't much of a crusader, and he didn't like empty gestures, so he just let matters slide.

***

He put aside those thoughts in the morning when he got up first to play tennis. Glen, who was not a player, found himself in the kitchen with Liz. Except for vacation trips, she hadn't spent much time in Hawaii, so she asked Glen what was happening there.

Glen answered, "The most exciting happening in the islands now is the sovereignty movement. What have you heard about it?"

"Almost nothing," Liz replied. "Of course there has been loose talk for years, but nothing has been organized that I know of."

"Well, things are starting to happen now. The hundredth anniversary of the overthrow comes up on January 17. There is a big push on that date to start the process of forming the establishment of the Kingdom of Hawaii."

Liz was surprised and reacted by saying, "Oh, come on, it will never happen. The state and the U.S.government will never give in to that."

"They may not have a choice. They have already recognized

the Native Americans as a separate nation and made reparations to the Inuits up in Alaska. Remember the Kingdom of Hawaii was a recognized entity the world over when a bunch of haole businessmen formed the provisional government, and with the backing of troops from the USS Boston, forced Liliuokalani off the throne. Then when President Grover Cleveland and his commission condemned the act, the provisional government thumbed their nose at them and held on to power. Washington didn't force them out, so a stalemate followed. When they finally did allow a vote, they rigged the registration rules so they denied most Hawaiians the vote. You had to hold land, read and write English, and swear allegiance to the republic. It was a farce, but it worked. Eventually, greed and self-interest prevailed, and the U.S. took on the republic as a territory and then as a state. Since, in their eyes, there was no more monarchy, they were also able to grab the royal lands for their own use, some of which are now military bases.

"Anyway, now we want a federal apology, money for rent on the land, return of the land, and the establishment of a sovereign Hawaiian Nation. Then we can decide if we want the monarchy back or another form of government."

Liz now had a question. "I notice you said we. Who is we? And how is this government going to be decided?"

The conversation then moved into the details of how this might or might not take place. At the end of it, Glen complemented Liz on last night's dinner. "It's almost impossible to get local style food around here. I don't realize how much I miss it until I taste some, and then it throws me right back."

Liz remembered her mother's joke about Hawaiian style breakfasts and said, "Maybe you like spam and eggs and two-scoop rice for breakfast, or I fix one bento box for you lunch? Maybe you one buggah like laulau for lunch?" They joined in easy laughter at the local style references.

Later, Mark showed up from water polo practice, and Dan returned from tennis. The rest of the day was a slow decompressing process. After dinner, wine, and sundowners, Dan could hardly remember his earlier concerns. In the rosy glow of the evening, the problems of the airline and his family receded into the distance. As the evening drew to a close, Glen asked Dan, "Do you ever get over to Molokai?"

"It's been years since I have done that. We used to talk about it, but we always ended up on Oahu, mostly because Manalani's folks are still there. Maybe someday."

"Well, you should do it. Now you have a special place to come to. If you want to see some of the old Hawaii, the Halepio Valley is the place. It takes a four-wheeler to get in, and it rains a lot, but there are almost no tourists. Nothing for them to do. Lots of taro fields. If you really want to get away, we always have plenty of space."

"Thanks, I really appreciate the offer. I don't know when it will happen, but I will make it happen. Let's drink to that, and then I want to head for bed, since I'm first tomorrow."

As they walked to their rooms, Dan had a good feeling about the next day and about Glen's offer. He knew it came from the heart. He just needed to allow a few extra days on his next trip to the islands.

***

Dan's next ride included wind shear scenarios. Rulley, the FAA inspector, knew this. He planned to be there to see the outcome. As he closed up his briefcase, he spoke to his partner next door. "Today's the day we nail this guy. It's our best chance since he got his medical back. They should have turned him down based on psychological tests."

"Hell, they're not about to do that. Ever since the Bob Hoover disaster nobody is about to stick their neck out on psych tests."

"Well, I'm going to make sure they run him through a take-off wind shear like he got in Hong Kong. It will be interesting to see how he reacts to that."

"Go get'em crusader. Let me know the results."

When Dan found out that his nemesis from the hearing would be on board, he objected strongly. The company check pilot replied, "Sorry, but as an A.C.I., he can show up any time he chooses. Don't worry about it. I'm still running the session. He's just here to observe." Dan requested and received approval for Dennis Silver to be aboard as an observer. That made Dan feel better; he had someone in his corner.

As the period progressed, Dan felt a nervous anticipation, but he put a lid on it and told himself it was unfounded. After all, he had successfully passed these scenarios before, and unlike his accident, he would have all three engines operating.

On take-off, after getting into the air, the airplane would not accelerate and began to sink back toward the runway. Dan called for firewall thrust and pitched the airplane up. Though his pulse was racing, he felt he had the situation handled, until the warning from the wind shear system blasted into his consciousness DON'T SINK DON'T SINK.

In that instant, Dan plunged back to the Hong Kong take-off. It was a bad dream recurring. He knew it wasn't real, but he was fascinated, a helpless witness to the recreation of a scene he never wanted to experience again. His delay in response caused the airplane to sink back toward the water. He fully expected to feel the tail strike the water and experience the crushing impact of the airplane breaking up. Instead, there was only the clicking sound of relays resetting and the motion of the simulator cab settling on its mounts.

Inside there was a long, awkward silence. Dan was in a state of shock, trying to adjust to his surroundings and what had just happened. An inner voice told him that his flying career was finished. He refused to acknowledge this message.

Dennis broke the silence in the machine. "It looks like maybe you had a flashback there, Dan."

"I don't know what it was, but I don't like it," Dan said.

"Seems like a good time to take a break."

They all agreed. Then they opened the door, crossed the bridge, and walked up to the break room. Dennis suggested that he and Dan walk down to his office. Dan's mind was a whirlwind of confusion. He was open to any suggestion. When they reached the office, Dennis poured two cups of coffee and said, "I wish I had some medicinal brandy to pour in these, Dan."

"Yeah. Thanks for the thought. I'm still in shock about what happened back there."

Dennis leaned back in his swivel chair and spun the props on a B-29 model plane for a moment before he spoke. "Dan, I hope this doesn't also shock you, but I wasn't surprised."

Dan scowled and braced himself in his chair. "It does shock

me. How would you know or suspect what would happen?"

"You aren't the first guy this has happened to. There even is an official label for it, PTSD, post traumatic stress disorder; shell shock if you want to use the old term."

"But I wasn't in combat."

"Doesn't matter. It's a normal reaction to extreme stress. Happens to fire and rescue folks, paramedics, police. They were the first to really examine it. You don't have to acknowledge this, but I would guess you are having sleep interruptions, bad dreams, maybe eating disorders, flashes of anger or depression from out of nowhere." Dennis paused and looked intently at Dan.

He knew Dennis was hitting close to home, but he wasn't about to go down this path yet. "So what does this mean to me and my career."

Dennis looked down at the model in his hands, then looked at Dan, and in an even, calm voice said the words Dan feared, "Your career as an airline pilot, Dan, is probably finished."

Dan was so mad and frustrated when he heard those words that he wanted to lash out at Dennis. Instead, he pounded the desk with his right fist, grabbed a piece of paper from the desk, crumpled it, and threw it into the wastebasket so hard it rattled. "Damn it, Dennis. You're supposed to be my friend. You're a stand-up guy. What is this garbage I hear coming from you? I thought I could depend on you to back me up in there. Why do you think I asked you to be there?"

Dennis raised both hands palms out in a gesture of defense and compliance. "Hold it, Dan. I am on your side, but you have to hear this from someone. Better me, than some goon from upstairs, right?"

"Okay, but I still don't like it."

"I don't expect you to, but here it is. We have learned a lot about this syndrome. Right now, the company and the union are putting together a program called the Critical Incident Response Program, CIRP. Anytime a critical incident or accident occurs, the crew members will be defused and debriefed by a team of their peers and a mental health professional with training in this specific area."

Dan said, "That's all very nice, but a little late for me."

"You're right, Dan. It was your accident that got us off the dime on this program."

"It's just too bad that a bunch of people have to get killed before a change takes place."

"You're right again, Dan, but that's human nature. It's always been that way. Don't expect that to change."

"But it looks like that leaves me out in the cold with my career shot down. Damn it Dennis, I've been doing this since I was a kid. It's the only thing I know how to do. Sure I can take a medical retirement, but what do I do with my life? I don't even have Manalani to help me. The kids try, but . . . well, it isn't the same."

"I know, Dan, nobody can replace her. It's tough to even think about."

"I never knew. I never knew how much she meant to me until I lost her. I don't think anybody can know until it's too late." Dan's voice broke and he had to stop.

Dennis took advantage of this break in the conversation. "Dan, you can do one thing. It's important, and the company will back you on it." Dennis paused to observe Dan's response. He knew he was pushing Dan emotionally and didn't want to go too far.

"Go ahead. Tell me what this is."

"You need to see someone, a professional that deals with trauma, PTSD, that sort of thing."

"Hold it there. You know that's one way to end your career for sure."

"This is different, Dan. You are already off flying status. The only way you stand a chance of getting back on is by showing that you have taken steps to counter the stress you've been under."

Dan wasn't satisfied, but he realized that Dennis was right. He said, "Yeah, but there's no guarantees right? In fact, nobody really wants me to come back on the line, do they? They would all just as soon see me fade away into the sunset."

"I won't deny that, Dan. It's not a question of you losing your skills, but there is a tremendous psychological aspect with an accident like yours."

"Yeah, nobody wants to fly with a pilot who has crashed, particularly one who has killed hundreds of people."

"I don't blame you for being bitter, Dan, but again, that's human nature. This is the best advice I can give you, and it's not just about flying either; it's about getting your life back together."

Dan relaxed a little and sat back down in his chair. "I know you have my best interests at heart, but it's a bitter pill to swallow. I will do it. There is somebody I can see, the same woman that worked with my family before."

Dennis smiled, relieved to get a positive response from Dan. "That's good, Dan. Somehow you've got to put all this behind you, and you can't deal with that all by yourself."

They stood up and shook hands. Dennis made an offer to Dan to come over for dinner sometime. Dan agreed, but knew he probably wouldn't follow up. That evening would be too full of pregnant pauses. He didn't trust himself yet in a social situation. Too many things could set him off into a funk of depression.

That afternoon he called Lydia Skoros for an appointment. She had an opening in two days. He put down the phone feeling simultaneously excited, nervous, and hesitant. That was the trouble these days. His life seemed to have no sense of purpose, and his emotions would lurch off into dark corners that frightened him.

***

When the FAA inspector returned to his office, he dropped his briefcase on his desk and said, "Got him! He had a flashback just like I thought he would. Now I'm going to the chief and ask for an emergency revocation of his license."

"Do you think that's necessary," his partner asked.

"I just want to make sure he's not out there risking people's lives."

When he returned to his desk, his enthusiasm was lower. "The boss said forget it. Apparently, he received a call from Intercontinental ops saying the captain would not be getting another shot at it. He's history as far as they are concerned. I get the definite feeling that they don't want to see him back either."

"That makes sense to me. So you relax on this one. You accomplished your purpose, and you've got plenty more on your plate."

"You're right, of course. Somehow though, it seems like an anticlimax, now that it's all over."

"Well, if you feel that strongly about it, you can keep dogging it. He might make an attempt to come back someday."

"He's not going to make it while I'm in this office."

"Yeah, yeah, yeah. I believe you, but drop it and move on."

CHAPTER 12

Two days later, Dan found himself again seeking some sort of advice and salvation from a woman he didn't like, and who he wasn't sure he trusted. Yet where else could he go? He didn't want to start all over with somebody new.

When he came through the door to her office, he noticed immediately that she was in front of her desk, her hands touching its edge, her upper body and head inclined slightly toward him. He took this as a good sign. She looked directly at him, unsmiling. "Hello, Dan. I'm really sorry this has happened. I hope I can help you."

"I'm sorry, too," was all he could manage.

Then she did something that surprised him. She walked up to him and put out both her hands. He instinctively put his hands in hers. Her hands were cool and surprisingly firm. She looked unwaveringly into his eyes for a few seconds and said, "You're in real trouble, aren't you?"

Dan wondered what she meant. Was it about the airline, his failure to requalify, or did she mean personally? What did it matter? "You're right about that. It seems like I'm drifting off course. I can't get my bearings." His leg ached; a deep breath sent sharp pain through his chest, but none of that compared to the hurt he carried inside. Just standing there looking at her, he felt that he was on the edge of crumbling. He had to hold himself together.

She took him by the hand and led him over to a plush easy chair. She sat in another chair with a floor lamp between them. He was aware she arranged this purposely to give the ambiance of a study or library in the home. As he eased himself into the chair, an involuntary sigh escaped him. She regarded him intently but said nothing.

He looked back at her wondering what should happen next. Then on impulse he said, "Everything has changed. Nothing is the same. I can hardly get through each day. I don't have any energy. I feel like I'm in pieces and I can't collect myself." He stopped suddenly. There was more, but it sounded like a list of complaints, and he didn't want to sound like a whiner.

She paused a few seconds before replying. "You are right, Dan. Nothing is the same. It won't ever be the same again. You will eventually pick up the pieces and regain your energy, but you will never be the same person again. A tragedy like the one you have experienced changes each one it touches. How it changes you depends on how you deal with it."

Dan didn't like the way that sounded. He shifted his weight forward in the chair, changing the pressure on his ribs and the position of his left ankle. "I don't want to deal with it. There is something really wrong here. I shouldn't even be here. We shouldn't be having this conversation. By all rights, I should have died back there with Manalani. If it was going to happen, that's what would have been right. All the other guys died in the cockpit; why am I sitting here talking to you? At least we would have been together." He had to stop talking; he was going to break up if he kept on this way.

Lydia looked away from him for a moment. Her face was in

profile. Her long straight nose and jaw line gave her a patrician look from that angle. When she turned to face him, her eyes were unblinking and intense. She delivered her words at a deliberate pace and in a tone that implied that she wanted their impact to remain in his mind.

"There is no satisfactory answer to that question, Dan. You are face to face with one of life's dark mysteries. People have asked that question through all of time. We all seem to think we have a pact, an understanding, with God or the universe, that we, and our loved ones, will not die until the proper time in old age has come. We see death strike like lightning in the distance, or even close by, but it will not hit us. And for most of us, it doesn't. But if it does, it can destroy our confidence in living. It rips the veil of assurance apart, and leaves us standing naked, before a power we cannot comprehend that shatters our world and its logic."

Dan said bitterly, "You got that right. It doesn't make any sense. Now I understand why people would commit suicide." He paused. Should he say it? Yes, she might as well know. "I tried to do it myself back in the hospital. I still sometimes think it might have been the best thing."

Lydia's eyes opened slightly; the dark irises became prominent. She shifted her legs and tilted her head. Dan could see that his statement had made an impact.

"That would have been the easy way out, Dan. Apparently, that's not the way for you. Like you said, you should have died back there, in the crash, or drowned in the wreckage, or died in the hospital. Don't you see? You are alive for some reason. There is a lesson here somewhere."

Suddenly, Dan was mad, and it felt good. "Lesson? Lesson?

Don't give me that new-age bullshit. I've heard that before. 'It's all karma. You create your own reality.' As far as I'm concerned, that's no better than saying it's God's will, or kismet. That may work if you are some yuppie cruising through life, but you are talking to a guy who has lost everything."

She seemed to gather herself up before she replied in a surprisingly powerful voice. "You have not lost everything, Dan. If you want to see someone who has lost everything look at television tonight or open a newspaper. You will probably encounter someone who has lost their entire family and their home, or possibly someone who has seen their children murdered in front of their eyes. You still have your children, your home, and probably a job with Intercontinental, if you choose to return to it. You have truly experienced a tragedy, but you have not been dealt the worst hand that life can give you."

"Well, that doesn't sound very helpful," Dan said.

"I just want you to know that you have a base from which you can start rebuilding your life."

"Right now, that seems like a goal too far away. I know I have to do it, but I don't have the energy. Little things can upset me so much. I did turn on the TV, and I did see just what you are talking about, and I just about broke up. I had to turn it off." The feelings involved began to flood into his mind again. His body began a slight involuntary tremor. He felt himself sliding off center. He shuddered and shook his head trying to regain control. Lydia observed all this before she replied.

"That's because you are a changed man. You have crossed over a certain line. You now know, in your own heart, what these people are feeling. You share their tragedy. In time these feelings will not be so acute. You will find your center, and you will regain your energy. But that is not now."

Again, bitterness flooded through Dan. "Yes, now is going through each day realizing that I killed a hundred-ninety-three passengers, including Manalani, and eleven crew members, some of whom were good friends. Now is knowing that I failed in my job, to keep them alive. Now is not being able to sleep. Or when I do, waking up suddenly thinking she is there, and then having to face the fact she'll never be there again. Or having one of those bad dreams that jolt me awake so badly shaken I can hardly breathe."

Lydia smiled slightly and said, "I don't know if it will do you any good, Dan, but there now is a label applied to the set of symptoms you are describing. It is called post-traumatic stress disorder, called PTSD in the trade. Have you heard the term?"

"Yes, I even skimmed through an article on it once, but I never thought it would apply to me. Ironic. Here I am, a laboratory case for study." This thought brought up some real doubts in Dan's mind. She probably didn't really care what happened to him. She sat around all day listening to people spilling out their problems, complaining, whining. How could she care? It would drive him nuts to do that all day.

Her reply broke into his concerns. "No, Dan, I'm not going to treat you that way. I just want you to know you are not the first to go through this, and there are common themes involved. Have you tried to recall the details of what happened?"

"Well, I did for the official company and FAA report, but the less said there the better. It's a matter of public record, and the attorneys will have a field day with it later. But there is a mystery there, a blank spot that is of no real concern to them.

I have no idea how I actually worked my way loose from the cockpit. My foot was trapped under the rudder pedal. The last thing I remember is trying to yank it out of there with no result and then running out of air as we sank under the water. Next thing I knew I was on the surface."

He wondered what she would make of that. He could tell by her eyes and the way she shifted forward that she was interested. "Dan, there are at least two areas where I can help you: one is with your recall of the details, the other is with your bad dreams."

"How can you do that?"

"By using hypnotherapy."

"Hold it. Hold it. As far as I'm concerned that stuff is just a couple of steps away from witches and goblins."

"Oh, come on, Dan. You should be more aware than that. Surely you have read about this procedure being used to aid witnesses in court cases."

"Yes, I have, and I have also read that it's not always reliable."

"It is true that it's not infallible, but in your case, with no motive to cover-up or create a screen memory, the results should be accurate. It's by far the best method to recover information in the mind that has been repressed by shock."

For the first time Dan felt that she was slightly on the defensive. She was trying to be convincing, very intense, as if she was delivering a sales pitch. The resistance inside him forced his reply, "I don't know. I guess I'm just old fashioned. Sounds like hocus pocus to me."

"Au contraire, Dan, it's been around for a long time. It's rather mainstream now days." She smiled at her little joke, and watched Dan to see his reaction. He wasn't sure about it yet and wondered aloud how this would help his dreams.

"Dan, there is something you can do to help yourself there. You are holding back a tremendous amount of emotion. You have to let it go. When is the last time you cried?"

Somehow, he knew this was coming. "I think I cried at the hospital when they told me—you know—told me—about Manalani." His voice was tired and strained. "I was in such shock, I'm not sure. And when I first went home, in the bedroom, that was hard."

"Dan, there is more, a lot more to let go. You have hardly started."

"Well, what do you expect? Do you want me bawling like a baby?" Dan didn't like the turn this conversation was taking. He thought he knew where this was leading, and it made him twist in his seat. Lydia waited until he settled down and looked in her eyes before she replied.

"No, Dan, not like a baby. Like a man, who wants to really have a life, and has a lifetime of repressed emotions to release. Dan, grown men do cry. It is a barrier you must cross."

"I can't do that. Not in front of you. Not in front of anybody. I feel like if I let myself go, I will break up into little pieces."

"I know you feel that way, Dan, but it will actually make you whole. Look, Dan, repressed emotions, stuffed inside, will find some outlet. Maybe as rage at inappropriate times. Or they can cause physical symptoms, or they can make your attention wander when you are jolted by a flashback, and you may have an accident. Believe me, this is a fact, not psycho-babble."

"So what am I supposed to do?"

"First, I want you to recognize where you are coming from.

You probably grew up in a family where 'grown men don't cry' was the implied credo. Then you were additionally trained by movies, particularly the cowboy movies in the John Wayne tradition. The strong, silent type. 'A man just does what a man's gotta do.' I'm afraid that Duke, bless his soul, has done as much to screw up men in this country as any single person. And he certainly didn't mean to. But now, you Dan, have a choice. You can bottle up your mind and emotions in an attempt at self-preservation, and you will become a cynical, hard, bitter, closed-off old man, disliked and barely tolerated by his friends and children. Or, you can go through it, all your emotions, holding back nothing, and cleanse yourself. If you do, you will gain a warmth and wisdom that will attract people to you and make them look up to you."

Her choice of words made everything seem so logical that Dan felt he was being taken down a path he wouldn't choose, but which he could not resist without seeming to be the stubborn fool.

"That doesn't give me much choice, does it, when you put it that way."

"Hey, it's not easy, but if you do it, some day you will love me for pushing you into it. That's where I get my satisfaction. That's why I do the work I do."

There was a pause in the exchange as she looked intently at him. The room was charged with anticipation. Dan felt suddenly exhilarated. Maybe there was a path, a way out of the darkness that had enveloped him. At the same time he was tense; he wasn't sure what came next. Lydia broke the silence, "I have an assignment for you to do tonight, if it is possible."

"Yes, it's possible, I've got nothing planned."

"You're a musician besides being a pilot. Manalani told me that. One good path to freeing emotions is through music, particularly if you are tuned into it.

"There is a singer named Sade. She has a CD out called Love Deluxe. On this disk is a cut called 'Pearls'. I want you to sit down, by yourself, in your library or wherever, somewhere you know you won't be disturbed. I want you to play this piece several times, put it on repeat. I want you to listen carefully to the words, and whatever feelings come up, let them out. Completely. No holding back. I want you to keep playing it until you can listen to it without anything coming up. Will you do that?"

"Well—yes—I guess so. What is it I'm supposed to be feeling?"

"Dan, this isn't a test. There are no correct answers. Whatever happens is correct. And by the way, if you feel like you are going to break up when it starts, don't worry. Just go with that feeling."

"Okay, I'll do it. I'm almost sure that Liz has that album in her collection."

"If you're not sure, get it on your way home. You can afford it. Then come back tomorrow and give me a report and we will do the hypnotherapy session. Can you make it?"

"What time?"

"I have eleven and three open. Which do you want?"

"I'll take the three o'clock."

"Okay, Dan. You're on your way. Believe me, there is light at the end of the tunnel."

As she said this, they both stood up. They were close together. To his surprise, she reached out, put her arms under his, and gave him a hug. He was so shocked he hardly knew how to respond. At first, he stiffened, but she felt so good, so warm, so encompassing, that he yielded. He started to choke up, his body trembled, tears formed at the corners of his eyes. He was afraid he would start sobbing right there. Oh, God, could he let himself feel that way again? At what cost? She must know the effect she was having on him.

She released him, smiled, took his hand, and led him to the doorway.

He looked at her and said, "If you don't mind me saying so, that didn't seem very professional."

"Oh, it was very professional," she replied. "I will do whatever my clients need to help them recover. What you needed right then was a little TLC, an inkling that you could feel good again. Right?"

"Yes, you are right about that. Thank you, very much. I hardly know how to express it."

"You just did. That's all I need. That, and your willingness to do the work. See you tomorrow."

As he walked out to the elevator, Dan was pondering what had happened. He did feel better, immensely so. And she really hadn't started to work yet. Maybe she really was a miracle worker. She did seem to know her stuff. He would pick up that CD on the way home and tell the kids to clear out tonight. They worried too much about him anyway. They needed a night out.

***

Dan sat in his favorite chair facing the fireplace. His dinner of leftovers was finished. A picture of Manalani was on a lamp stand to his left. A small fire drifted the smell of wood smoke into the room. His attempt to relax with a sip of Sandeman Port was not successful. Feelings ebbed and flowed without his volition. His fingers opened and closed around the ends of the chair arms. He knew that once the music started he would be swept into a tide of emotion. It would take him into uncharted waters. The realization that he was afraid shocked him into action; "Pearls" began to play. The dirge-like but strangely beautiful opening motif created tightness in his chest and began to choke him up. The lump in his throat expanded until it filled his whole neck. Then it began:

There is a woman in Somalia

Scraping for pearls by the roadside.

There is a force stronger than nature.

Keeps her will alive.

This is how she's dying.

She is dying to survive.

Don't know what she's made of.

I would like to be that brave.

When she cries to the heaven above.

Tears began to roll down Dan's cheeks. The words were touching him at some point deep inside.

There is a stone in my heart.

She lives life she didn't choose…

The stone in his heart suddenly broke open. Waves of grief rolled over him. He began rocking back and forth, his breath coming in gasps, his body wracked by unleashed forces over which he had no control.

There is a woman in Somalia.

The sun gives her no mercy.

The same sky we lie under,
burns her to the bone.
Long as afternoon shadows
gonna take her to get home.
Each grain carefully wrapped up.
Pearls for her little girl.

Listening to these lines, Dan could see this woman of the desert walking her lonely road. Somehow, that image was suffused with one of Manalani, her face, her movement. A series of montages, half vision, half-feeling, swept through his mind. They were beckoning to him, calling him. He felt their message deep inside him—let it go, let it all out.

It came out as an animal cry, a howl of anguish that shocked him to the core. He was coming apart at the seams, but after the feeling passed through him, he felt released. When she repeated the line, "There is a stone in my heart," he realized that the stone in his own heart had been broken. It was still there, but it was in pieces.

He remembered Lydia's instructions to replay the song until he no longer was emotionally shaken by it. He took a long drink from his glass of wine. Could he do this? Could he go through this catharsis again? Yes, he could. He pressed repeat on the player.

This time he was not racked with emotion as the waves of grief passed through him. The tears continued, but by the end, he just felt empty, drained of all emotion. He turned off the light and staggered off to bed. He was too exhausted to puzzle out the process that had just occurred. It would have to wait until tomorrow when he would see Lydia.

**

In Lydia's waiting room, he found he was eager to talk to her. Last night had been his best night of sleep since the accident. He woke up full of questions, and without the accompanying dread that often rose with his wakening consciousness. An enveloping sheet of sadness that pervaded most of the day, but he could deal with that.

When her receptionist waved him on through, he found her in front of her desk again. She extended her hands, looked at him intently, and said, "You did it! Good. And it helped didn't it?"

Dan smiled and said, "Yes, it did, in an entirely surprising way. At least to me. I guess, like you said, I had a lot to let go of."

She motioned to the chairs again. "Do you want to tell me about it?"

Dan wasn't sure how to express himself. "It was like a dam burst inside of me. I was out of control." He noticed her smile at the word control. "There was a mystery, too. It was like Manalani and the woman in Somalia merged in some manner. I could see or sense them both. They were both telling me to let go."

"And you did?"

"Oh yeah. I did all right and thought I was going to howl the house down."

"That's all right, you needed to do that."

"I know that now, but it was a frightening experience at the time."

"Of course it was. You were pushing into unknown realms. That is frightening for anyone."

"There is still something that bothers me. Why would a song about a woman in Somalia affect me that way? Her experience and mine are entirely different. And somehow, you knew it would work. How did you know?"

Lydia managed to laugh and look mysterious at the same time. "A woman's intuition, Dan. You have heard of that."

He laughed in reply.

She continued, "For someone else I might have suggested a country and western song, or a Mahler symphony; it just comes to me, and it always works. I can't say why."

"You're not kidding then; it really is a woman's intuition." Dan looked at her, puzzled. At times, there was a feeling about her, that she was ancient and in touch with a body of knowledge with which he had no connection.

"Yes, that's right. To answer your other question, the wounds of grief are universal, anger, pain, abandonment, terror, loneliness. The external cause may vary but the result, the feeling, is the same. A woman from Somalia, a pilot from Palos Verdes, there are certain core feelings that are the same. Strip away all the veneer and you are not that different at the core. That doesn't mean that her experience and her reaction to it are the same as yours. But at the core, there is a shared feeling that can be transmitted. Somehow a good artist, Sade in this case, can translate that. You will hear others, a song that cuts to your heart, which moves you. When you hear one, let it happen."

That made Dan uneasy. She was asking him to go with an emotional flow that was against his nature. "I'll be bawling in the streets if I let that happen."

"No you won't, Dan. I know you better than that. If you find a song like that, take it home with you. Play it. You still have more to release, though last night was a major move."

"Last night was a revelation to me. I didn't realize that I

could let out that much emotion all at once."

"That's because you have a whole lifetime of repressed grief to let out, your father's and mother's death, the puppy that died when you were a kid. All of that is stored up in there somewhere. Given a chance it all comes spilling out."

"Is that good?"

"Do you feel better?"

"Yes, but…

"Yes, but what? Look, it takes energy to hold any emotional stuff inside. Going through it releases that energy to be used in other ways."

"Yes, but we just can't go around spilling our guts out all the time, or venting our emotions randomly." Dan could see the veins standing out on the backs of his wrists and forearms. He took a deep breath to settle down,

Lydia watched this process with no comment.

"Of course, there is a time and place for everything, Dan, but your problem is not inappropriate display of emotion. It's getting it out where you can see it. Get that?"

"Got it, I guess."

"No guessing. God, you are hard headed. You just had a mind-blowing experience, and now you are trying to shunt it aside. Do you want to go back to where you were before?"

"NO!" A mixture of anger and excitement rose in him.

"Then keep open. Don't shut down. Let's see. What was coming up next?"

"You were going to hypnotize me back into the accident scene. You know, I'm not really sure I want to go back through that."

"Don't worry, Dan, you are not actually going to relive it. It will be more like watching it as a movie with you in the primary role."

"Okay. It seems like you know what you are doing, and I really do want to know what happened when I blanked out."

She had him transfer to the couch and started the standard induction technique - fractional relaxation, warm heavy body, descending staircase, counting backwards. After his curiosity died down, he found himself drifting, sometimes even losing track of her voice. She asked him to respond verbally to some questions. That jarred his relaxed state, but it quickly became part of the continuing refrain. She got around to suggesting that he was in the MD-11 at Hong Kong preparing for take-off. He stumbled over the first verbalization but then quickly found a rhythm as he described the familiar process unfolding in front of him.

Eventually, the events seemed to unreel effortlessly. He was there, watching himself go through the motions of flying. As the moment of impact approached he began to feel tense, but there was no fear. In his peripheral vision he saw Dick Borman hit the ditch switch. He grunted and felt his body jerk in response to the forces at impact. As the water rose in the cockpit, he again sensed panic and the struggle to release his foot. That immense void, his death, rose up to meet him. At that moment, just as he thought he blanked out, he heard a powerful yet calm voice break through.

STOP

Stop what?

STOP STRUGGLING

EXTEND YOUR LEFT LEG FORWARD

ROTATE THE FOOT TO THE TWO O'CLOCK POSITION

LIFT YOURSELF OUT OF THE SEAT
NOW GO FOR THE LIGHT

He could see light over his shoulder. Desperately he pushed and kicked his way through an opening, cutting his hands and hitting his head on some part of the structure. Then he was on the surface.

The shock of this revelation snapped him into a normal waking state, eyes blinking, head shaking, confused.

"What the hell was that? What was that voice? I don't remember that. Did you suggest that?"

"No, Dan. That was not a suggestion. That really happened."

"What happened? You mean to say that I actually heard a voice giving me the correct commands to get myself out of there? Where did that come from?" Dan's stomach churned; his jaw clenched. *Voices?* He thought, *Doesn't that mean I'm at least mentally unbalanced?*

"Dan, have you ever heard of or read about this kind of thing happening to someone else?"

"Oh sure, I think I have. But it was always third or fourth hand kind of stuff, or in a book. I figured it was just the author's way of getting himself out of a corner he'd written himself into."

"That could be true, but this voice, coming to a person in crisis, has been known about for thousands of years. In fact it's only fallen out of favor in the last few hundred. Before that time, people actively searched for the voice to guide them. Whole disciplines and religions were based on that search."

"But what does that have to do with me? I don't believe that stuff."

"It should be obvious to you that belief is not required. You have encountered another of life's great mysteries."

"Enough already. I had enough mystery happen to me last night. I don't need any more. How does this fit in with the rest of my life? Just tell me, where does this voice come from?"

"Look, Dan, I'm not your guru. I don't want to influence you. I can give you several possible ways to view this. It depends on your world view."

"Okay, go ahead. I'm listening."

"If you were a conscientious, church going, true believer Christian, the answer would be obvious; it's the voice of God or Jesus. If you were Muslim, it would be Mohammed. If you were Hindu, it would be Krishna, or Shiva. In any case the voice of your personal god. If you were a member of a tribal culture, such as one of the First Nations, it would be the voice of your ally, or in Hawaii your aumakua. If you were one of the new age people, it would be your spirit guide or higher self coming to you, since it was not your time to die."

Lydia leaned back in her chair. Her eyes flitted sideways.

"If you don't like any of these ideas, you might consider Jung's construction based on the collective unconscious. We do know that there is a large portion of our brain that is generally quiet. Jung, and others, postulate that this quiet portion is the repository of memories that extend back through our genetic line to a pool of information common to all humanity. In times of crisis, this unconscious information or intelligence can become particularized, arising in the form of a voice, a hunch, a feeling that some particular path should be followed. Warriors go out on extended vision quests seeking just such guidance. Families of aborigines in Australia can receive this information simultaneously forming a type of group mind. So you see, what happened to you is unusual, but not unique or crazy. It's been around for a long while. Is that comforting to you?"

"Well, yes it is. But, I'm still puzzled. I mean, which one of those theories is right?"

With a wave of her hand, she dismissed his question.

"Come on, Dan. This is not an exam. There are no right or wrong answers. The one thing you can know for sure, is that at some level, the world does not work the way you were taught it does, or the way you believe it does. I like to use J.B.S. Haldane's statement, 'The world is not only stranger than you think; it is stranger than anything you can think'"

Dan puzzled over this, but he wasn't ready to let her off the hook. "Look, I'm still the one who has to face this voice from the twilight zone, and I have enough things to think about already. Can't you give me some source to go to for more information?"

"Yes, I can do that. Get *The Power of Myth* by Joseph Campbell, an interview with Bill Moyers. It's also available on video if you don't like to read. This is a wonderful introduction to a way of looking at the world that is ancient, but new to you."

"Thanks. That sounds like a good place to start. Now, do you think going through this stuff will put an end to the dreams I've been having?"

"I can't guarantee that Dan, but it should. Can you describe the dreams to me? That will give me a clue."

Dan hesitantly described his flying and falling dreams. He felt very self-conscious about this. He had never discussed any of his dreams with anyone except Manalani. Lydia, of course, could see the symbolism in them, and suggested techniques and practices that might eliminate them. This was strange territory for Dan. He shifted uneasily in his chair. By now his ribs ached and his ankle was throbbing again. "I'm not used to thinking in these terms. You make it all seem so logical, but I know when I walk out of this room, I'm going to wonder if we really had this conversation."

Lydia rose from her chair, extended her hands to him to help him out of his chair, and said, "Dan, just do it. It doesn't take faith, but it does take courage to try something new."

Though part of Dan felt very self-conscious about a woman helping him get to his feet, another part of him enjoyed the physical contact. When she gave him another hug in parting, he was very conscious of her warmth, her softness, and her femininity. It excited and disturbed him simultaneously. At least he knew that in her presence he felt more alert and alive than at any other time. Was he becoming too dependent on her? It didn't matter now. The important thing was that she could see a way out of the mess that he was in. That was a comfort.

CHAPTER 13

During one of Dan's trips to the Long Beach offices of Intercontinental, he ran into Glen again. When he mentioned he was planning a trip to Oahu to see Manalani's folks, Glen insisted that he take time to visit his home on Molokai. At first Dan declined, but as they talked longer, he realized that a period of rest and relaxation at a remote location might be just what he needed. The names Glen gave him offered an entree to a friendly but tight knit community. When Dan described the problem he was having with his ankle, Glen also recommended that he see Otsuka Roshi at the Zen Center in Kaunakakai. He said that the Roshi had an amazing reputation for healing people with problems that seemed intractable. At this point Dan's mood was such that he was open for help from any source.

Liz and Mark could take care of themselves with the help of the housekeeper he had hired. Liz would come out to join him after he had been there a week. Mark was going to be involved with school and sports activities. Dan had finished his dealings with Intercontinental for awhile, so there was nothing holding him back. His hesitation came because he did not want to face Takeshi and Nona.

On the plane ride to Honolulu, he envisioned various scenarios that might occur, none of them pleasant. Picking up the box at baggage claim that contained the urn with Manalani's ashes did not help his mood. A low-pressure area that had anchored itself just west of the island chain pumped low clouds and rain into the area. The weather conspired to push Dan's mood to the edge of despair. What could he possibly say that would be adequate? Even though she was his wife, what could he say when he had killed their only daughter? How could he present them with the urn that contained her ashes? Again, he wished they had died together.

When he reached the beach park at Haleiwa, he stopped. He could go no farther. He walked the wet sand. The waves lapped at his feet. Nothing in his life had prepared him for this burden. The billowing clouds allowed sunlight to illuminate the surf pounding on the reef. Plumeria and ginger layered the moist air with scent. Wrapped in his problems, Dan hardly noticed. Finally, he gave up trying to sort out his emotions or plan his opening words. He called from a phone booth in the park. Takeshi answered, "Come ahead, we are both here. Ain't gonna be going nowhere." From that response, Dan could not glean any inkling of his reception.

Driving up the hill along the row of shack-like cottages, his sense of dread was unabated. When he pulled in the drive and parked under the mango tree, he could see the screen door open to the carport. By the time he was out of the car, they were almost at his side. Nona spoke first. "Hello, Dan. How is your leg? Why don't we go inside?"

"Oh, the leg is coming along okay. I guess it's not much of a day to be outside, is it." Should he get the box out of the trunk? No, that could wait until later.

At the door, Takeshi waited, as Dan walked up the steps to the kitchen. He sat at the kitchen table. As usual, there was a small vase of local flowers on the table. The morning newspaper was at Takeshi's appointed spot. The smell of soup cooking and wet, smoke-permeated wood provided an undertone similar to incense.

In spite of Dan's unease, he could immediately appreciate the sense of solidity and calm they had established in this simple home. Everything was in exactly the right place and had been there for years. It helped to settle him down.

In the island way, the conversation drifted around subjects of little consequence. For once, Dan appreciated their leisurely approach to any important matter. First Dan drank an iced tea offered by Nona. and then Takeshi brought out two bottles of beer, then two more.

While describing his ankle injury, Dan said it could have been much worse. He was almost trapped in the wreckage. There was a pregnant silence. Dan knew he had to take the plunge. "I suppose I should back up and tell you the whole story. I'm sure you want to know."

He could see Takeshi grip his bottle tighter as he replied, "Of course you right Dan, but we no want to push you. You tell in own good time. It must be hard for you." Nona did not speak, but nodded in agreement.

"It is hard for all of us," Dan said. "I can hardly imagine what it must be like for you. Sometimes I still find myself believing that none of it really happened—like it was a bad dream."

"Buddha say, this life here is a dream," Takeshi replied. "We all here to play out roles, like in one movie."

"Well, if this is a movie, the plot has turned ugly in a way I can't comprehend."

"Buddha say, life is full of sorrow. Come from desires and

attachment to those desires. No attach—no loss—no sorrow."

"That's a nice philosophy, but I don't see how anyone can do it."

"Buddha say that. I no say I can do it. But you go ahead. You talk story. You no worry about us."

Dan gave them a shortened version of the crash and its immediate aftermath. Only flickers of emotions passed over their faces at the points where he expected them to be shocked. They asked no questions about the details. At one point, Dan expressed remorse at allowing Manalani to come along. Nona said, "You not know future. It was one natural decision. You not at fault." This gave Dan more comfort than he could have expected.

When Dan finished, Takeshi went to the refrigerator for more beer. On his return to the table, he stood behind Dan for a moment, placed his hand on Dan's shoulder, and gave it a short but powerful squeeze. Nothing was said, but that physical contact was so strong that it set off a flood of emotion in Dan. His body began to shake slightly; his throat tightened up. He knew at some level he had been forgiven. Then Takeshi asked, "You have brought Manalani's ashes to us?"

"Yes, in the car."

"Please, you would bring them to us."

"Of course."

Dan could hardly talk. He was glad to have the release of physical action. On the way to the car, he settled down. He gave the enameled box to Takeshi, who carried it into the house. Inside, he and Nona opened the box and took out the urn. They looked at it for a few moments, then Nona said in a low controlled voice, "Good."

They both turned from the kitchen table. Takeshi took the urn. Nona said, "You come with us." They walked down the hallway to another room. When Dan reached the doorway, he was staggered. He did not anticipate what he saw. The room was empty, except for a small shrine on the far side consisting of candles, flowers, incense, a small statue of Buddha, and a framed picture of Manalani. They had left a space for the urn. The impact of this scene so shook Dan that he was glad they were facing away from him.

They both knelt down and said a few words Dan could not understand. Dan clasped his hands, rocked back and forth, uncomfortable, awkward. Part of him wanted to kneel with them, but he couldn't do it. If he did, he knew he would find himself prostrate on the floor. How could they do it? How could they accept this loss with such equanimity? It wasn't an act performed for him. He knew that with some inner certainty.

They rose to their feet, and Nona took his hand as they returned to the living room. A few minutes of silence existed, except for the sound of rain, wind, and mynah birds outside. Nona spoke, inviting him for dinner. He accepted. The emotional pitch lowered, and conversation returned to normal until he made his exit. Dan had a good night's sleep in his hotel room. The following morning, on the short flight to Molokai, his mood was much lighter than on his arrival at Honolulu.

Lack of business at the terminal, and the slow taxi ride to the Zen Center, indicated a change of pace on this island. The low buildings making up the compound were nestled under tall trees on a mountain slope facing southwest. He paid the driver and walked under an archway. The grounds were immaculately groomed. The whole arrangement reminded him of pictures he had seen of temples in Kyoto, but on a smaller and simpler scale. Several shaven headed students were working in the area. One of them approached Dan and said, "You are Mr. Swanton?"

"Yes."

"Remove your shoes and put on slippers please. Otsuka Roshi is expecting you."

They went through a large high-ceilinged room with benches along the sides, then down a short hall. The student opened a sliding screen and motioned Dan into the room beyond. The room had a western-style desk and chair in it. There was a framed piece of calligraphy on the wall and a window onto what looked like a vegetable garden. Dan had no idea what the protocol was in his situation.

The Roshi came through the door at the other end of the room. He was shorter than Dan, as Dan expected. He wore a loose black robe, cinched at the waist, which made it difficult to determine his body type. His face was round, small nose, dark eyes, large ears, a shining forehead with a large domed skull. Dan noticed that he appeared to glide as he stepped toward Dan to shake hands. His voice came from deep within his body. "Aloha, Mr. Swanton." His hand was broad, flat, and callused like a farmer's. This surprised Dan. "I do a great deal of gardening. It helps to settle the mind." Dan was shocked. Was the Roshi reading his mind? "You are surprised. No, I'm not a mind reader. I just observe very carefully. I have studied the human body and mind for many years."

Dan recovered. "Yes, I expect that would be a useful skill for someone in your position."

"It is useful for anyone. Like a pond disturbed by a strong

wind, we are all different on the surface."

Dan said, "One thing that impressed me as soon as I entered your compound was a sense of calm or tranquility."

"Calm surroundings help to induce a calm mind. The chatter of the little mind in each of us must be stilled before one can know what lies beyond."

"It seems so obvious when you say it, and I feel it in these surroundings. I have not felt at peace with myself or my world for a long time."

"Yes. Glen Miyashiro called me to say that you had a serious accident and suffered severe injury from which you are recovering."

"Yes, it was a disastrous accident. I have both physical and mental recovery to make. That is one reason I am here."

"Come with me into this next room then. We can begin."

As they walked into the other room, Dan realized that already his emotions were smoothing out. Something about this man instilled immediate confidence. Again, he noticed the Roshi's smooth gliding walk that seemed to produce very little vertical motion. The room had two cushioned full length tables in it and very little else. It was noticeably warmer than the other rooms.

"First, I would like you to strip down to your shorts and stand facing me."

This might have made Dan nervous elsewhere, but here it seemed like a natural request. He laid his clothes on a bench.

"Now, turn ninety degrees. That's right. Now face away from me. Have you seen a chiropractor?"

"No, I've never really believed in them."

"Hmmm. Besides the obvious damage to your ankle, your

lumbar vertebrae have been twisted and your hips have taken a set off horizontal. Not surprising—it is a compensation your body makes to take weight off the injured leg."

"Can you do anything about it?"

"Yes, we can. Quite a lot. Lie down on the table face up."

As soon as the Roshi placed his hands on Dan's ankle, it felt as though a heating pad had been applied there. He asked, "What are you doing now?"

"I am transferring ki to the injured area. This might seem to be mysterious to you, but it is an ancient practice in much of the world."

Dan then thought he could hear the Roshi humming. It seemed to course into his body at a vibrational level lower than he could hear. At the same time, he could feel fingers pressing deeply into the joint. He was surprised there was no pain, but at that instant, there was a sharp jolt, and he could feel the foot twist in relationship to the ankle.

"Relax again," the Roshi said. "It was necessary to do a manipulation there. Roll over onto your stomach."

Dan could feel the Roshi's hands move up his legs to his pelvis.

"I am going to work on your pelvis. You may experience some pain. I need to loosen the fascia that are locking your hips in place. Breathe into the pain, if it occurs, and keep your mind and thoughts under my fingers. Do not pull away from the pain."

Dan was glad he was warned, because soon the pain was enough that he was grunting and breathing in short gasps.

The Roshi's only response was to say, "That's good," and to begin humming again.

Suddenly the pressure was gone and he told Dan to breathe deeply and relax. Then he worked up and down Dan's back, rubbing, pressing, and twisting at various points. He stepped back, told Dan to roll over, placed a blanket on him, and small pillow under his neck.

After resting a few minutes, Dan stood up. He could not believe the difference he felt in his body. It was as though someone had taken a great weight off him. A sudden flash of well being and excitement coursed through him. "I can't believe it! It's like you performed a miracle! I feel like a different person. I can walk without limping."

The Roshi smiled benevolently at Dan. "It's hardly a miracle. The body wants to restore itself when given a chance. I merely provide it with a pathway to do so."

Dan could not stop grinning. "Well, I'm sold. I still think you are a magician."

"Hardly. You may need to see me once more."

"I'd be glad to if you can make this much difference."

As they moved to the other room, Dan had several questions in mind. "What do you use the big hall for?"

"We sometimes hold our meditations there. It is also our dojo."

"Dojo? What's that?"

"We have certain disciplines that help to train the mind and body. I practice Tai Chi and Aikido and archery."

Dan was surprised at the term practice, and said, "I'll bet you mean teach rather than practice."

The Roshi shrugged. "It is true that I teach, but in these arts or disciplines one never stops practicing. There is no final goal or endpoint. When you fly, do you ever feel there is nothing more to learn?"

"No, you are right. That's what keeps it interesting. I can see the parallel. There is always another lesson to be learned."

The Roshi replied by doing that deep hum again. This time Dan felt it was a sign of approval. Dan decided to cross over into an area that really bothered him. "Otsuka Roshi, I have been in turmoil since the accident. Over two hundred passengers were killed, eight flight attendants, three pilots who were my friends, and my wife."

Dan paused, expecting a response, but the Roshi said nothing, just looked at him with a level unblinking gaze.

"I can't make any sense of it. I mean is fate a hunter that plunges out of the sky like a predator, destroying lives without meaning? Or is this some kind of payback, karma as I think you call it, for something I did in a past life. And if so, why should these other people die. Why didn't I die back then? More than once I have thought it would be better if I had."

"You ask many difficult questions," replied the Roshi. "Men have asked them since ancient times. Those who say they have the answers may not have looked deeply enough into their implications. Let us go outside while I consider my answer to you."

The Roshi led Dan to a doorway that opened to the garden in back. Its structured beauty immediately struck Dan as a perfect design. It looked natural, with its small brook, trees, rocks, bamboo, and a few flowers, each one strategically placed to produce a feeling of harmony and peace. Beams of light descended from the overhead canopy. The bamboo whispered as the breeze passed through. A few birds called. Carp swam in a pool made by the brook that bubbled quietly. Moss and zoysia grass covered the ground. One flowering tree and a few lilies provided a counter point. The word sanctuary sprang into Dan's mind, and it fit perfectly.

Dan said, "This is amazing. Unless I knew better, I would think that all this had happened without any planning or planting."

The Roshi smiled his benevolent smile again. "Yes, that is the aim of this garden, to produce a feeling of nature in a small area. This has been done in Japan for hundreds of years."

"It certainly has a soothing feeling."

The Roshi said, "I have spent many hours here planting and sitting. A retreat like this is helpful when one needs to contemplate difficult questions. Let us sit over here."

He led Dan to two small benches facing each other at an angle. They sat silently for a few moments. Dan had the impression that the Roshi was an immovable object, as if he had become part of the rocks around him. He commented on it.

The Roshi laughed quietly and said, "There is an old Zen principle. When sitting sit. When standing stand. But above all, don't wobble."

Dan smiled. Another silence ensued. Finally, the Roshi began, "You may be surprised to find out that Zen Buddhism does not speak directly to these questions. Other branches of Buddhism have sprung up that attempt to do this. In Zen, we feel that to focus on the present moment is always the task. The mind tends to flit away from the present like a bird or insect. We call this mind, the little mind. It is what we use to deal with the world of appearances. Behind all this, lies another state we call big mind. It is quiet, unchanging, and eternal. It exists in everyone. Our practice in zazen is primarily to enter this state. We use a koan to shock the student into this state, sometimes called no-mind, because in it, all the fluttering of the mind stops." The Roshi frowned slightly and said, "This is difficult to place into words; it is a wordless experience by its nature."

Dan said, "I can see that. I may only get part of it, but go on."

"When one enters this state, one realizes that all questions coming from the little mind, even those of the type you are asking, cannot be answered directly. In the world of appearances, answers shift constantly with mood and circumstances. What satisfies you today will be inadequate tomorrow. Our practice is to go past that, into the state that lies beyond, and yet is here in every present moment, in the space between our thoughts. Unfortunately for you, this may not be what you had hoped for."

"You are right," Dan replied. "And yet as I sit here and listen to you here in this garden, I feel you are correct. I feel at peace right now. But when I go out there, and get into that world, I'm afraid it will all come flooding back."

"Yes, that is true," replied the Roshi, "but it is good you have had this experience here. It is also good you are going to the Halepio Valley. There are people there who will help you with your questions."

"How will I meet them or know them?"

"Ah yes, another old saying, 'When the student is ready, the master appears." The valley is a small community. In a short time, everyone will know your history and needs. You will receive help."

Dan said, "That is interesting. You seem very sure of it."

"I am. You are on a good path. One benefit of your tragedy, it has stripped you of all pretense. There is a friend of mine there, a Hindu recluse. If you find him, he may give you more satisfying answers than I have."

"I'm not complaining," Dan said. "You have given me some insight, but I do have one more question, if it is appropriate."

"Any question you ask is appropriate. As you have experienced though, I may not have the answers you wish."

Dan shifted his position. He noticed that the Roshi had remained absolutely still during this conversation. "I keep wondering what has happened to Manalani. I am no longer a Christian, so I don't think she is in heaven or some other glorified place. And yet, I feel that she hasn't completely evaporated or disappeared. Maybe that is just wishful thinking. I don't know."

The Roshi smiled again. "I think I can help you there. I am asked this question often. My answer comes not so much from the Zen tradition, but from a story my master gave me.

"Before we are born we are like droplets in a stream. We flow with the current; we exist, but not individually. When the stream plunges over a precipice and forms a waterfall, thousands of tiny droplets form. They each shimmer in the light, believing absolutely in the importance of their individuality. At the bottom of the waterfall, they suddenly merge into the river again. They have not disappeared. They have only changed back into the river and are part of all of it. There may be countless waterfalls as the stream seeks its path to the ocean. Each time, thousands of droplets form again, always different, always the same. Does this help you?"

"Yes it does. At some level that has no words. More of a feeling. Intellectually it means that nobody is destroyed or annihilated; they just change state. But the feeling runs deeper than that. I can't explain it."

"You do not have to. Just stay with that."

The Roshi rose from his bench and said, "Now we must part. I think you will find an adventure ahead Mr. Pilot. Pay attention. Stay in the present moment, whatever it brings you. Don't think too much."

"Thank you very much," Dan said. "You are very kind."

The Roshi turned toward him and said, "Actually, I am not kind. I am merely a sign post, pointing out a way for you."

They walked silently along a path by the buildings and out to the archway. Dan saw the taxi waiting there. How had that happened? He had not called him or told him to wait.

The Roshi observing his surprised expression said, "One of my students probably called for him." He raised one hand, palm outward, in a salutation as Dan got in the taxi. Dan nodded.

As they pulled away, Dan asked the taxi driver if he had received a call from the Zen Center to pick him up. The driver said no. He just had a break between fares. He knew Dan would need a ride, and on impulse, came up to see if he was right. He liked to drive up to the Zen center anyway. Coincidence? Dan wondered.

Glen had told Dan to contact a man named Tiny, a driver for Menehune Tours, to take him into the Halepio Valley. The taxi driver took him to their office. He met Tiny there, a three-hundred-pound giant of a local boy with a singsong high-pitched voice that seemed out of place in such a huge body. Tiny said it would take him about an hour to be ready. Dan could use the time to pick up groceries and last minute supplies. Kaunakakai had only two grocery stores, one hardware store, and one liquor store, all within two blocks of each other, so Dan's task was simple.

Watching the people in town going about their business, Dan could see that local Hawaiian people outnumbered the haole population. Many friendly smiles and shaka signs flashed about as he sat outside watching the street scene. He remembered a line from an Olomana recording, "Here we have rainbows and midmorning showers. People are laughing and loving their hours. The young and the old men—we are all brothers." Sitting there in front of the shops, with the trade winds rustling the banana leaves and palm trees, it all fit together. The events of yesterday faded into the background of his mind.

When Tiny reappeared, there was a sudden flurry of activity. Supplies, bags, and camping gear stuffed in the back of the jeep, and they were on their way. Tiny was a human dynamo. A continuous stream of comments and questions flowed out of him. Pidgin and laughter sprinkled through his commentary causing Dan to miss parts of it. Tiny didn't seem to care, and would laugh harder when Dan asked him to repeat or clarify some point.

"You bring extra lamp oil and stove fuel?"

"Yeah. I got that."

"Mosquito punks, DEET, toilet paper?"

"Yeah. I got that too."

"So, how you know Glen?"

"We are both pilots for Intercontinental Airlines."

"Hey, you one lucky buggah. You fly all over. You get free ride all over, right?"

"You're right, at least on my own airline."

"So, you evah been dis island before?"

"No, I've been to Oahu a number of times. My wife, Manalani, came from there. But I've never been here before. Talked about it, but it never quite happened."

Tiny looked at Dan. He guessed that Tiny was considering a question about Manalani. Instead, Tiny said, "You lucky. Not many haoles get to stay in Halepio; most tourists just come for a day. No hotels. Rain too hard for good camping."

Dan asked, "How do local people take to an outsider like me staying there?"

"No problem, brah. You know Glen. You okay. Just slow down island style. No electricity, no phone, no car, no big thing. Throw away watch. Live by sun. That's the way life should be."

"That is going to be a big change for me. Working for an airline, everything is determined by the clock and schedules."

"It take you maybe three, four days to adjust. You stay more than a week and then come topside, you want to go back, not come out. You see."

This was going to be quite an adjustment, Dan thought. He was glad he brought along some books and a battery-powered CD player. What about extra batteries? Had he brought enough? He asked Tiny, "If I forgot something, or need more, how do I resupply myself?"

"I come down valley almost every day. You see me or leave list on gatepost. I get for you. Sometimes your neighbor, Keone Kanahele, may go topside. He can do."

Dan remembered, "Glen said I should meet him."

"Oh, you will. No problem. He look after you."

At this point, the rocking motion of the car and the warmth of the sun caused Dan to drop off to sleep. Eventually, he felt the jeep come to a stop and heard Tiny say, "Hey brah, you wake up. Look out. See valley where you go stay."

Dan saw a massive U-shaped amphitheater, three or four miles across and three thousand feet deep, with the open end toward the ocean. At the end of the valley, clouds capped the steep walls cut by ribboned waterfalls. Toward the ocean, shafts of light speared through the rain and towering clouds. The valley floor shimmered in reflected light from taro fields and multiple streambeds. The various levels of trees and undergrowth represented all shades of green. Encompassed by trees and water, a few simple houses clung to the high ground.

Dan turned to Tiny and said, "This is amazing. This must be what all the valleys looked like in the old days."

Tiny replied, "You right. But more people—plenty more in old days. Forty thousand Hawaiians live here before haoles come. It was place of great power. Hawaiian spirit gods lived here. Kamehameha and Kahekili fought battles over valley. People died of disease or moved out to towns, so population dropped. Final blow come when tsunamis hit valley. Last one in 1964 wiped everyone out. Now with sugar mill shut down, local people move back, clean up fields, grow taro and vegetables."

Dan asked, "How many people live here now?"

"Oh, maybe a hundred. Hard to say. Some people live topside part time for make money. So now we head down, okay?"

"Sure, lead on."

"You like this. Better than roller coaster ride."

Dan had never seen a steeper, narrower, hair-raising road. It was also muddy and deeply rutted. To raise the risk, in places a side slope leaned toward the drop off.

Dan asked, "Has anybody ever gone off the edge here?"

225

"Oh sure, but not for a while."

"What happened to them?"

Tiny looked over, squinted his eyes and said, "They die." Then he laughed with that high-pitched giggle and said, "You can see wrecks down below, if you want, but they mostly covered with vines."

"No thanks. I'll just be happy when we are down there in one piece."

"No worries. I never fail. This road really not made for cars; it for mules and horses. For years, we use them to haul out taro to town, and then let them loose. They come home on their own."

"I sure can see why you need four-wheelers down here," Dan said. "I bet the roads must wash out here a lot."

"You bet right," Tiny replied. "Sometimes no road at all. Watch this." As he said this, the jeep was descending into a streambed with a vertical bank on the other side. Tiny cut the wheel to the left and they were driving upstream with water almost to the floorboards.

"Do you always do this?" Dan asked.

"Only when water is low. Better crossing upstream, but several miles out of our way. Look up left."

Dan could see a pair of waterfalls disappearing into the jungle growth. One was a mere ribbon, the other a torrent of water.

"They main source for this stream. Legends say they two lovers who turned themselves into waterfalls so they always be together. Small one that way because the sugar company ditched away most of it for water cane fields."

"I should think there would be plenty of water with all the rain," Dan said.

"Not always in summer. Besides, they run ditch for miles to places where it no rain so much. In old days, during times of little rain, people from other villages come here, trade for food. Now we get food in store, come from mainland. Not so good."

Tiny turned out of the streambed to the right, giving Dan his first view of the taro fields. A light breeze ruffled the water in them. The leaves of the plants danced in unison with each passing gust, giving the impression of dancers standing in one place swaying. Dan could see where some hula movements were similar. As they passed by, a few workers straightened up from their tasks and waved. Almost all of them pressed at the small of their backs as they did so.

"Looks like hard work," Dan commented.

"Yeah, back breaking, hot and muddy, but good work. It keeps you connected to the land, the aina, the source for everything that Hawaiians love."

They again forded a stream. This one had cement approaches at both sides. A truck waited to cross on the other side.

Tiny turned to Dan and said, "That's your neighbor, Keone. Good luck. You meet him."

As they approached the truck, Tiny and Keone gave each other the shaka sign. Dan knew that it was the local way of showing everything's cool, hang loose. Tiny said in greeting, "Howzit brah? How you stay?"

"I go topside. I got a load of da kine to sell. Pick up supplies. You know. Usual kine stuff."

"Hey, I got your new neighbor with me. You know, the pilot, Glen's friend."

Keone smiled, flashing a set of impeccable white teeth that contrasted with his broad dark face and intensely black hair and beard. "Greetings there, Mr. Pilot; I heard you were coming. Welcome to our valley. E komo mai. What is your name?"

"Dan's my name. Glad to meet you."

"Take time to settle in, Dan. I see you tonight or tomorrow morning."

"Thanks," Dan said, "Be glad to see you."

Keone gunned his engine, which was running roughly. Tiny said, "Okay brah. See you in Kaunakakai."

As Keone rolled by, Dan got a good look at him in profile. It reminded him of pictures he had seen of King Kamehameha. He was impressed. Keone was big-boned and powerful; his broad back seemed to fill half the truck. Beyond his size, Dan sensed a certain presence about him, a centeredness similar to the Roshi's, and a confidence that projected outwards. In military terms, it could be said he had command presence.

Dan commented on this to Tiny. He replied, "Yeah, he da kine all right. Pure Hawaiian as far as I know. Plenty mana."

"How's that?"

"It come from three sources, your lineage, your spiritual connection with the gods, and your personal power. To be one chief in old days you had to have all three. His place there on your right."

Dan saw a simple house with several outbuildings. There seemed to be nothing remarkable about it, though he noted it was very organized—no junk cars or trash, no collapsing buildings that were so common in the country, trees all spaced out, and vines cut back. In this climate, there was an expenditure of energy necessary just to keep the jungle under control.

"And here your place across the road on the left."

Dan could see that Glen's house was more modern, post

and beam construction, raised up off the ground, with storage underneath, a new red steel roof, green paint, and white shutters. Very country looking, but just a little bigger and newer than most places he had seen.

Tiny stopped the jeep next to the stairs and said, "Here your happy home. How long you stay?"

"About two weeks. My daughter is going to join me in a week. I'll probably need to have you drive her out here."

"No problem. I come all time. We get your stuff upstairs. We so lucky. No rain now."

Together, they got him settled in—windows and shutters open, gas water heater and refrigerator started, lamps lit, and a fire going to dry out the dampness.

As Tiny drove away, Dan tuned into the sounds of wind, water, and birds. A melancholy mood, tinged with an edge of excitement, settled over him. It was a familiar feeling to Dan, similar to what he experienced as a boy when he was left alone to take care of the farm.

He took a short walk around the property and started down the road, but the rain came down heavily, and he retreated inside. The rest of the evening, he spent reading by the fire with the sound of the rain drumming on the roof. He made split pea soup, ate some bread, drank two glasses of wine, and fell asleep soon after.

At dawn, he awoke to the sounds of roosters crowing and dogs barking. Then birds started calling, and light filtered into the valley and the house. He lay in bed, feeling warm and lazy, content to observe the day as it began to unfold. His view from the bed extended out over the taro fields to the valley walls on the west side. There, the oblique rays of the rising sun turned the apparent grayness of the dawn into splashes of brilliant green interspersed by slivers of water cascading down cliffs.

He got into his sweats and warm socks and made coffee, toast, and papaya for breakfast, and a tuna sandwich for later. Outside, the sounds of voices mingled with a tractor starting. Again, that familiar connection to his boyhood coursed through him.

He decided his main event for the day would be a walk out to the beach and a search for the beginning of what locals called the Z-trail. He put on his hiking shorts and boots and selected a walking stick from several by the stairs. His daypack contained rain gear, food and water, a small camera and field glasses, a compass, knife, flashlight, rope, whistle, waterproof matches, and a book.

He started off in good spirits, a new adventure beckoning, his ankle feeling better than ever. Most of the time, he hardly needed the stick for support. Before long, he encountered mud and water to the tops of his boots. He wished he had brought along the tabi shoes that he had seen under the house. These were preferred footwear for stream hopping and reef walking.

He did not see Keone, but that probably meant that he had not returned home from town or was in another part of the valley. The trail to the beach quickly left the taro fields and intersected a muddy, potholed, four-wheel track. It took almost twenty minutes to reach the beach, which surprised him, but he wasn't in a hurry.

The beach itself was a surprise. Over the years, wind and water action had raised a high berm, so that the beach was not visible until he was nearly on it. It certainly did not resemble the beaches in postcards—dark sand, no palm trees. Instead, there was a forest of ironwoods, many damaged by an earlier windstorm. A strong onshore wind backed big surf crashing offshore. This wind predominated. It twisted and bent the bushes and trees along the shore. Since the ironwoods had long needles similar to pines, the overall impression was similar to that of northern California or Oregon.

On the right side of the bay, a waterfall tumbled directly into the ocean. A river, formed from the collected waters of the valley's streams, cut the sandy berm in the center of the bay. The current was strong, but did not appear to be deep. At one place, the river and the surf contested each other, and the water surged back and forth with the period of the surf.

Dan was content to observe this primal meeting of the land, water, and air. He pulled out his glasses to check out details on the canyon walls. On the west wall, the Z-trail slashed upwards leading to a series of uninhabited valleys. Other than by sea, it was the only access to them. He pulled out a book, *Stories and Legends of Hawaii*. The sun came out, and within minutes, he dozed off.

He woke up hot and slightly dazed. Across the river, there was supposed to be the remains of a rock temple, called a heiau in Hawaiian. He decided to ford the river to search for it. The cool water would feel good. He took off his boots and socks and hung them around his neck in preparation. He eased out into the current, testing the bottom with his hiking stick. He was surprised at the pull on his legs. It was only slightly above his knees, but already he could feel its potential to sweep him off his feet. With every step he took, it pushed him diagonally out toward the ocean.

Only a few feet remained to the far bank, but his left foot

came down on a rock at an angle that wouldn't support him. Suddenly, the current swept him downstream in water up to his chest. For the first few seconds he just felt stupid for making a bad decision, but then he discovered he could not regain his footing at all. He bumped along the bottom. Then he plunged into the arena where the incoming surge from the ocean met the river current. For a few seconds, the forces balanced, and he was able to stand. Then the ocean receded. The water was too deep to make any progress, and the current began pulling at him with renewed force.

Now he was worried, and for good reason. If he lost his stance now, the river would sweep him out to where the surf was pounding. He jammed his hiking stick in downstream to form a tripod with his legs. The current pulled the sand away from his feet. He thought about the casting off his pack and shoes, but he needed both hands to brace with the stick. Rocks carried by the current were hitting his legs. One of them dislodged the hiking stick, and he was at the mercy of the river and ocean. The pack hampered his attempts at swimming. One of the boots wound around his neck and was choking him. Just as he was about to take a breath, a wave smashed into him, and he choked on water. There had to be a way out of this. It would be a stupid way to die.

The thought flashed through his mind that if he did die, he would be with Manalani, but instinctively he fought against the forces pounding him. Several times his feet touched bottom, but each time the river current and waves working in concert sucked him back under. He wasn't defeated, but he wondered how long he could keep this up.

Suddenly he felt a strong pull on his pack taking him sideways. A voice said, "Hey, haole boy. You like swim?"

Within seconds, they were in calmer water, and he could see his rescuer was Keone. As they staggered up to the beach, he thanked him and said, "How did you know I was out there?"

"We finish work in field. I go look for you. Friends say you head down toward beach. I come down just in time for see you swim. So, I come out and join you. Next time you go for swim, take-off pack and leave boots."

Now Dan was feeling truly stupid and chagrined. "It didn't really look that bad when I started out. I feel really stupid that you had to come out for me."

"This is very special river. It eats at least one person a year. I no like you be next sacrifice to Mano. If you like cross, you have to know how."

Dan was going through the things in his pack. Keone offered him a towel from his truck to dry out the camera and field glasses. Dan asked, "How should I have done it?"

"Probably on a day like today, no way," Keone replied. "Upstream, more spread out and shallow. But very rocky there, hard to keep footing. You try here, timing is important. You wade in shallow until surge from ocean comes in to meet river. Then push across before current starts up again. Sometimes you no can do. Then try wait."

"I guess I try wait, next time," Dan replied.

Keone laughed, "You look like one wet puppy now, but you okay, right?"

"Yes, I'm okay, except that I feel really stupid about having to be rescued."

"Oh, I think you make it after a time. You are one fighter. I can tell."

"Well, thanks anyway. What a way to start my time here."

They placed Dan's pack and boots in the truck. Dan thought they were about to leave when Keone turned toward him and said, "Now you ready for one lesson?"

Dan said, "What? What lesson are you talking about?"

"We going cross river together. You learn how."

"Hold it," Dan replied. "I'm not sure I'm ready for this."

"Yes, you are," Keone said. "It's a good time. We are both wet right? Sun's out. It's warm. If you no go now, you stay scared of that river. Like falling off one horse. You need for get back on."

Dan realized Keone was right and agreed. They crossed over four times together. Dan gained confidence in his training and led off the last time. Afterwards, he realized how right Keone was. It turned a humiliating incident into an adventure and formed a bond between them.

By the time they reached their houses, Keone had regaled him with stories of other mishaps and tragedies brought about by nature's forces in the valley. Dan realized that by living close to the earth and nature, the people of this valley gained a wisdom that could not be learned from books. Once again, he was back to his roots as a farm boy, and a knowledge that he thought he had left behind.

Dan lit the fire and spread out his things to dry. Both the camera and field glasses were waterproof, so no problem there. After his clothes were dry, he cut the draft to the fire. Keone had invited him for dinner, so he cleaned up, picked up a bottle of wine, and headed down the steps to the road.

When Dan crossed into Keone's yard, the hunting dogs caged in back started an uproar. Two small yard dogs ran out to greet him. One dog got under his feet and he almost stumbled. The day's events set him back a bit; both his ankle and ribs hurt. He had thought his ribs were repaired but the thrashing he had taken showed they weren't 100% yet. He again needed the cane or a stick for support. The doctor had warned him about the length of time for recovery, but he thought he was out of the woods. Not so.

Keone came to the door as he was hobbling up and said, "Hey, brah, you all bust up?"

Dan was surprised it was so obvious. "No. Just set back a bit."

"Come on in. We talk story before dinner. Laulena, here's Dan."

Dan faced a woman that was a match for Keone. She was as tall as Dan, and weighed more, at least 190 pounds. She was big in all dimensions. She wrapped him in a hug and said, "Aloha. You come stay for while?"

Dan wasn't sure if she meant tonight or his time in the valley. "Uh, yes. For a couple of weeks, I think."

"Good. You be here long enough, you no want to go back."

She took the bottle of wine and thanked him saying, "Tonight we going have Onaga, and taro hash done special kine way, and taro leaves steamed, and black rice pudding for desert. Show Halepio home-style grinds. You like?"

"I'm sure I will," Dan said.

Keone motioned to two chairs facing the fireplace. "Get comfortable. You like beer?"

"Yes, I'll take one."

When Keone returned they began talking about the valley and the importance of growing taro. "Taro is a symbol of our culture. It is more than food. In the ancient legends, it was the older brother of mankind, and from it came all the peoples of the land. The stalk is called Haloa, and the corm is what we pound to make poi. Growing it is one gamble. It is a fifteen-month crop, and a flood or drought can wipe out a crop. Still, I wouldn't want to live anywhere else. I feel connected here, to the aina and my ancestors."

Dan commented, "It must be like what people feel in Europe where families have lived for many generations in one village."

"I'm not so sure," Keone replied. "The difference I see between Europeans and Hawaiians is that Europeans see everything around them as dead, or at least below them in importance. Hawaiians, and Native Nations see everything around them as alive, and themselves as part of it, not separate. That one big difference."

Dan agreed, "You know that is a side of Manalani I appreciated, but I never fully understood."

Keone said, "I don't expect you could. It's something that comes from your bones. What you live with and grow up with."

"Hey, you can sound pretty philosophical if you want to," Dan said.

"I went to college at University of Hawaii for a few years, but I came back to the land. College was all just talk. I'm like a chameleon. When I'm wit' da blalas, I talk da kine. When I'm with you, I talk the king's English. No big thing."

Dan thought it was interesting, how Keone could do that, like being fluent in two languages. At that point, Laulena called them to dinner. As they ate, she asked for Dan's background, so he gave them an abbreviated story of how he arrived in the valley. He discovered they had four children in school topside.

They stayed with aunties and uncles and returned on weekends and holidays. Keone had a sister who was visiting relatives on Oahu. They were happy to hear Liz would be joining Dan and wanted to meet her.

Keone and Dan retired after dinner to their chairs in front of the fire. The rain and wind beating against the house gave him a strange sense of dislocation. It was certainly not the Hawaii of Hula shirts and mai-tais. Their conversation drifted easily into the area of Hawaiian views on death and afterlife.

Keone said that most of the knowledge and beliefs were handed down through chants since there was no written word. "Those people whose life was to learn chants, they learn exact memorizing, subject to many tests of accuracy by kapunas. Oldest of these chants, called the Kumulipo, is about creation of the world." After a pause and a look at Dan to see if he was getting this, Keone went on to say, "Like the bible, I don't think it should be taken literally. Most Hawaiians believe that spirits have ability to assume multiple forms. Each family has an aumakua, a totem animal that can advise or protect them. It contains part of the spirit of their ancestors."

Dan asked Keone if he believed that literally.

Keone replied, "I don't have an easy answer to that."

Dan could see that Keone was troubled about how to respond. After a few seconds, Keone rose from his chair. Taking it by one leg and back, he pressed it against the rock hearth. Dan could see the muscles of his forearms stand out like cords of rope. His head sank between the bulges of his shoulders. The firelight flickering across the darkness of his scowling face, with only the whites of his eyes showing, gave him a demonic appearance. Dan wanted to tell him to stop. He had no idea what Keone was up to, but he was frightened into silence.

With a loud crack, the chair back and legs snapped into pieces. Keone threw several of them into the fire. He turned to Dan and with a broad smile said, "It was an old chair. On its last legs," and then laughed at his pun.

Dan laughed also and said, "That may be, but there is something else going on here."

"You're right. It is a little demonstration of our personal beliefs. Death is simply a change of state. The body returns to the earth. But that is just a changing state. If you live with nature, you realize that nothing is wasted. Every death creates a beginning. At one time, that chair was a seed, then a tree, then lumber, then a chair—all changes of state. What is that chair now?"

Dan said, "It is smoke and ashes and light and heat."

"You are correct of course," Keone replied, "A change of state or form. It hasn't disappeared. And what can you say about the heat and light?"

Dan was a little puzzled. "Well, it has radiated out into the room and…" Dan's eyes widened as the realization hit him.

Keone smiled triumphantly and said, "You got it, brah. It became part of us. Literally. Just like food or water. Part of that chair is with you until you die. Then you and chair become something else."

Dan was stunned. In different surroundings, he might have rationalized some of his feelings. But, in this house, in this valley, with these people, with the chair burning in the fireplace, and the rain coming down, and the wind rustling the trees, and the light in Keone's eyes, he felt he had received an insight that went beyond words, something that settled into the core of his being.

Laulena brought them desserts. The emotional tone of the evening dropped several notches, but the impact of Keone's demonstration remained with Dan.

CHAPTER 14

The days began to fall into a routine. Dan would wake up with the sun, have breakfast, do some stretching, and read while listening to music. In the middle of the day, he would hike or ride horseback around the valley. Sometimes he would help Keone, but the stoop labor in the fields left him sore very quickly. He found rock walls and signs of old Hawaiian villages all over the valley, usually covered by trees or vines. Even to his untrained eye, it was obvious that thousands of people must have lived in the valley in the past.

On a trip up towards the head of the valley, he ran into the Hindu, or Swami as some of the locals jokingly called him. He was a source of amusement; they hinted that maybe he had fried his brains with drugs in the seventies.

Dan took a turn up a side trail when he saw a primitive shelter to one side. At first, he thought it was deserted, but then he saw a man working in a garden off to the side. He thought that he might slide by unnoticed, but then the figure turned toward him, waved him over, and said, "Aloha there pilot. Enjoying your walk?"

"Yes," Dan replied, "I find the whole valley interesting. How did you know who I am?"

"This is a small valley. I'm not a hermit. Everyone knows who you are. I assume you know about me."

"You're right. You seem to be known as the Hindu, but I don't know your name."

"I use Ananda. I dropped my family name years ago. Do you have a goal on your hike today?"

"No. Just getting exercise, working my injured ankle out."

"Oh, yes. You had the accident where you were injured."

"I'm surprised how much you know about me," Dan replied.

"People here like to know what is happening in the valley. What might be nosey somewhere else can be self-protection here. If you're not in a hurry I'll make you some tea."

"Thanks. I'm just wandering about."

Ananda had a two burner stove set up under a tarp behind his one room shed. Dan observed him as he went about fixing their tea. He certainly looked like a Hindu, skinny, long boned, bearded, and hair wrapped in a turban. His brown eyes sank deep in their sockets, but they reflected light with a jewel-like intensity. His movements were quick and agile, resembling a bird. He hummed quietly as he worked. Dan was surprised at his hospitable manner.

"I thought you were pretty much of a recluse. I didn't want to intrude on you."

"Oh, I like being by myself, but you are an interesting addition to our little insular community."

"So, how did you end up being here?"

"It was a long route. I started out as a particle physicist at Stanford working in non-linear quantum dynamics. Then I became interested in holographic aspects of the brain and got a degree in molecular biochemistry. Eventually I became disillusioned with that field and headed off to India and Nepal to see if that ancient repository of knowledge could be merged with western thought. What I learned made me perform the classical dropout maneuver. In my wanderings, I found this valley and immediately felt at home. Hah! An indication of how far I have to go is revealed by my desire to show off my fancy background to the first person that comes along."

"Well, I'm impressed," replied Dan.

"That's the point," said Ananda. "I'm trying to impress you. I don't want you to think I'm just some mind-blown hippie. Why should I care?"

Dan said, "Seems natural to me to let people know who you are or your background."

"Ah, yes. But then, we are dealing with maya, the world of surface appearances, ego and all that. It is a game that I want to drop, but apparently not quite yet."

"So, what happens if you drop it? What's your goal? Do you expect to get to the state of nirvana?"

Ananda didn't answer Dan directly. He handed him a teacup and motioned to a space underneath an orange tree nearby. Dan sat on a stump. Ananda sat cross-legged on the ground. He rolled his eyes and gave out a low whistle. "Even though that seems like a logical question, it's not an easy one to answer if I'm going to be honest. There really isn't a goal; it's more of a process. If there is an end point, a finish line, then we are starting off on the wrong foot."

Dan said, "Yes. I can see that this is one of classic splits between eastern and western thinking. Western thinking is almost always goal oriented."

"It goes further than that. Even on the material level, there's no bedrock reality. Reality is only shared perceptions. I'll give you an example. What is light?"

Dan bit on this question. "It's a wave, a frequency, part of the electromagnetic spectrum."

"Yes, but is that all it is? What about photons, packets of energy you can measure with a light meter?"

"Well, of course it is that too." Dan began to feel hesitant.

"But which is it, a wave or a packet of energy? The answer is that it is both. It depends on how you measure it. But what is it when you are not measuring it? The truth is, we don't know. Quantum physics says it is a field of potentiality, of all possibilities, until it is measured or observed, and then it collapses into one form, as if to please us.

"What is in this space here?" Ananda held up his hand with the thumb and first finger forming a circle and pointed to it.

"A circle of course—space." Dan answered.

"If we were primitive people we would both agree on that," said Ananda, "And that would be our reality. But think a minute. We are more sophisticated than that. At any instant what is passing through that space?"

"Radio waves, television programs of course," Dan answered. He had thought of these already.

Ananda added, "And how about x-rays, gamma rays, neutrinos—a whole quantum soup of vibrations and particles. Now we take a receiver, pluck out just one of these frequencies, and hear a Mozart concerto, or maybe some slack key guitar. Is that music in the radio receiver? If so, you could break it down in pieces to get it out. Is it still with the instrument that played it? In the radio station? No. It is in your mind. That's where the music exists. It has potential as music, traveling as electromagnetic waves, but it takes the right receiver, and your brain and mind to make it into music. When Natalie Cole sings a song with Nat King Cole, and you hear them singing a duet together on the radio, and he has been dead for many years, what kind of reality is that?"

Ananda sat back and smiled. He looked like an elf or wizard to Dan, who found himself in a very strange mental space. He had heard all the words that Ananda had spoken, but the effect left him speechless. He sat there staring back at Ananda, just listening to the sounds of the birds and wind around him—noticing the way the light filtered through the trees and made a pattern on the grass between them.

After a few seconds, Ananda said, "HAH! It happened. Your mind came to a stop. For a few seconds at least you were in touch with reality. You can't do it when you are talking. You can't do it when you are thinking. It comes in the space between thoughts."

Dan laughed nervously and said, "Is that what my kids mean when they say they are spaced out?"

Ananda brushed that thought aside with a quick, "Maybe. See, in the space between thoughts there is part of each of us that is pure potentiality. That part is called the witness; it is with us all the time. It is infinite. But it can only be contacted when the mind shuts down. This state of no-mind is the state from which everything arises. It is part of the self, with a capital S.

"This infinite part of us is not material, does not die, is always present. The Bhagavad Gita speaks of it: *For that which is born, death is certain, and for that which is dead, birth is certain. You should not grieve over the unavoidable...The Supreme Self, which dwells in all bodies, can never be slain...Weapons* cut it not; fire burns it not; water wets it not; the wind does not wither it. Eternal, universal, unchanging, immovable, the Self is the same forever…Therefore, you should not grieve for any creature."

When Ananda was finished, Dan said, "This is really interesting. I've always thought that the Hindu concepts of reincarnation and karma were just too weird to consider seriously, but what you have said makes sense to me, in a strange sort of non-linear way."

They both laughed, and Ananda said, "There is a lot of weirdness in the way the basic conceptions are interpreted and expressed. That weirdness in India is what the media picks up, which further distorts it. But, you can see why I'm out here, and why people go to ashrams for retreat. You cannot come in touch with this state of existence when you are rushing around, picking up on all the nervous yamayama in the world of maya. Not unless you are a Buddha or Krishna."

There was a pause. Dan decided to take advantage of it by veering towards the subject of Manalani's death and the mystery of his survival.

"Ananda, do you know I was the pilot in a crash where most of the crew, many passengers, and my wife died?"

"I had heard that."

"That event has almost destroyed my life as I knew it. I don't know why I lived. I think, except for my kids, it would have been better if I had died. If there was a god that did it, he is capricious and unknowable. If it was fate, a bolt from the blue, it makes life meaningless. We are all just pawns in a game of cosmic chance. If it is some part of my karma, what did I do to deserve it? Where is the lesson? To learn to survive without her? What about all those other people that died, and their families? I can't believe they were put there for some special purpose. That is just empty rhetoric, looking in the dark for any light, grasping at straws to stay afloat. I know this question has been asked for eons. I just never thought I would be asking it."

Ananda did not immediately answer. He looked past Dan, over his head, and started an almost inaudible humming sound.

"You are humming!" Dan said. "You're humming. The Roshi hummed. What is this, some sort of humming conspiracy?"

They both smiled in spite of the seriousness of the moment. Ananda said, "I guess it's what we both do when we are presented with a difficult question to answer."

He stood up and poured them both some more tea.

"Here's one thing I can tell you that doesn't come from the Hindu tradition. Whatever doesn't break you will make you stronger."

"Ananda, I had a psychologist tell me something like that not long ago. I didn't find much comfort in it then, and I don't now."

"But it's not about comfort, Dan. It's about strength, the ability to endure."

"Okay, I'll buy that. I can endure. But what about these other questions."

"The Hindu concept of Karma is unpalatable for most westerners. That is why we find so many variations of it. You don't have the cultural background and history to absorb it, and I'm not even saying that it is right in an absolute sense.

"Karma is a Sanskrit word that in its most general sense just means action. Hindus speak of being on the wheel of life and death; that it keeps rolling through countless reincarnations. Where you are on the wheel is determined by your actions in the past. At any moment in time though, you have the free will to break out of that moment of inertia. When you die, any unfulfilled wishes or desires will bring you back, until you finally give them all up. You have an infinity of time to accomplish this, so from the viewpoint of the soul or Self, you can't fail."

Ananda paused for a moment, took a sip of tea, and looked quizzically at Dan. "I'm giving you a capsule version with many gaps. Are you getting any of this?"

"I am," Dan replied, "But it doesn't seem to apply to the question I asked."

"I'll get to that. I just needed to give you some background. Nobody can really answer to your satisfaction why this event occurred in your life. From a strict karmic view, it may have to do with past lives. There also is group or cultural karma, in which you and everyone in our society is enmeshed. What is important is what you do with this experience. You have already made a good start. You are asking questions that are important, looking for a new path, a new way of living. Everything is called into question. The old paradigms are gone. You are adrift.

"It can be unsettling, even agonizing. You are swept away by strong feelings. Don't deny any of it. Accept it. Go with it. But watch it. Watch it. Step back. Become the witness as it is happening. Become the Self that is always there. Know that there is always part of you that is infinite, ever present, not sucked into the movie that we play parts in. Don't fall for the idea that you are just a player in that movie. You have been sold a bill of goods, a paradigm that says you are a skin-encapsulated ego, squeezed into the volume of a body and a span of a lifetime. Step out of that belief. When your mind stops, and the ego drops away, you come in contact with the part of you that is infinite."

Ananda paused. Dan said, "Like when I was with the Roshi, sitting here with you right now, your words and what I have experienced give me a feeling of peace, of non-attachment. But, when I walk away from here, I will start to wind up again. And there is still the question of Manalani. What has happened to her? I can't believe that she has just dropped out of existence, into the void, or some impersonal state. But is this just wishful thinking?"

Ananda put his chin on his hand looked at Dan for a few seconds before answering. "I can give you this from the Vedic tradition. Those writings, which have been around for several thousand years, say that we have a subtle body that is non-material and does not die with the physical body. It can stay around this place if there is a compelling reason, often because of a sudden unplanned departure. Needless to say, there is plenty of anecdotal evidence for this."

Dan said, "Of course I've heard about this, but how much of this might be fantasy?"

"Wrong question, Dan. If someone has the experience of meeting their loved one, and it seems real, and they believe it, who cares? It satisfies the need that is inside them. It gives them a feeling of peace or resolution. That is what is important, not if it can be reproduced in a laboratory."

"There have been times when I felt Manalani's presence around me," Dan said, "but I repressed it, regarding it as irrational. And yet, I looked forward to it happening again. At least I feel better now that there is a conceptual framework that it fits into."

Ananda began to hum again and looked off into the distance. Dan waited patiently this time. Eventually Ananda said, "Here is one more thing, Dan. It is an intuition, but if it feels right to you, you should do it. You should go up the Z-trail and camp out on one of the headlands up there. Being a pilot, I think that any inspiration or revelation you might have is likely to occur in a high place."

"That's interesting. I have been looking at the Z-trail all week, a sort of fascination with it, but without any clear intent. Of course, I don't know about making it with my ankle screwed up. It looks like a tough trail even if you are fit."

"You should know that the hero's journey is never easy." Ananda looked at him with a sly smile.

"I don't feel like a hero"

"We're all heroes, principal actors in the story of our lives"

Dan said, "My daughter, Liz, will be coming here in a few days. I know she would like to do it. Maybe we will."

Ananda nodded in agreement, picked up Dan's cup, and walked over to his sink under the tarp. Dan realized it was time to go. They shook hands. Ananda gave him some advice on the trail, and Dan was on his way. The rest of the day, each time Dan looked at the Z-trail, a feeling of anticipation bubbled up, lending a tinge of excitement to his mood.

The next day was sunny and warm with little wind. Dan decided to walk to the beach. The river was low, and he crossed over to the other side. Near the west wall of the valley, on a grassy bank above the sand, he discovered a memorial to a young boy who died trying to save his surfing companion. It included a photo mounted on fiberglassed wood with a caption, a cross, flowers, and various trinket offerings added by passing hikers.

He clenched his fists as the lump grew in his throat, choking on the emotion flooding his body. He knew that it was because Manalani had no memorial. They had all agreed to this, but now he wondered about their decision. The sun was hot at this site, so he moved down the beach to a shady spot. Waves breaking on a rocky point off to his left drew his attention. When he looked back to his right, he could see a woman just entering the water. He was shocked to see that she was nude. She looked Hawaiian, with dark skin and long hair down to her ample hips. She paused for a moment, and then plunged directly through a breaking wave swimming with strong clean strokes to the calm waters outside the surf zone.

After swimming parallel to shore toward him, she rolled over onto her back, putting her arms over her head. She floated effortlessly like a seal. From Dan's viewpoint, he could see her breasts protruding above the water.

He felt self-conscious about watching her, but he was fascinated and did not stop. Eventually, she rolled over and swam back to her starting point. As she came out of the water, it was obvious that she was a large woman without being noticeably fat. She wrapped herself in her pareo and shook out her hair. For the first time since Manalani's death, he felt a twinge of libido rising in him.

He was sitting there mesmerized when it suddenly occurred to him that she was walking directly toward him. Self-conscious and embarrassed, he thought of moving away, but it was already too late.

As she came closer, she looked at him and smiled. He smiled back but his mind was racing. Should he feign nonchalance? Look away? Wave to her? Say hello? It was decided when she spoke to him. "Aloha, Dan. A fine day for swimming. Have you been in the water yet?"

"Umm, no. Not yet. How do you know my name?"

She laughed. It came from deep inside her, her whole body shaking. "Dan, everyone in the valley knows your name. I am Haunani, Keone's sister."

"Oh, that's right; he said you were visiting friends on Oahu. So you are back."

"Yes, I am. And it feels good. To me, Oahu and Honolulu represent everything that has gone wrong in these islands."

"I can understand that," Dan said. "I don't even like it there."

"I'm afraid you cannot even begin to feel the way I do. You don't have a hundred years of being displaced in your own country." She saw Dan recoil from that remark and said, "Sorry. I don't want you to start feeling guilty for what other haoles have done. You have enough problems of your own. Actually, I'm here to comfort you. I will save my militant attitude for when it serves a purpose." Dan wondered what she meant by comfort. It appeared their meeting was not an accident. "When I return, I always go for a swim. I guess it's a ritual cleansing. Did you enjoy watching me?"

Dan was speechless. He could feel himself blushing. He mumbled an inaudible reply. This made Huanani laugh again. "You so funny. Why you look guilty? You are a man. Men like to watch women swim. Hah! Why you mumble? You look like little boy. I'm sorry. I shouldn't laugh. But you haoles so funny about bodies. Come on. I show you secret place. You will like."

Her infectious good mood won Dan over. How could he resist? He felt emotionally adrift and she swept over him like a wave. She grasped his hand, pulled him to his feet, and led him down the trail leading into a forest of tall trees. A few houses stood on stilts near the border between the trees and fields full of water. They seemed empty now. Some were well kept; others were broken down. Haunani told him the history of each. Then they walked into a wilder section, under a canopy of trees with little undergrowth. At an opening toward the water, she suddenly stopped. She grasped his arm, pulling him to her and pointed. "See—Aukuu, fishing."

He could see a gray heron, very close and very still. He was also very conscious of his arm caught between her arm and the softness of her breast. Another flash of libido passed through him.

As they penetrated farther into the woods, it became very quiet. Very few birds appeared here. Tree ferns grew in the wetter spots. Impatiens formed a carpet of white and pink flowers. A brook tumbled down from their right. They crossed it on a fallen log. The undisturbed moss on its upper surface revealed that few people traveled this route.

Suddenly Haunani turned right off the trail. She bobbed and weaved through the underbrush. She was amazingly agile for a woman her size. He had observed the same trait among Hawaiian men on the tennis court. Was it genetic—that ability to move a large body so quickly and in balance? With his ankle limiting his flexibility, he had a hard time keeping up. She sensed this and slowed down.

After several minutes of this, she suddenly stopped. Her body blocked his view. She reached back, grasped his hand, and pulled him up to her side. His view enclosed a tropical fantasy come true. A waterfall thirty feet high plunged into a large black pool ringed by kahili ginger in bloom. The scent penetrated the whole valley. Small fusia and orange lilies sprang up between the rocks in the shallow water. The sun beat down on the open water giving it a burnished metallic sheen. The melodious call of a shama thrush echoed from the rock faces. Dan was transfixed. He entered that timeless space of which Ananda had spoken.

Without speaking Haunani led him to a small grassy spot. Within a few minutes, he began sweating in the warmth of the sun. Haunani suddenly stood up, and in one quick motion slipped out of her pareo and into the water. Breaking the surface near the center of the pool, she called out, "You get da clothes off now and come in water, or I come get you and drag you here."

Dan realized she was not bluffing. It would be embarrassing to have that happen. It seemed he had no choice. She swam away from him toward the waterfall. He untied his shoes, pulled off his pants, and stepped in. Near the edge, where there was little circulation, the water was warm. Near the center, it was deliciously cool.

For a few minutes, they swam in circles. At one point, Haunani stood under the waterfall. With the water breaking into a silver cascade over her black hair and strong dark body, she was the embodiment of the archetypal Polynesian woman, Gauguin's painting come to life. Dan was in conflict. Part of him wanted to experience her, but he resisted that urge with strongly conditioned guilt.

She swam over and floated next to him. He was treading water, and commented that he had never been able to float like that. "That's because you don't have water wings," she replied, and slipped down into the black water.

Dan was slowly swimming on his back when he felt her slip up underneath him and throw an arm across his chest. As she did so she said, "I have enough floatation for both of us. Relax; let me be your guide."

Dan relaxed somewhat, but he was very conscious that her body supported and enveloped him. Then he felt a slight feathery touch along his groin. At first, he thought it might be a mistake. Then he knew it wasn't. He was aroused and growing hard, but he couldn't let this happen.

"Haunani, you'd better stop this. I like it, but it's not right."

"Hah! You so haole again. Why you think it not right."

"What about your brother? What would he think?"

"What would he think? He knows already. We talk about you. If you going to make change, you gotta open up. Get unfrozen. Feel everything. So that's my part. Free you up. Good idea. Fun for me, eh?" Laughter bubbled up from inside her.

"I don't know that I'm ready for this yet." Dan felt ridiculous protesting and yet felt that he should. He realized that there was some sort of role reversal going on.

"Hah! You nevah be ready if I wait. I know what you think. You worry about Manalani. Think you be faithful to her. I tell you, Manalani approve. She no want you be frigid old man. Manalani send me. Spirits send me. You think all this kine stuff happen in valley to you by chance? No. That's why you here. Relax, go with it."

As she was saying this, Haunani guided them to a rock shelf that was like a seat in the shallow water. She floated Dan onto it and slipped her legs around his hips. In the water, her large body was weightless, and she moved like an eel, somehow able to assume any position she desired. Her arms slid under his armpits. Her large breasts floated under his chin. He felt her hips moving against him and realized with a shock that he was already inside her.

What had Ananda said? Don't deny your feelings. Go with them. But watch it. He was certainly swept up in a tide of feelings now. Then the dance of Shiva began—coiling and uncoiling, pressure and release, thrust and recoil. She lifted them off the seat and into deeper water. The light reflected off her eyes. They changed from obsidian to polished ebony, to black tar, and back.

She lifted him upwards into her—lips parted, head thrown back, hair flailing the water. At one point, he grasped her by her breasts then her hips. Then all sense of where he ended and she started fell away. They became a single organism, pulsing electricity, discharging in unison.

Timeless.

Mindless.

Gone.

He may have lost consciousness. All he knew was that he slowly came back to awareness wrapped in her arms and legs in shallow water. It was an oceanic feeling, like being born again.

As they lay there, he spoke first. "I don't know where we went, but it was amazing. Have you ever been there before?"

She pressed up close to him and said, "No, not quite like that, Mr. Space Pilot. We were out there somewhere, weren't we?"

"You're right. I feel like I have been on some enormous voyage."

As they put their clothes on, Dan began to feel self-conscious and guilty. Haunani sensed this and said, "Now don't start going haole on me. You feel better, right?"

"Yes, but…"

"No buts. Now you ready for next step."

"What do you mean, next step."

"I don't know. It's whatevas. What you think?"

Dan considered whatever might be next. "Liz is going to arrive in two days. Ananda and I talked about going up the Z-trail."

Dan looked up to his left. He could see it above where they were walking. Haunani broke into his thoughts, "Now that's a good idea. I think you do that."

"What about Liz?"

"Take her too. She like hike?"

"Yes, she does. We haven't done something like that for a long while. You're right. I think it is a good idea."

Haunani smiled broadly and said, "See, it all work out okay. You a free man now."

"What do you mean by that?"

"You come to valley carrying lots of baggage. Much pilikia. Many worries. Maybe you leave a lot lighter."

Haunani gave Dan's shoulder a squeeze as she said this. She was as tall as Dan and looked directly into his eyes. The dark glitter of her eyes seemed to hold a knowledge and passion that Dan found unsettling. He felt he should thank her in some way and said, "Haunani, I don't know how to say this…"

Haunani cut him off. "Then don't say nothing. No need. You owe nothing. What I give, I give with no strings. Besides, I like you. Some fun back there, eh?"

They both laughed. Dan didn't reply. It wasn't necessary.

CHAPTER 15

On one of Tiny's trips into Halepio, he gave Dan the flight number and time of Liz's arrival. Dan arranged to go to the airport in the morning with Keone.

When he saw her coming down the air stairs, he was surprised at the rush of emotion that flooded his body. He could hardly wait for her to get through the gate. When she did, he swept her up in a hug that almost lifted her off her feet.

"It looks like your time here has really given you some relief," she said.

"More than you could guess,"

"Well, what's the plan, Stan?"

"First, we pick up your stuff. You did bring your camping gear?"

"Sure thing. Where are we going? What is the house like? What have you been doing?"

Dan began to fill her in as they walked to the baggage area. Part way through, she broke in. "Hold it, Dad. I almost forgot. Glen called me. He wanted you to call him on his cell phone if you had any problems or questions about the house."

"I don't. Everything's working fine."

"He also said that the flight service here, across the field, has a motorglider you must absolutely go to see. It's called a Stemme Chrysalis. He gave me the owner's name and phone."

Dan paused a few seconds; he wasn't really sure he wanted to do that. "I'm not sure, honey. We have a lot of other things on the fire."

"Glen was pretty insistent," Liz said. "He said you don't want to miss it."

"Oh, what the hell, we're not in that big a hurry. I know it is a really beautiful, high performance ship. Expensive, too."

When Tiny arrived, he drove them over to Rainbow Aviation. When they introduced themselves to the owner, Masami Dugent, and dropped Glen's name, he insisted on taking them out to the flight line to see the ship.

Dan became enthusiastic. "She is a real beauty, I'll have to admit. Looks like a competition ship. What kind of lift to drag ratio does she have?"

"50 to1" replied Masami. "Cruises 135 knots using 5 gallons per hour. Can't get much more efficient than that. Stressed for 6g's positive and 3g's negative."

"How much does it cost?"

"About $170,000 on the mainland, but with shipping and the trailer, it was almost $200,000 to here."

"Wow. That's a hunk of money for a sport machine."

"Yeah, but look at it. And you should fly it. Hell, people pay over $200,000 for a piece of art that doesn't even fly. They just stick it up on a wall and look at it. Think of it as a piece of fiberglass kinetic sculpture where you can peg your joy meter if you are a real pilot, and not some candy-ass airplane driver. Besides, I became the Hawaiian state dealer, so it's a write-off for me."

"I'll have to admit, I'm jealous."

"You don't have to be. I'll check you out. Fly it today."

"That's tempting, but we are committed to another plan today, going with Tiny here, down to Halepio Valley for a few days."

Like any good salesman, Masami would not be diverted, and said, "Look, when you come out, save some time for a flight. As a matter of fact, I need to take it over to Oahu for some demos in a few days. If the timing is right, you can fly it over there for me, and that won't cost you anything."

"That sounds like a deal," Dan replied. "We'll see if it works out."

"Hey, we'll make it happen," Masami said, as they walked back to the jeep.

After they were underway, Liz tried to encourage Dan. "Dad, that would be really exciting—to fly a plane like that over to Oahu."

"Yeah, I know. It's a tempting idea. But that is an expensive machine. I wouldn't want to prang it, and I haven't been flying gliders lately."

"Oh, I bet you would slip right back into it." Liz said.

Dan still hesitated. "Well, we'll just have to see how it works out."

Tiny broke into their conversation to ask about supplies. They picked up a few things in town. On the way to the valley, Tiny kept Liz amused and informed with his nonstop travelogue on the area.

Dan spent the next two days showing Liz around the valley. She was enchanted, both by her surroundings, and by the people she met. One afternoon she tried planting Taro. Like Keone warned her, it was hot, dirty, backbreaking work, but she stuck it out, coming home exhausted and muddy. They decided to rest the next morning and then hike up the Z-trail to spend the night on one of the ridges.

They spread out their gear on the deck of the house. To lighten the load they decided to eat only trail mix, dried fruit, and some chocolate. At first, Dan was determined to carry the lion's share, but Liz convinced him that was foolishness considering his ankle and ribs.

The next day, it took them nearly an hour to get to the beach, cross the river, and reach the base of the trail. Keone told them to allow two hours to make it up the steep switchbacks to the top. The lower part of the trail was in the trees and brush. The air was hot and still and mosquito laden. They had to stop every few minutes to wipe the sweat out of their eyes. Dan's first handkerchief and sweatband soaked through. The sweat caused the repellant to wash away, and the mosquitoes were having a feast.

On the first dogleg above the trees, they left the mosquitoes behind, but the sun beat down relentlessly. When they reached the first switchback on the ocean side, Dan was already exhausted, and was glad for the break. They dropped their packs gratefully, shared some fruit, and leaned into the wind that whipped around the corner of the cliff.

The surf crashed onto the rocks three-hundred feet below. Across the valley, the waterfall plunged off the cliff directly into the ocean. Back in the valley, two falls were plainly visible. Clouds and mist covered the higher reaches. A gray rain shaft, extending below a cumulus cloud, appeared to be headed for them. They both hoped they might receive a little rain to cool them off, but the cloud felt the effects of the cliff walls and veered off to the west.

They picked up their packs and moved upwards. As if the trail had been toying with them, the obstacles became serious. It was so steep that each step became a one-legged knee bend. In places, the rocks that formed steps were sloping and wet from recent rains. At other places, the slick red clay mud was like oil. Dan was using two sticks for balance, but the trail was so steep and narrow, that in many places only one was useful.

His ribs ached. Several times his ankle needed to support his weight at an odd angle, and he could feel the joint grinding painfully. By the time they reached the next inner switchback, he considered defeat in the recesses of his mind. He slumped to the ground sucking eagerly at his water bottle. Liz could see he was in trouble and said, "How are you making it there, old soldier?"

"Not very well," Dan admitted. "I feel like I have just spent an hour on the Stairmaster with a thirty-pound load on my back and a heat lamp over me."

"That's really a good description," Liz said. "I don't feel real chipper myself. What about your ribs and ankle?"

"I can take the pain in my ribs, but I'm worried about the ankle. It's really not up to this. One wrong move, and I'm history. I'll have to be carried down, and I don't want that."

"Well, let's slow the pace. We have the rest of the afternoon to make it. The sun will be moving, so we'll be in the shade. At least we won't be roasting."

Dan agreed. The more hot and tired he was, the more likely he was to make a disastrous mistake. When they finally reached the next switchback, they took a long break in the cool breeze. Dan wiped down and put on a clean shirt.

On the next leg, the temperature was definitely cooler. Dan

gained his second wind, and thoughts of defeat receded. They rounded the last turn and entered the upper forest of ohia, koa, eucalyptus, and paper mulberry trees. The trail still sloped upwards but it was manageable.

Dan had just gained confidence that they would reach their goal when disaster struck. Dan's good foot caught on a root; his bad one came down on a patch of mud-covered rock, and he was immediately down, twisting in pain, gritting his teeth.

Liz rushed to his side. "Oh no! Not now! How bad is it?"

"I don't know," Dan said, "It ain't good. Hurts like hell, but I don't think I broke it again."

He pulled off his boot and gingerly felt the area. It looked ugly around the stitches, blotched white and red, but it always looked that way. He could rotate the joint, though it was painful and seemed to be swelling. They had a cold pack with them and wrapped it in place with an Ace bandage. He couldn't put any real weight on it. Liz found a tree branch with an L-shaped joint that he could use as an improvised crutch.

She asked him if he wanted to go back. "Hell, no!" he replied. "Too far down. Besides, I'm not giving up now. We must be fairly close to the campsite on the first ridge. Look honey, you run on ahead and check it out."

While she was gone, Dan took two of the pain pills he had been given. She was back in twenty minutes. "The campsite's just ahead on a branch off the main trail."

They loaded up. Dan could hobble slowly with the aid of the crutch. At this pace, it took thirty minutes, but when they arrived, the spot was so magnificent he felt the whole effort was worth it.

The site was in a clearing, below which the ridge dropped

away abruptly. Other ridges to the west protruded like giant shoulders into the ocean where the sun was setting through layers of clouds. Bands of light and dark caused the ocean below to turn from green, to metallic gray, to a blinding flash of silver. Towering white cumulus clouds with black bottoms marched like bands of brothers into the distance, withering away into little clumps as they lost their source of energy, the heat rising from the island itself.

Liz busied herself with setting up the campsite under the trees. Dan found he was no help there. He hobbled a few short steps out to a grassy area where a tree provided a perfect backrest. He used his foam mattress as a support and leaned back, exhausted. The pain had subsided. The pills had taken effect. He slumped into unconsciousness, and a vision enveloped his mind.

It began with Dan running down the brow of the ridge. When he gained sufficient speed, he arched his body and threw himself into the air. With his arms outstretched into a sweptback V, and his body in an airfoil shape, he was able to lift off and fly out over the edge of the cliff. It all seemed familiar. He had done this before in a dream.

Then he felt a tingling along his shoulder and arms. Looking out at them, he realized they had transformed into wings. Simultaneously his body felt lighter, and he sensed he had a long tail streaming out behind him. He had morphed into a tropic-bird. He felt slight changes in the wind currents. He could predict where the lift would be best and reflexively change the shape of his body and wings to take advantage of it.

He soared along a ridge top, gaining altitude, rolling from side to side, observing the world below him. Then, with a flick of his wingtips, he rolled over into a dive, picking up speed until his entire body thrummed and vibrated. He careened down a cliff, only a few feet away from its pockmarked face, pulling out into a long high-speed arc across the valley floor.

As he began his pull up, three other birds joined him, and the game started. He knew the game was to see who could ride the rising columns of air to the highest point. It was done as a form of training and to show dominance, but he also sensed that it was done out of an expression of pure joy.

To get the best lift, he needed to fly in circles very close to the ridge. Two of the birds were younger and were tentative in their approach. They began to fall back. The other bird used a radical approach, flying straight into the cliff and hugging its contours. He sometimes picked up big gusts of lift that way, but he was blown about wildly, and the erratic nature of his flight path would lead him into dead spots.

Near the top of the ridge Dan found just the right combination and was able to gain enough of a lead that he could make a celebratory dive on the others. They all peeled off for another round, but as Dan picked up more speed, another bird shot across his vision traveling horizontally at high speed. On impulse, he jinked left to follow. He could see it was a female.

She pulled up into a vertical-climbing roll. Near the top, she took several strong beats of her wings and came almost to a pause. His momentum carried him up to meet her. At that moment, at the apogee of their arc, perfectly matched in equilibrium, he recognized her, and his heart surged. With every atom in his body, he knew absolutely that Manalani's spirit was contained in that bird. He could feel her calling out to him.

Then they were off, dancing the great wheel of the universe. Rolling, diving, climbing, only inches apart, sharing that instantaneous single-minded communication that birds have, all the repertory of maneuvers that Dan had watched and envied from the ground. She showed him secret places known only to birds: a dive through an archway in an interior canyon—a crevice box canyon, where the compressed updraft shot them upward like corks out of a bottle into the base of the clouds above—a five level waterfall where scarlet and black I'iwi's came to drink.

At last, they returned to the hill where he started. From a great distance, he could hear Liz calling him. His time in the avian world was ending. In the same moment, he transitioned back into his body. There was no time for regrets or goodbyes.

"Dad! Dad! What's happening? Are you dreaming?" He could hear Liz's voice clearly now, but he didn't know how to answer.

"I'm okay Liz. It's hard to explain. It was more than a dream. Were you worried?"

"Not exactly. But your whole body was moving, and you were making strange sounds."

Dan wondered if he should tell her. Would she think he was crazy? He had to trust that somehow he could translate the experience to her. "Liz, the best I can say is that what I experienced was like a dream, but it had an intensity and clarity unlike any dream I have ever heard of. I just met Manalani's spirit in the form of a tropic-bird. We flew together."

He filled her in on the details. The wonder of it excited her. They both agreed on the vision's reality at some level, and they tried to fit the experience into some familiar framework.

It contained elements of lucid dreaming and out of body experiences. Dan had usually dismissed these stories as wishful thinking. Now, confronted with the intensity of his own experience, he needed to reconsider all of his previous opinions. He found great comfort in Amanda's words when he had said, "If someone has the experience of meeting their loved one, and it seems real, who cares?"

In the end, it mattered little to Dan where experience came from. The intensity and emotional content made it real for him. It was late into the evening before he fell into an exhausted dreamless sleep.

By morning, the swelling in Dan's ankle had reduced to the point that he could wear his boot. The return down the hill was a tough slog, but the exhilaration remained with him, and the effort and pain involved seemed a small price to pay.

***

Dan and Liz decided to leave in two days. He needed at least a day to recover. That night, Keone invited them to dinner. The dinner, and winding down as they packed the next day, gave a sense of closure to Dan's experience. The following day, when they arrived at the airport, Liz pointed out that the motor-glider was still there.

I'm surprised," Dan said. "I thought it probably would be in Honolulu by now."

Keone drove them to Rainbow Aviation's hanger. On the way, Liz got excited. "Are we going to do it, Dad?"

"I'm not sure we should. Let's see if Masami is here, and what he has to say."

"I'll bet he wants us to do it."

"What makes you so sure?"

"Otherwise, the plane wouldn't be here. Since it's here, that means that we should fly it."

As Liz expected, Masami was there, and he was glad to have Dan deliver it. During Dan's checkout, Masami dropped a few hints about a partnership or sale with lease back. Dan would not commit, but Masami made it sound interesting. Since their gear would not fit in the limited luggage space, Masami arranged for Mahalo Airlines to fly it over.

Liz and Dan strapped in side-by-side. One good feature of the Chrysalis was its seating. Most soaring airplanes were tandem and required an intercom for communication. Because of the long wingspan, taxiing out to the runway was a slow careful process. The acceleration on take-off roll was hardly breath taking, but once in the air, the ship handled beautifully. They made a turn and began a climb toward Halawa Valley on the east end of the island. Masami told them since the tradewinds were blowing, they should cruise the north shore sea cliffs, which extended up to three thousand feet. Cruising one-hundred-forty mph at five-hundred feet they could see all the details of the country alongside them. Halawa itself looked a great deal like Halepio, a large amphitheater with waterfalls at the end. When they rounded the corner and turned west they entered the updraft area where the tradewinds blowing in from the northeast were forced up over the sea cliffs. The ship came alive in Dan's hands and began immediately climbing a thousand feet-per-minute.

He switched the engine off. As the propeller slowed to a stop, the folding mechanism pulled it inward. The nose casing slid back over it, providing a perfectly smooth surface.

They entered stronger winds. Their rate-of-climb increased further. The variometer almost pegged off scale. "Whooee! We are on the up elevator now for sure." Dan was excited. He had almost forgotten the thrill of the free ride. They appeared to be rising vertically. They shot up above the cliff top into the clouds above. Dan peeled off to his right toward the ocean, building up speed to the red line, the max speed allowed in the airplane. In the smooth air over the ocean, out of a sheer feeling of joy, he pulled up into a vertical climb, arcing over the top with rudder, nearly weightless. Then with the nose pointing vertically down, he made a smooth pullout.

Dan and Liz looked across the cockpit at each other, both of their faces split by grins they had no desire to stop. Dan said, "Masami was right. If this doesn't peg your joy meter, you're just not a pilot. It's all yours honey. Have a go at it. It handles beautifully. Just remember to use enough rudder."

After a few tentative banked turns, Liz gained confidence and began performing lazy eights. She dove the airplane to pick up speed, then pulled up in a steep left climbing turn until at the ninety-degree point the airplane was just above the stall speed. Then coming down the backside she rolled continuously to the right until the airplane was wings level at its original speed. Continuing to roll and pull up to the right, she performed a mirror image of the first half. Done perfectly, it would look like an eight lazily lying on its side. The airplane rolled and pitched in a long sinuous arc never stopping at any point.

Dan caught sight of a ribbon waterfall and took the controls again. "Look at that!" He pointed with his left wing. The wind up the cliff face was so strong that it took the spray leaping out into space and flung it upwards until it disappeared into the clouds above. "Take us on up the coast," Dan said. "I want to look at Halepio. Then we will fly over the Kalaupapa peninsula."

"Dad, look at that view. It's totally awesome."

"You kids use that word too much, but I agree with you this time."

Ahead of them huge mountain buttresses shouldered into the ocean, their faces sheared off by ancient landslides. Cumulus clouds capped the mountains. They were extensions of the upward thrust of the earth. Shadows filled the valleys except where the sun pierced shafts of light into their depths. Waterfalls plunged thousands of feet down these cliff faces onto the rocky shores below.

A few isolated rock islands, resembling breaching whales, dotted the near shore region. Waves from a large north swell threw themselves at these rocks endlessly. On the peninsula's leeward side, the wind tore huge manes of spindrift from the waves. When the angle of the sun was correct, these plumes of spray refracted into the colors of the rainbow. It was a scene of primordial elements—sky, wind, rain, earth, and ocean—the forces that shaped the islands. All this could only be taken in from an airplane's or a bird's point of view.

As they turned into the valley, Liz said, "Look, there's the Z-trail, and the waterfalls. I can hardly see the houses; they're so tiny and hidden among the trees."

The air was sinking in the valley. They raced to the far side to regain lift. "I bet I can see our campsite." Liz pointed ahead over their left wing.

Dan rolled into a steep bank, circling over the clearing. "I think you are right." He rolled out heading west, still looking down to his left.

Liz squeezed his arm and in a quiet intense voice said, "Dad. Look on the right wing."

There, just off their wing and slightly higher in tight formation, was a tropic-bird, its wings swept back to keep up with them, long scissored tail fluttering behind, head cocking back and forth, bright eye clearly outlined.

"Oh God," Dan said, "It has happened; what I hoped for. It's her. It's got to be."

"Of course it is, Dad. She has been waiting for us to return. Somehow, she knew it would happen." Dan realized he was holding his breath. He wanted nothing to disturb this moment. With a flick of her wings, she rolled over the canopy and arced down off their left wing. Instinctively Dan peeled off after her. Just as he got to her level, she pulled in closer to the cliff and began a soaring climb, challenging Dan to match her. At first he could do it, but as the lift died out near the top of the cliff, she easily out-performed him.

As he staggered close to the stall, she swooped down on him in a spiral. He rolled in with her, pulling in as tight as he could. No matter how hard he tried, she kept inside of him just a few feet from the canopy, her tail and wings flexing as she made tiny adjustments to her flight path. The wing of the Chrysalis buffeted and the airframe trembled. It was all he and the machine could do.

"Dad, she's playing with you! Showing you she can outperform you! Isn't it great?"

"Yeah, I can't believe it." For a moment, in the intensity of their performance, he had been determined to match her. Now he relaxed, laughed, and threw up his hands in a gesture of defeat. For a few seconds she drifted in even closer. Then she made a slight change in path so the sun hit him directly in the eyes. A shadow flitted over his face, and she was behind them. He racked the plane into a vertical reverse, but she was gone.

Dan's heart sank. Then he thought, *What did you expect; she was going to fly over to Honolulu with you?* He turned back on course and looked over at Liz. Her eyes were glistening. Was she crying? He reached over and took her hand. She squeezed it so hard it hurt. For several seconds they said nothing. Then Liz said, "Well, Dad, you got your confirmation. Now do you believe?"

"Yeah, I'm a believer now. It's as though this was laid out as a lesson for me. Each question I asked has been answered in some way."

"I'm so glad I came along," Liz said. "I was the one that talked you into flying the Chrysalis. Now was that fate, or what?"

"That's what amazes me," Dan said. "It's like it was all planned out. It had to be this way. I've heard of this kind of thing happening to other people. I just never thought it would happen to me. Now that it has, I feel as though I have stepped though some doorway, and things will never be the same."

As Dan looked around him, he realized that this experience of elation and wonder was coloring all his perceptions. Everything he saw, heard, or felt resonated with some significance beyond its outward manifestation. For the first time since the crash he felt truly alive and at peace with himself. He didn't know if this was a temporary state, but he wasn't about to question it.

He tried to express this to Liz. "You know, for the first time,

I feel ready to move ahead with my life. Whether or not I get back on the airline hardly seems to be important. I don't have to push those big buses around the sky. I really am a stick and rudder man at heart."

"Boy, I'm glad to hear you say that. I wanted all along to say something like that, but you were so obsessed with getting your captain's seat back, I was afraid to."

"The idea that Masami talked about might make sense. I would really enjoy demonstrating a plane like this, checking people out, letting them see a new approach to flying. If not this, there are probably dozens of other possibilities for an old dog like me. With my retirement coming in, money shouldn't be a real problem."

Liz grinned at him, happy to see a positive outlook coming from him. "Let me throw out another idea, Dad. If you could collect your thoughts on what has happened to you, it would make a good book. It could be an inspiration for some people."

"Oh come on, Liz. I'm no writer. I might have the experiences or ideas…"

Liz jumped in at his pause. "You can get it ghost written by an experienced writer. You know, the as-told-to kind of book."

Dan pondered this possibility. "I don't know. It's a pretty out there story. Do you think anybody would believe it?

EPILOGUE

What did happen to Dan after his flight in the Chrysalis? He and Masami entered into a partnership to promote and sell motorgliders. However, Dan wasn't willing to move to the islands, and the time and effort of commuting there made him slowly lose interest.

He discovered flying in the northwest, that area extending above Seattle towards Canada. He fell in love with floatplanes, and the new landscapes and adventures they opened up. When he gained enough experience, he took some of his pension and bought into a small charter operation. They flew people and gear into the islands dotting Puget Sound and up the west coast of Canada and Alaska. Eventually, he sold his Los Angeles home and moved to Orcas Island.

Many of these islands and areas are only serviced by boat or airplane. These communities depended heavily on operators like Dan's for life-giving support. He found great satisfaction in this. He introduced youngsters to flying through the Experimental Airplane Association's Young Eagle Program.

As you might expect, his attitude toward life changed. He was much less demanding and more open with his kids. Mark and he became friends, a status that was only possible when Dan dropped his authoritarian and judgmental attitudes. In general, Dan became more sympathetic to other's problems, less solution oriented, and a better listener. Even when they didn't know his story, fellow pilots and friends knew they could talk to him about things they felt were important and controversial.

Liz became an accomplished pilot. She spent each summer with Dan. When she obtained her commercial ticket, and enough time in floatplanes, she flew as a reserve pilot for Dan's Island Wings operation. When she finished college, she still needed to build up her flying time to three thousand hours before any major carrier would consider her. She took off to southern Africa. In Zimbabwe and Botswana, the bush/safari operators were looking for young pilots eager to fly a hundred hours a month, taking their clients into remote jungle and desert strips. But that is another story.

So why is this fiction? Because Dan really isn't a single person. He is a synthesis of pilots I have met during my career. What about the crash and its aftermath? It happened, but not at Kai Tak in exactly the way described. It would not be fair to the pilots I have interviewed and reports I have read to expose them this way. Therefore, Dan stands as their straw man. Only in this way could I get to the story that lies behind those glaring headlines you occasionally read in the newspapers or weekly magazines.

GLOSSARY

AVIATION TERMS

ALPA, AirLine Pilots Association, the union of airline pilots.

CAD, Civil Aviation Department of Hong Kong, similar to the FAA of the United States.

"Cleaned up", gear and flaps retracted.

DFDR, digital flight data recorder, commonly referred to in the press as the 'black box' even though it's usually orange or red depending on the manufacturer.

EAD, engine alert display, an annunciator panel that alerts the crew of any failure or discrepancy in the engines.

EPR, engine pressure ratio, on a turbo fan engine this is the primary indicator of power.

FAA, Federal Aviation Agency, regulates and promotes civil aviation in the United States.

FADEC, full authority digital engine control, a computerized device that alerts the pilots to any discrepancy or failure in the engines.

FLIGHT DIRECTOR, a guidance bar on the pilots flying display that indicates the correct attitude for the task selected. If the pilot follows this bar, it will lead him to the correct flight path.

FMS, flight management system, with the correct inputs from the pilots the system will guide and navigate the airplane through its entire enroute flight plan.

"Ground returns", reflections from buildings and mountains that prevent the radar antenna from locating clouds and rain. This sometimes can be cleared up by rotating the antenna to an upward angle.

ICAO, International Civil Aviation Organization, the international regulatory agency that promulgates the rules for international flying.

MD-11, a three engined airliner, designed by McDonnell Douglas Aircraft Company to compete with the Boeing and Airbus long distance airplanes on international routes.

NOTAMS, notices to airmen alerting them to any recent changes affecting their flight.

NTSB, National Transportation Safety Board, the agency that investigates all civilian airplane accidents.

"TAKEOFF CLAMP", this is a mode of the FADEC that locks the throttles into their takeoff position. The pilots can override it if necessary.

TOGA, take off and go around, it is both a command, and a button when punched, will cause the FADEC and AUTO FLIGHT systems to pitch the airplane up with full power to the best climb attitude.

V_1 is called the takeoff safety speed. This is the last point, if there is an engine failure, where the pilot can decide to stop within the runway distance, or climb out and clear a 35 foot obstacle at the end of the runway.

"Walk around", pilot's slang for the safety inspection before each flight.

WEIGHT & BALANCE, the calculation of the correct weight and center of gravity for each flight. This affects both performance and flying characteristics.

HAWAIIAN/PIDGIN

First a disclaimer: I am not a Hawaiian language expert and pidgin being a patois, varies greatly in its sound and interpretation with each ethnic group. All that said, this may help the reader who is not familiar with either form.

Aina, the land, which has both physical and spiritual connection for Hawaiians. For them, the land is sacred and alive and supports them. The loss of their land over the last century has been a disaster for their culture.

Aumakua, traditional family spirit guardian, usually residing in a particular animal.

Brah, this would be bro in city street/surfer slang.

Da kine, this can mean any kind of thing, as long as both parties know in common what it is. This can result in some amusing conversations—"You know, da kine bra, da kine." "Yeah, I know da kine."

E komo mai, welcome.

Haole, white man or woman, the origin of this term may never be determined, but there's no doubt about its use.

Heiau, A rock altar dedicated to a particular spirit or god. Some of these are huge, and all of them are important to Hawaiians no matter what their outward condition seems to reflect.

Kapunas, elders, teachers held in high respect. These are the people who still hold the knowledge of the old ways.

Mana, spiritual power or force exhibited outwardly or inwardly. To traditional Hawaiians everything is alive and has mana to some degree or more. The complexity and depth of this word can take a lifetime to explore.

Mano, shark god, the aumakua for many Hawaiian families.

Onaga, red snapper[Japanese], ula ula in Hawaiian.

Pake, Chinese person.

Pareo, a shift or wraparound worn throughout Polynesia.

Pilikia, troubles, worries.

Shaka, hand sign that means hang loose, everything's cool.

BOB TRIPP